THE AERODROME

REX WARNER

The Aerodrome

a love story

ELEPHANT PAPERBACKS
Ivan R. Dee, Publisher, Chicago

THE AERODROME. This book was originally published in 1941 by The Bodley Head Ltd., and is here
reprinted by arrangement. Introduction copyright
© 1982 by The Bodley Head Ltd.

First ELEPHANT PAPERBACK edition published
1993 by Ivan R. Dee, Inc., 1332 North Halsted
Street, Chicago 60622. Manufactured in the United
States of America and printed on acid-free paper.

Library of Congress Cataloging-in-Publication Data:
Warner, Rex, 1905–
The aerodrome : a love story / Rex Warner. --
1st Elephant paperback ed.
p.   cm.
"Elephant paperbacks."
ISBN 1-56663-025-8
1. Fascism—Fiction.   I. Title
PR6045.A78A37   1993
823'.912—dc20   93-11245

Contents

To John and Pam

Philosophers have measured mountains,
    Fathomed the depths of seas, of states, and kings,
Walked with a staffe to heav'n, and traced fountains:
    But there are two vast, spacious things,
The which to measure it doth more behove:
Yet few there are that found them; Sinne and Love.

GEORGE HERBERT

Author's Note

AUTHORS often place at the beginning of their books a disclaimer to the effect that 'all characters and scenes hereafter described are entirely fictitious'.

In my case anyone who has read my other books will know that such a disclaimer is unnecessary. I do not even aim at realism. And in this book my two worlds, 'village' and 'aerodrome', are of course not intended to describe any village or air force in existence.

For the purpose of my story I have made both these worlds somewhat repulsive. Let the story, if it can, justify itself. But, in case it should be misunderstood, let me here assert that both for the Air Force and for the villages of my own country I have the utmost affection and respect.

Introduction

BY ANTHONY BURGESS

THE AERODROME appeared when the phony war, or Great
Bore War as an Evelyn Waugh character called it, was over
and the real war was beginning. For those of us engaged in
fighting that war overseas it had to be a book that we merely heard of; the reading of it had to be long deferred. When
I say 'we' I mean the members of what Arthur Koestler
rather disdainfully called the Thoughtful Corporal Belt:
'Read for pleasure, man,' he wrote to an imagined representative of it, 'and forget Joyce and Péguy.' The fact is that
there was not much time to read for pleasure, whatever
Koestler meant by the term, but there had to be time to try
to learn what the war was all about, and this meant reading
not only Joyce and Péguy (and Koestler for that matter) but
also Kafka. When we started learning about Kafka we began
also to learn about his British disciples. One of these was
William Sansom, whose *Fireman Flower* was a brilliant exercise in the technique of Kafkaesque fantasy, and another was
Rex Warner. *The Wild Goose Chase*, we read in such literary
magazines as came our way, was a sedulous Kafka allegory
with a strong political theme, but *The Aerodrome* was something different—an intensely original work which was
Kafkaesque only in its use of allegory or large-size metaphor,
whose subject-matter was too complex to be merely political and which, despite a strangeness relating it to Kafka, was
very much in the English fictional tradition—meaning that
it had three-dimensional characters (which Kafka does not
have), humour and irony, and the smell of the English earth.

I shall never forget my first reading of *The Aerodrome*. A thoughtful sergeant-major rather than corporal, I was being sent home to England from Gibraltar on a derelict ship of French provenance with a monoglot Chinese crew. We slept on the deck and rats jumped over us all night long. Rats also turned up in the savoury stews which, along with apple jam in cans the size of petrol drums, formed our three-week diet. There was a small ship's library and in this I found three, repeat three, hardback copies of *The Aerodrome*. I stowed one in my kit bag and it became the first item in my post-war library. One of the others I devoured at once; I was, as I had expected, enthralled. I have reread *The Aerodrome* several times since and am, at each rereading, progressively more amazed at its prophetic qualities. Eight years older than *Nineteen Eighty-Four*, its claim to be regarded as a modern classic is as sound as that of Orwell's novel, but one can see clearly why it has to be rescued periodically from popular oblivion. It lacks the 'popular' elements of Orwell's book—sex, overt brutality, explicit and recognizable ideology. It is subtle, ambiguous and restrained. It is also optimistic.

The basic scenario is a brilliant invention in itself. There is a thoroughly degenerate village, which represents fallen man. Men literally fall dead drunk, sluts fall backwards in the hedgerows; the local rat-catcher earns pints by biting off the heads of live ratlings. The pub is the centre of gruff or maudlin sodality; the manor house, with its decrepit squire, is the centre of secular authority; the church, with its imperfect rector, pretends to look after spiritual needs which are not much in evidence. This is the wretched or joyful human condition; the village is the human family with its palimpsest of interlinked atomic families. Outside the village there is a great aerodrome dedicated to cleanliness and efficiency. It is a self-sufficient totalitarian state with its eyes on the air, not on the earth. The earth is dirty, and so are the men who work on it and live off it; the future lies in the unsullied empyrean. The aerodrome absorbs the village, converting the manor house into a club and the rectory into a gymnasium, turning agricultural land into airfields, exerting inhuman discipline on what was once a free society but itself, in the person of the Air Vice-Marshal, preaching the doctrine of freedom through self-control and the eschewal of brutal instinct. *Arbeit macht frei.*

Roy, the hero-narrator, is a much more convincing character than Orwell's Winston Smith in that he is capable, which Winston Smith is not, of switching without exterior compulsion or brainwashing from a liberal to a totalitarian view and then back again. If no man in his right mind could voluntarily accept the principles of Ingsoc, there is something in all of us which finds the Air Vice-Marshal's doctrine of non-attached working for the future fairly attractive. 'What a record of confusion, deception, rankling hatred, low aims, indecision,' he says of the old imperfect society which has to be destroyed, and, thinking of the dishonest decade which World War II brought to an end, we have to agree with him. We are prepared, with certain qualifications, to accept too his denunciation of filiality and paternity. Huxley's *Brave New World* presented a society in which family had been abolished as responsible for all our complexes and repressions and, indeed, manias (Our Ford speaking as Our Freud) and, without benefit of official ectogenesis, the Aerodrome proposes to free men from the slavery of wives and mothers. A brave new world indeed, in which sex is a toy and the breeding of children an abomination.

But the brilliant irony of the book lies in its theme of the inescapability of family ties. There is high comedy in Roy's gradual discovery of who his father and mother really are, the revelation that all the major characters of the story are shamefully, even criminally, related. The unnamed Flight Lieutenant kills his own father, also Roy's—the Air Vice-Marshal himself. This comic Oedipism is completed by rumours of incest. The death of the father means the end of the Aerodrome, though we cannot be quite sure that it will not rise again. After all, an Air Vice-Marshal presupposes an Air Marshal, and him we never meet. But Roy voices the philosophy which ensures that neither he nor ourselves will ever be tempted again to put on the uniform of the Collectivist State: the imperfect life of the village, despite the Sophoclean dangers that lurk there, is, by reason of its formlessness, its lack of a cut-and-dried philosophy, exciting and adventurous; the Aerodrome, despite its firmness of purpose and its superhuman technology (pilotless planes, for instance), is a negation of life.

This is a symbolic novel rather than merely an allegorical one. I mean that it functions, in spite of the author's disclaimer, as a realistic work with larger overtones. The scene at the agricultural show indicates what I mean. The Flight-Lieutenant, the paradoxical badge of whose complexity as a character is an air force slang which both sounds and does not sound authentic, unleashes a prize bull which stands for the coming totalitarian brutality as well as the primal forces that resist it. He kills, through an accident which is also a deliberate act, the rector whom Roy has believed to be his father: cynically filling his place as air force padre (a rector is a mere ruler; a padre is a true father), he is enabled to find, through a negative road, the truth and the light. The drunken old grocer puts on an act which makes a grotesquerie of the mother-son nexus: 'Oh mother, I see you in your poor little cottage, poking the fire, thinking, ah, thinking of your wandering son. I thank God you cannot see him. Among the burning globes, in the din and degradation, mother, of a gin hell he is to be beheld. A gaol-bird, mother, a broken reed: and the woman at his side is not his wedded wife.' The comedy of the book, a quality altogether missing in Orwell's dystopia, is not to be discounted. But it is a comedy of high seriousness.

The value of *The Aerodrome* as literature becomes increasingly apparent at each rereading. I mean that one finds new involutions, new paradoxes and complexities at the same time as the solidity of character and of place strikes with renewed force. But the mystery of the work does not dissolve. 'The national flag' and the 'capital' remind us that we are in a location that is universal, not just English. And yet the language breathes England—not just the flowers and the grass but also the common-sense pragmatism and decency which will defeat, we think, any encroachment of totalitarian aerodromes. But we must not forget the quite uncommonsensical complexity:

I remember that night as we looked over the valley in the rapidly increasing darkness that we were uncertain of where we would be or what we would be doing in the years in front of us. I remember the valley itself and how I saw it again as I had seen it in my childhood, heard a late-sleeping redshank whistle from the river, and thought of the life continuing beneath the roofs behind us.

'That the world may be clean': I remember my father's words. Clean indeed it was and most intricate, fiercer than tigers, wonderful and infinitely forgiving.

Like the book itself.

THE AERODROME

CHAPTER I

The Dinner Party

IT WOULD BE difficult to overestimate the importance to me of the events which had taken place previous to the hour (it was shortly after ten o'clock in the evening) when I was lying in the marsh near the small pond at the bottom of Gurney's meadow, my face in the mud and the black mud beginning to ooze through the spaces between the fingers of my outstretched hands, drunk, but not blindly so, for I seemed only to have lost the use of my limbs. The tough damp marsh grass tickled below the ear and around the eyes. The mud smelt good, and I pressed my right cheek down flat upon it, seeing with my left eye the dim shapes of trees, like giants guarding beneficently the field of a dream, at the upper end of the meadow, and beyond the trees a few small stars, jolly in the immense darkness. Oh, I could have cried for joy and peace! I dug my toes into the soft ground, then raised myself a little on my elbows because the point of a long reed had penetrated one of the interstices of my hard dress shirt. Then I bit off a portion of another reed and sucked the white pith. I rolled over on my side, and some water squirted cool over the collar at the back of my neck.

The other two were on their feet by now and, either because they imagined the marsh to be dusty, or for some reason which I did not understand, were smacking each other's shoulders and buttocks with their hands. We had all three tripped over the wire at the same

moment, and: 'God set fire to the Duke of Ireland!
Who'd have thought it?' Fred was saying. 'Roll along!
Roll Along!' Mac sang, and then they turned to me,
wishing me to proceed with them, but I refused to move
or to say a word, so that in the end they stumbled away
together though, as they went, I could hear them de-
bating whether or not they had done well to leave me.
'Good old Fred! Good old Mac!' I said to the grass,
and then pressed my forehead for a few moments into
the mud, lying perfectly still and listening to the gurgling
and sucking noises all round me swelling from the
plashy ground.

When I heard the fierce broken snarl of an owl from
the upper end of the meadow it was as though my very
bowels were pierced with a sudden excitement, like a
lancet, of joy. That almost painful delight passed and
left me drowsy. I began to think, but not yet of what
had happened to me that day. Slowly, and almost yard
by yard, with a sense of the most delicious ease, I began
to set before my mind's eye, since it was too dark to
see, the familiar meadows, tracks, slopes, hills and trees
that surrounded me. I imagined our village as it had
been and as it still was, the land on which I lay; and
then the people, and the rapidly accelerating change or
threat.

Below me the fine meadows gently swept downwards
to the river. They were intersected by narrow ditches
where water-rails are often to be seen, stepping more
delicately than racehorses. At this time of the year the
redshank come inland from the coasts and estuaries to
nest here, and all day in a fresh wind I have listened to
their confident whistle mingling with the outlandish

scream of lapwing twisting madly in the air above the wide valley and the running shadows of April clouds, so that the birds' wings and voices seemed a part of the restless sky and the moving world.

The river itself is narrow and runs fast in twists and loops, for it has much room to cut its own way in this valley. There is sedge which rustles dreadfully both in the stream and the wind, and several islands with willows growing upon them, places where both swans and otters nest. Beyond the river are meadows, at first rather flatter than they are on our side; but they are soon drawn up like a blanket into folds and creases to cover the shoulders of the further hills, and here and there one can see the big tufts of woods, the smaller hair of copses. There are no villages in sight, and the bridge is several miles upstream, out of sight too.

But on our side of the river, away on my right hand, I hear the church clock striking eleven. The village street runs down the hill sharply to the church, and there stops. Along the street, at both sides, are the grey stone cottages to which Fred and Mac will by this time have returned. Polyanthus and honesty are in full bloom in their gardens, and the huge lilac bush at the corner cottage where the Squire's chauffeur lives will soon be in flower. In the churchyard there is one tall tree, a libocedrus, which runs up into the air like a black flame, and which, when I was a boy, I used to worship, visiting it regularly after morning service, thrusting my head and hands through its dark foliage, fancying it to be some goddess or divine creature, not uninterested in myself. Though embedded in earth it seemed a visitor from another world, like the people at the aerodrome, for it was the only conifer in the churchyard and stood most purely among the gigantic horse-chestnuts whose sticky huge buds were now peeling into leaf.

The church I envisaged now from the outside, a compact and solid mass, with its short square tower, gravel paths circling the building, daffodils on the graves. And on the left of the church, if one were facing downhill, one would see the tall Manor with its cedar tree and large well-kept lawn. On the right was the Rectory, where my guardians lived and whither by this time I should have returned.

In the Rectory garden the grass is somewhat unkempt; heavy bushes of laurel and laurustinus droop over the paths; there is one tall tree by the disused stable, a lime tree, in the topmost branches of which I once fixed a small platform to be used in my solitary games as a look-out post. I know every inch of this garden; the feel and taste of branches and twigs; the smell of leaves and grass in rain and sunshine; the consistency and colour of the soil in different parts.

There are no other large gardens and only one other large house in our village. This house is the pub where I had been drinking that evening, and it is at the top of the village street, so that between it and the church all the small village extends. They would be polishing the glasses there now, sweeping the floors, setting away the darts in their separate stands of cork; and soon the landlord, his wife and daughter, after turning out the one light still shining in the big bar, would go in procession up the narrow stairs to their beds.

I was friendly with the landlord's daughter and now thought with a feeling of resentment of some attentions which had recently been paid her by the Flight-Lieut-enant. At the same time I became conscious of drops of water running down inside my shirt collar to the warm hollow between my neck and collar-bone. I shifted my position, no longer so much enjoying the mud and damp, and began to think of the aerodrome on the summit of the hill, almost a mile beyond the public-house.

This was an institution which, so we were informed, was of great, even vital importance to the defences of our country; but it was so well concealed that many visitors to our village have gone away from the neighbourhood without ever having suspected its existence, although the sight and sound of perhaps fifty planes in the air at one time must have convinced them that some such a concentration of force could not be far distant.

The long hangars were set not in rows nor in any regular order, but were so disposed and camouflaged that even from quite close at hand they appeared merely as rather curious modifications of the natural contours of our hills. The living quarters for officers and men were equally well hidden, some in natural indentations of the ground, others in thick groves of evergreen trees which had been specially planted for the purpose. Many of these buildings also, where visible, resembled older landmarks. One of the main depots for the storage of arms had been constructed so as to appear indistinguishable from a country church; the canteen where, I had been told, champagne was drunk as freely as beer is drunk in our public-house resembled, in spite of the luxury within, an old barn. So with the officers' quarters, or those of them which were not buried underground or hidden completely by coniferous trees.

The wealth of the inmates was, we knew, immense. Sometimes their wives and mothers would be seen clearly as some huge car slowed down for a moment at one of the entrances to the aerodrome from the main road. These women were richly and tastefully dressed. They seldom turned their pale hard faces to look through the windows of their cars towards the edges of the road where the villagers, if any happened to be there, would be standing and touching their caps as a token of respect and admiration. Such feelings must always be provoked by a display of power and beauty that appear innocuous; but they were not, as I shall show, the ordinary feelings of the villagers towards the aerodrome as a whole. Jealousy, I think now, was always mingled with our respect, and fear and a kind of meanness with our admiration.

Moreover certain events had taken place which could leave no one indifferent. Old Tom, who had worked close to the aerodrome ever since it was built, had been driven mad by the roar of the engines as all day the planes took off with their undercarriages almost grazing the hedge of his field. Many of the villagers, also, had been fined for infringing minor military regulations, for setting snares on Government property, or for leaving their carts in inappropriate places. There had been, too, some cases of the rape or abduction of young girls carried out by aircraftsmen or junior officers; but as these occurrences were common enough amongst ourselves, no great importance was attached to them.

So I imagined to myself, as I was lying in the meadow, the appearance from a distance of this powerful institution, for no unauthorized person was allowed on the premises, and, at this time, I had never been nearer to the aerodrome than the main road which runs along the top of the hill above our village. Moreover I had only met one of the officers, though I was not, I had fancied, their inferior either in birth or upbringing.

But now, as these words reiterated themselves in my memory, I became conscious of dull pain spread over me which, becoming intense enough to seem localized, I began to feel as an emptiness in the stomach—pain, dismay, and a hardening of the eyes as I pressed my forehead into the grass and mud, remembering with peculiar vividness the lights and shadows in the Rectory dining-room that evening, the faces round the table, the tones of voices, and what had been said. Now I turned my eyes again to the shadowy elm trees, darker than the sky, and they seemed no longer kindly, but like dreadful moving pillars, forcing me from my place. For these hills and woods and meadows were not mine as I had thought them, nor was I myself what I had been brought up to believe myself to be. Also, that evening, an act of extraordinary indelicacy had taken place.

I know well that to many readers of this story the grief and destitution which I felt at this time will seem extravagant. All my memories were of this place—the churchyard, the gardens, the paths and hedges—and of its people, the Rector and his wife, the Squire and his sister, our gardener, and later the landlord's daughter and the young men with whom I had played football against neighbouring villages or darts in our own public-house. I had believed myself a native of this country, had acted and grown up as such. Should an accident of parentage make all this difference then? Is not the fiction that has been firmly believed as good as true? I can only

19

say that I did not find it so. When I lay drunk in the mud I had been able to forget my sorrow, but now it returned upon me, in pangs of uncertainty and desperation, like the wounds of love. I sat up and stared over the dark pool before me, remembering what may seem to others such a trifling point—that I did not know who I was.

That evening, in order to celebrate my twenty-first birthday, a dinner party had been given at the Rectory. It had originally been intended to invite only the Squire and his sister, who were our closest personal friends; but at my urgent request there had also been invited the young Flight-Lieutenant with whom I had become acquainted only recently, and who, alone of the personnel of the aerodrome, was a not infrequent visitor to the village pub.

This young man was remarkably handsome, and dexterous in all his ways. I soon began to look up to him with the kind of admiration which a young and inexperienced person will often give to one who excels him in beauty, knowledge, and ability, and who is yet kind enough to acknowledge the admiration and treat the admirer as a friend. Nor was my affection for him at all lessened by a consideration of the faults which certainly marred his character; for in spite of the extraordinary charm of manner which he could so easily display, he was often bitter, moody, and vindictive. I had sometimes met him out walking along the main road by the aerodrome, when he would refuse to speak a word, far less suggest that I should accompany him. Often, too, in the course of a general conversation he would shock me by some brutally expressed criticism of our way of life. His actions were sometimes entirely irresponsible.

He would play the most absurd and often cruel practical jokes on perfect strangers. On one occasion in our public-house I saw him throw a dart deliberately so that it penetrated a man's hand. But all this, shocking as it was, seemed to me rather the symptoms of some disease in him than an expression of his true character, which I saw as distinguished by so many virtues and graces which were wholly absent from my own. And even after what had happened that evening I still could not but more than half approve of the man, though I pitied with all my heart those whose hospitality and whose feelings he had so mercilessly outraged.

It was not until the end of the meal that there was made to me by those whom, up to now, I had assumed to be my parents a disclosure important enough to unsettle the whole basis of my thoughts and feelings; and it was the Flight-Lieutenant who, more than any other of those present, had seemed to understand how important to me this disclosure was, even although all his views on the subject were, I could see at once, wholly different from my own. The others expected me to receive the news as though it were some surprise packet almost bound to please and certainly not likely to alter in any way the general tenor of my life. And it was with the air of one who has something quite pleasantly momentous to say that the Rector, he whom I had always regarded as my father, but to whom I must now refer as my guardian, rose from his place at the head of the table after the port had been passed round once, and began to propose, on this auspicious occasion, my health.

His wife, my female guardian, was sitting opposite him, her hands folded in her lap and a look of placid contentment spread like butter over her somewhat flat face. On the Rector's right hand sat the Squire's sister, a tall thin woman with most remarkably clear grey eyes. She was greatly interested in charities of all kinds. Opposite her was the Flight-Lieutenant, and I can remember now how extraordinarily handsome he seemed to me when the Rector rose to speak. The candlelight was caught and twisted in the tight curls of his yellow hair. His jaw was thrust rather further forward than usual as he held the stem of his wine glass between two fingers of his right hand and explored the liquid with his keen eyes. The Squire was sitting next to him and had just been discussing with me, whom he faced, the prospects of our village cricket XI for the coming season. When he spoke of village sport or of church affairs the old man's deeply pitted eyes took on a look of confidence and persuasive kindliness, though at other times his eyes would waver or seem to withdraw from the face into a kind of ghostliness. People said that since the building of the aerodrome he had never been the same. Now he seemed to me very old, amiable, but in weak health.

The Rector tapped on the table and cleared his throat. His wife, leaning towards me with a smile in which I seemed to detect even then some sorrow, said: 'Listen, dear, to your father. He has something important to say.'

I turned my head quickly and saw most vividly the candlelight gleaming on the mahogany table, the glasses and the hands. Then I looked up at the Rector's pale face which was made more pale still by the black beard which he had grown, so I had been told, to cover a scar from a wound which he had received when fighting as a young man in his country's service. His eyes were so piercing as to seem fierce, although he was in reality, as I well knew, the gentlest of men.

'With your permission,' he began in his clear mild voice, 'I will make a few observations on the occasion of our young friend's coming of age.'

'Hear! Hear!' said the Squire, and I caught his eye looking gravely on me.

The Flight-Lieutenant flipped the edge of the table with his finger-nail. 'We are doomed,' he said, and then made a face at me. His behaviour was deemed by the others eccentric, but not unpardonably so.

The Rector continued. 'But first of all I must, in fulfilment of a resolution which I have made with myself, give you, who are all close personal friends' (here he glanced rather timidly at the Flight-Lieutenant), 'some news which you ought to know and which will, I feel sure, surprise you, although it need, I think, distress no one.'

He paused again, and the Flight-Lieutenant leaned across the table towards me. 'That's all he knows about it,' he whispered, and winked.

'Sir, sir!' said the Squire.

The Rector proceeded, not having heard or not noticing the interruption. 'Twenty-one years ago to this day,' he said, 'a little stranger, a baby, came to this house. We gave this little friend of ours the name of Roy, and we have kept him with us ever since.'

Here I observed that the Squire's sister was looking at me with approval, but I felt too disquieted to smile at her. I could feel a pressure of blood at my wrists and a rush of blood to the heart, though what could have caused this premonitory turmoil, unless it were the curious note of hesitation in the Rector's voice, I should not have been able to say. I paid hardly any attention to the Flight-Lieutenant who had pronounced in an audible whisper the words: 'About as silly a name as could be found.'

The two ladies looked sternly at him, but the Rector continued as though he had heard nothing. 'It is indeed twenty-one years ago to the day when this stranger, now as I think you will agree with me a fine young man, first visited us; but it is not the fact that this day is his birthday. Indeed the lady whom he has called "mother", and I, who have been proud to bear the name of "father", cannot say on what day of the year he was born. We are not, you see, his parents, however much we may love him as though he were our child.'

'This is monstrous,' shouted the Flight-Lieutenant, jumping to his feet. 'It makes no difference at all.'

The Rector turned his penetrating eyes upon the interruptor. 'So these are the manners of the aerodrome,' said the Squire's sister. 'They are certainly not ours,' while her brother, his face already somewhat flushed with wine, grew redder, thumping the table, and said in a gruff voice, 'Down sir!' as though he were addressing some domesticated animal. Only the Rector's wife preserved an expression of unbroken placidity.

As for myself, I was filled with such a deep inner perturbation that I hardly observed the general embarrassment. 'Who am I then?' I said, and the Flight-Lieutenant made another face at me and then sat down.

The Rector continued, still in a somewhat hesitant manner, but almost as though no interruption had taken place. 'This little stranger,' he said, 'was in very deed and truth a stranger. He was found in a basket lying at the top

24

of the village at about the place where the main road now is. At that time the aerodrome and the main road itself were in course of construction. A good woman, now the wife of our village publican, brought the little child to us, trusting that we would welcome it out of charity. Of its parents nothing, naturally, was known. It may indeed be considered possible that at least one of them was a person from another district, perhaps even from another county, employed temporarily on the construction of the aerodrome. But in this we can be guided only by the purest conjecture.

'Now by a most strange coincidence, so strange even that in it I have often seemed to detect the hand of Providence, my wife was returning that very evening from a six months' stay abroad, whither she had been forced to go for the treatment of a serious illness. To cut short a long story, we decided to bring up the child as our own, and so we have done. He is sitting with us tonight, respected and loved, if I may say so, by us all. His education, though it has been given him at home, is, I think I may say, a sound one. His athletic capabilities are well known. His character, though undeveloped, seems likely to develop on sterling lines. Roy, my dear fellow, I raise my glass to you. And though, as truth demanded, I have had to inform you that we are not your real parents, trust me, my boy, that you can rely upon us as though we were indeed what you have called us.'

There was some applause at this, and the chairs slid back as guests rose to drink my health. The Flight-Lieutenant remained seated. His lips were compressed in a smile that had no warmth in it. His voice too was cold. He said: 'Though this particular subject is, we

25

all know, not of the least importance, it is a fact, is it not, that for the last twenty-one years you have been telling lies ? May I ask what is your authority for this ?'

He spoke in a remarkably quiet voice, and yet the intensity with which he spoke seemed to command among his audience something almost of respect; although anger and embarrassment very quickly supervened. I saw that the Rector's eyes were blazing with anger and that his hands were trembling. 'Have the goodness now to drink your friend's health, sir!' he said. 'If you want my authority for the care I have taken of him, it is love, sir, justice, sir, and pity.'

The Flight-Lieutenant sprang to his feet. 'To Roy!' he said and, draining his wine before any of the others had so much as raised their hands from the table, he flung the empty glass over his shoulder. It broke into fragments against a picture of a Greco-Roman sculpture of the huntress Diana. Then he crossed the room quickly to the window and, jerking back the curtains, displayed a view of the sky and many stars shining there. 'Love!' he shouted through the window, 'Justice! Pity! Oh, very good indeed, sir!' Then he turned and ran out of the room.

I followed him, with all my thoughts so confused as not to know whether by following him I intended to extract from him an apology, to sympathize with him, or to pick a quarrel. As I left the room I saw the pale perplexed faces of my guardians and of their guests. No doubt but that the party had been wholly unsuccessful.

I reached the front door and the garden path, but soon heard the sound of the Flight-Lieutenant's motor bicycle as he went away from me up the hill that leads to the aerodrome. Then I followed slowly to the top of the village, and spent the rest of the evening in the pub. Not that I felt anything but gratitude to my benefactors, but merely that I lacked assurance. Now I was sitting in the mud.

CHAPTER II

The Confession

'O LAMB OF GOD, have mercy upon me! Root of Jesse, hear my prayer! O Light, guide me! O Way, lead! O Truth, purify me! O Lamb, wash me in thy blood! O Dove, O Branch, be not far distant, I beseech thee!'

The words were thrown through the still thin lips above the jutting beard, as though each word were swung like a hammer to descend finally on some anvil inside or outside the mind. The Rector's head was tilted backwards, his chin resting on his clasped hands as he knelt in prayer at the little desk in the alcove at the far end of his study. His eyes stared upward to where a religious picture hung on the wall, dim to see except where running irregular blobs or stains of firelight spread across it, like the effects of stones flung into an obscure pool. But the Rector seemed to be looking at something beyond the plunging light and the indistinct figure of a man with bent knees attempting to hold up a cross. His eyes, and indeed his whole body, with no tremor in his clasped hands were motionless, except for the small movement in his lips through which the words came emphatically and without hesitation as though he were some delicately adjusted machine, now perfectly fulfilling the task for which it had been designed.

I stepped back quietly on the soft carpet away from the rigid kneeling figure of my guardian, for I shrank from interrupting his devotions by squeezing past him to the door which was close by his right elbow. So I moved back again to the window through which I had entered the house, and, though I disliked occupying the position of an eavesdropper, I shielded myself with the curtain, fancying that I should have only a few minutes to wait before the prayer was ended, and the Rector would retire to bed.

On my return to the house from the meadow I had found the lights out and the front door locked. Although it was likely that they had left the back door open for me, I decided that a quicker way of entry was through the study window, the fastening of which I knew to be broken. And, since I was still somewhat embarrassed at the thought of my own part in the unsuccessful dinner party, I had entered the room as quietly as I was able, not wishing to encounter my friends until the next day. Now I did not care to run the risk of making a noise by opening the window again from the inside, but considered it best to wait where I was, even though I was trespassing on another's intimate thoughts. I could have had no suspicion at the time of how intimate they were. So I remained uneasily listening, with my eyes straying from the tense kneeling figure to the fire flickering at his back at the far end of the room, the curtain that covered the window next to the one where I hid, the large writing desk in the centre, and beyond it the rows of theological volumes which filled all the wall space opposite me.

The words came in a steady uninterrupted stream and, if it had not been for the fervour and intensity with which they were uttered, would have sounded like the recitation of some lesson learnt by heart. 'Where is the hyssop, O Lord God?' he was saying. 'Where is the hyssop to purge me? My sins are a river. They are great boils, O my Healer, corruption, God, and running sores. I am become a stench, my Saviour, and a place of howling. But thou, O Lamb, can'st take away the howling and make it calm. Thou can'st put frankincense in my nostrils, frankincense, O thou Righteous One, and cassia, so that all my transgressions may be even as a sacrifice and as a windless calm.'

I observed that, although the night was cool, great drops of sweat were standing on his forehead, and yet his words were pronounced more calmly as he continued: 'Lamb, let me tell you again my sin. Every year I have told it to you, and every year you have listened to me. You have understood. You have not been unduly vexed, O Most Merciful. And this is the twenty-second year. Listen again then, I beseech you. Hear thy servant, O Holiness. Give ear, O Most Mighty, O Prince of Peace.'

Here he unclasped his hands for a moment and paused. When he continued he seemed to me to be speaking more rapidly but with less agitation. 'I was thirty years of age, O Unchangeable One,' he said, 'and had just completed my course of study at the Theological College. My great friend Anthony (O, let him be a saint in thy sight) was with me, and thou knowest, Lord, of what plans we two made together for the furtherance of thy Kingdom on earth, that thy Will be done. Lamb of God, let me remind thee of Anthony. Thou knowest, Lord, his rough and honest face, his great intellectual gifts, his lack of any kind of nervousness, his spiritual integrity. Light of the World, what wonder was it that he was preferred to me and given the offer of this living, of this house, O God, of this pleasant heritage in which to do thy Work? And what wonder was it that she who is now my wife

(Guard her, O Keeper! Save her in her goings in and in her comings out!), what wonder was it that she should have preferred his love to mine, even though, before she met him, she had pledged her troth to me, to me thy most unworthy servant? Were these occasions for pride, O Most Humble One? For backbiting, Magnificent? Thou knowest my sin. Pride, O God, Deceit, Saviour, Malice aforethought, thou Blameless One, Covetousness, Disloyalty, and, O Spotless, at the end, Murder.'

He stopped speaking and seemed to shake his head as if in nervous relief at having uttered his last difficult word. I saw his hands clasp and unclasp, and in involuntary horror at the scene at which I found myself a witness I stepped forward a little from my place of concealment. Whether or not I should then have revealed my presence I do not know. I had perhaps some such idea in my head, but quite possibly I should still have shrunk from interrupting with my ordinary presence a mood of such agony that it seemed not to belong to my previous experience either of the man or of the place. But whatever resolution I had was driven out of my mind by the new sight which I saw as I stepped from my hiding place. For, from behind the curtain that covered the window next to mine, I saw another head protrude. It was wearing a night-cap, and at first this unfamiliar article of clothing together with the expression on the face prevented me from immediately recognizing my mother or, I should say, the Rector's wife. Her face was very pale and her thin yellow hair was drawn up under the night-cap, baring a greater expanse of white forehead than that which she showed when dressed and ready for the day. Rarely did she reveal in her expression any feeling at all beyond placidity and contentment, but now her eyes were narrowed, and she was staring at her husband with a look that seemed to me to show no pity or distress, but something more like triumph, and something too of contempt.

Perhaps I had made some noise, so great was my astonishment both at her presence at all and at her appearance, for she turned her head towards me, smiled as though she were welcoming me to some pleasant and normal scene, the breakfast table perhaps, or a Sunday School treat, and pressed her fingers to her lips. Then she withdrew again into her hiding place so that I could see nothing of her but three gleaming finger nails on which the light flickered, as she held with an unseen hand the heavy folds of the curtain.

'Thou, O Lord,' said the Rector, 'who hast told us that whosoever looketh after a woman to lust hath already committed adultery, when was the beginning of my treachery, when did I murder first? Was it that shameful notion that my mind so instantly and indignantly rejected, the notion that came to me on the Manor lawn, when we were playing croquet, and I saw Anthony's beautiful head laid close to the head of my betrothed, close to the handle of the croquet mallet, God, and the shining hoop beneath, and the cedar protecting them from the sun? Lion of Judah, I thought then of blood, and I was horrified. I drove back the thought like iron into the ground of my mind, but in the terror and fury with which I drove it back there was still something tremulous, My Saviour, something delicious. O have mercy upon me, Most Merciful! Pity me, Supreme! O, after thy great goodness, shine upon me, the filthy one, the abomination.'

Here I saw that he let his head fall upon his forearms while his thin bent back was shaken with sobbing. This lasted for some moments, but when he began to speak again his voice was very much calmer.

'Let me be exact, Righteous One,' he said, 'and admit with shame that even now, after twenty-two years of contrition, of tears, of repentance—even now these unholy thoughts stir me: with loathing, yes, God, (for I am a sink) but also with a kind of fascination. Purge this from me, Redeemer, that I may be clean. This is my desperate wickedness, and, Lord, thou knowest it. Lord, let me begin.'

He took a deep breath and continued unhesitatingly, as though he were reading a narrative from some novel or newspaper. 'Perhaps, thou best Inquisitor, it is not of consequence when first the thought came to me of killing my friend. The thought came. It was rejected. It came again. It persisted. Both on the croquet lawn and in other places I was filled with unreasoning jealousy. Pride, of a most perverse character, drove me into hatred when Anthony was preferred to me and given the parish, this parish, my God, which I had so long coveted. As though each corner of the world is not filled to overflowing with thy work to do! As though I were worthy to pick and choose, Christ, among thy vineyards! And I kept my hatred against my brother close covered in my deceitful heart. I congratulated him fervently on his new appointment. I smiled into his winning eyes. I accepted thankfully his suggestion to accompany him on a mountaineering holiday, and, even as I accepted, the thought came to me that would afterwards be translated into most dreadful action. At that time, too, I most

33

distinctly remember, I thrust away the thought as a temptation of the Evil One, but I thrust it away gently, as a soft and cherished thing. God, do I delude myself when I think that even then I might have been, not guiltless, thou knowest, but not so wholly stained, if only that scene had not taken place on the night before our departure?

'You saw it all, Most Holy One of Israel. You were in the moon. You were behind the trees. You were above the blackened grass. You were with me as I hid at the corner of the veranda in the heavy smell of the tobacco plants. You saw them, Saviour, in each other's arms, and you heard the whispered words that I could not hear, for they were removed from me. In perfect uprightness, Redeemer, you watched most mercifully over your own children, over me, too, Stainless, and my black heart.

'It was then that I became resolved to sin by murder. Not without qualms, thou knowest, not without groanings and beatings of the breast. In my arrogance I calmed my conscience (thy voice, Great Friend) by fancying myself to be an instrument of justice, claiming actually righteousness for myself, O Light of Humility, Meek King. Lord, you say: "It is I that will repay." Lord, you do repay.

'Let me pass over quickly, God, my journey to the mountains. You know what turmoil was in my heart as the train carried me north and I gazed across the carriage at my friend who was sitting opposite me. He was reading a work of light fiction and from time to time setting the book down on his knees while he smoothed back his hair, inspected the countryside or smiled at me. Then I smiled back and began to foretaste the pains that were to come. But I was resolute, O God of Battles. Even then I knew that I should return alone.

'I will not tell you now, my Saviour, of our first evening at the hotel, our apparent gaiety and of the discussion which we had over the wine about the fulfilment of your holy work on earth. By then I was wholly corrupt and spoke, I remember, with particular fervour of a certain reredos in which were depicted white doves ascending from and descending into a chalice of wine. But next day, O Splendour, among the mountains, could I not then, in the gentle sunshine among the towering heights, emblems of your mercy and enormous power, could I not then have repented? When I looked from high down upon the farms and cottages of the plain, the mild cattle in the fields, the sheep on slopes below me, might I not then have heard thy voice which never, O Hound, never for one moment, I know, had ceased to pursue me? God, I was deafened by my blood and by the roaring of my pride.

'O Infinite Compassion, we ate our sandwiches together within a thousand feet of the summit. By this time the wind had veered round and the sky was becoming overcast. I looked hungrily at the gathering clouds, since in dirty weather an accident will always seem more credible to outsiders who, in most cases, are ignorant of the real dangers of climbing.

' "I don't like the look of the weather," Anthony said. He had a crumb at the corner of his mouth.

' "We'll risk it," I said. "It's not going to come to much."

'Then he looked doubtful, but I was the leader and he trusted me. Saviour, my friend's goodness, his evident

35

confidence in me, added to my fury. I was lightheaded and laughed, but my heart was frozen. We went on together without ropes till we came to the eastern arête. You know the country well, God. It is a difficult climb, and was very difficult then when the storm was gathering and the cloud already beginning to drift down to us from the summit and to sweep past us in skeins and rivulets between the hills. But I still laughed, as though my excitement was in the climbing, and Anthony, though he was obviously puzzled, would not, I knew, refuse to follow me.

'I knew the place where I would do the murder. There is a small ledge, Saviour, with fingerholds where a man may stand spreadeagled against the rock-face at the top of the arête. From the ledge there are holds high up that can be reached and from them it is easy work to the ridge above; but if once one loses one's footing on the ledge there is nothing but rock so smooth that one can hardly scrape one's nails upon it.

'I reached the ledge and stopped to take breath. I could see Anthony below me and could see that he thought this climb foolhardy, though he was determined to follow me. "It's not far now," I shouted, and he smiled grimly. Then I reached for the high and difficult holds; but then they seemed easy to me. I swung myself off the ledge and found at once the crack for my feet. It appeared a matter of moments before I was at the top of the arête, listening to Anthony who called "Nice work" from below. I looked back, and now the damp cloud came pouring down on us, so that I could see Anthony's shape, which seemed somehow magnified, but could hardly make out the expression on his face.

"Hurry!" I shouted. "It's going to be nasty for a bit."

'I braced myself against the rock and, peering forward and downward, watched him scramble to the ledge. Here he paused for a moment as I had done. Most merciful and divine Lord, in the mist and cold the blood was beating in me like hammers. I felt his body at the end of the rope as one might feel a fish. I threw myself sideways, jerking him from the ledge, as I knew from his whole weight on the rope and the short cry which he uttered.

'Redeemer, very quickly I fastened the rope to the jut of rock that I knew was close to my right hand. Then I looked down and could see his body swinging scarcely eight feet below me, near enough, God, but with no holds for fingers or toes, and sheer rock for two hundred feet. The cloud was now dense over the face of rock. I reached down as far as I could, though still out of reach of Anthony's hands. It was difficult to see his face, but when I glanced at it, before I took out my knife, it seemed to bear a look rather of bewilderment than of anything else. I did not look at him, O God, while I was cutting the rope. Had I looked, O Great Dove, would I have desisted? Lord, thou knowest. I only know that it was at this moment that my excitement began to ebb and that I felt myself to be doing something unpleasant and almost dull. So, in an awkward position, I tussled with the thick strands of rope, as if it were a necessary task which I had unwillingly undertaken, and I never looked at him once, nor did he utter a word, till the rope parted and I saw him drop away from me into the mist. I threw the knife after him, scrambled to my knees and let out another three or four feet from the rope which I had belayed round the rock, so that it would appear that

37

it was he who had used the knife himself while standing on the ledge. Merciful God, I spared neither his life nor his honour; for my story would be that in the mist he had lost his nerve while he was on the ledge, that I, unable either to inspire him with fortitude or to haul him up the cliff face single-handed, had made the rope fast and gone to get help; that in my absence his panic had got the better of him and that he had severed the rope himself. O God, have mercy! Christ, have mercy! Son of God, save! Spirit, Ghost, Thrones and Powers, do not utterly reject me, but look from your great height with pity upon my wasted heart!

'My Dove, there is little else to say, little else but once more to implore you to extend over me your compassionate and healing wings. My story was received as true. The body was recovered by Doctor Faulkner, a great friend both of Anthony and myself. I never saw it, but I attended the funeral and, though it may seem odd to you, my Saviour, I wept as the coffin was being lowered into the ground. It was not for weeks and months, God, not till my ambitions had been realized, not till I had received the offer of this living and had married the lady who is now my wife, that the veil and mist of my deliberate sin fell from me and I began, O too late, O Hope of Jacob, to repent. And thou knowest, Lord, that even now, after twenty-two years in which I have endeavoured to do thy work, that even now my repentance is incomplete, my soul foul and unwashed, mere filthiness, my Love, and desolation.'

Here there succeeded a long silence, and I peered out again into the room from behind the curtain. The Rector had let his head fall upon his arms and, though his lips were moving, he uttered no words that were audible. I looked to the right and saw his wife's head, with the night-cap on top of it, protruding from the other alcove. Her eyes were clouded in a kind of mistiness, though not from tears, and I thought that her face expressed sorrow and, mingled with it, something peaceful. She was gazing at the kneeling figure of her husband, but not as though she took a great interest in the sight. For myself, I was too shocked and alarmed by what I had heard to pay any minute attention to her. I had now no thought of leaving the room, no consciousness of the dishonest position in which we were both placed. I listened as the Rector began to speak again, more slowly and in a low voice.

'Even tonight,' he was saying, 'O God, my God, when I was speaking to that boy, even then I was unable to tell the truth. The reasons for my silence, Lord, were weighty, thou knowest; but in thy sight is not truth the weightiest thing? Might I not have told him?'

He paused, bowed his head, and then raised it as though about to speak again. My heart was beating quickly as I strained after the words that were never spoken. For, just as he had opened his mouth to speak, I saw his wife slip from the alcove where she had been hidden, steal quickly across the room and take her stand by the door close to the Rector's elbow. She stood there motionless, with her hand on the doorknob, so self-possessed in her manner that even I might have imagined that she had that instant entered the room from the corridor outside. The Rector turned to her with a start, and I saw him looking sternly at her. She spoke first and said: 'I am so sorry for disturbing you, but won't you come to bed now, dear?'

He remained kneeling, looking at her as though he had awakened from a dream. She carried on her face that calm and contented smile which I knew so well, and so they gazed at each other for some seconds, until there was heard the sound of stumbling feet and voices from outside the study windows. It seemed, to judge from the noise, that several men were gathering into a group. Feet stamped; there were whispers, gruff ejaculations, and then silence. We in the room still listened and suddenly a peal of hand bells sounded shrill and cold and loud at such a short distance.

The Rector's wife turned to her husband. 'It is the bellringers,' she said, 'who are doing this in honour of Roy's birthday. Someone told me that we might expect them.'

She still smiled as the Rector rose unsteadily to his feet. 'Go and see if he is in his room,' she said and, opening the door, she laid her hand on his shoulder as he went through it. Then she crossed the room to the curtain which concealed me. She smiled at me, with one hand patting my cheek, and said: 'When he returns I'll tell him that you have just come in through the kitchen window.'

The bells pealed out, often discordantly, and I guessed that the ringers must be mostly drunk. The Rector came back into the room. His face was slightly paler than usual, but his expression quite different from that which I had recently observed. Without waiting for any explanation he clapped me on the shoulder and said: 'Well, Roy, so you're back at last. Now just listen to those bells.'

We listened, and I have seldom heard our village players give a worse performance. Soon we drew back the curtains and opened the windows. A final jangling, and the bells were still. Outside I saw the big figure of George Birkett, the chief ringer. Behind him were the others, among them were Fred and Mac, red-faced and grinning, both swaying slowly on their feet. They and some of the others guffawed apologetically, while George touched his cap and said: 'Long life to Mr Roy, Your Reverence! And to you, too, and to your lady, Sir.'

We asked them into the hall and gave them beer and sandwiches. There was much laughter, I remember, and both the Rector and his wife played their parts well. Finally Mac had to leave the room hurriedly, and the others began to follow him. We all shook hands, and when they had gone the Rector's wife kissed me on the cheek, and then took her husband's arm.

'Quickly to bed everyone now,' she said. 'Remember that tomorrow we have the Agricultural Show.'

CHAPTER III

The Agricultural Show

IT WAS, oddly enough, the expressions I had seen on the face of the Rector's wife, her resource and self-confidence, that I thought of most when I had retired to bed, and during wakeful intervals of the night, and when I woke up in the morning. The fact that my guardian was a murderer neither shocked me much, nor, when I came to think of it, greatly surprised me. The crime had been done at least a year before I was born, at a time when the Rector was a young man, before he grew his beard. I could not imagine even his appearance at this time, and so could not connect with the man I knew the scene on the mountainside and its passion and deceit.

Yet I knew the Rector to be a man of strong feelings, in spite of the gentleness which he had always shown to me, and I saw that if he had sinned he had certainly suffered for it. I might feel horror for the crime, but I could feel no enmity against the criminal. Had I still believed the man to be my father, I might perhaps have felt differently. As it was I saw the situation as one in which I could not possibly be of help and in which I was myself not even remotely implicated. With the Rector's friend, Anthony, I had not, I reflected, anything whatever to do, and it was difficult either to pity or to condemn a person whom I had never seen and of whom previously I had not heard.

I was much more interested in the light which the confession had thrown on the relations between my two guardians, and it was a shock to me to realize that the Rector's wife, so docile in my experience, had ever been, even if ever so slightly, unfaithful to her husband. I began to see that, just as in the case of my assumed parentage, I had been taking things very much too much for granted. Instead of the orderly and easy system of relationships with which I had fancied myself to be surrounded, I began now to imagine crimes and secrecies on all sides, the results of forces to which previously I had given little or no attention. Were even the Squire and his sister, I began to wonder, all that they purported to be? And how much had the Rector's wife already known of the story to which both she and I had listened that night? To judge from the expression on her face when I had first seen her from behind the curtain she was not hearing anything either new or particularly horrifying; but I was wholly unable to account for what had seemed to me the look almost of satisfaction with which she was listening. And again and again my mind went back to the Rector's last words, before he had been interrupted; for these words seemed to indicate that at the dinner party he had not told me the truth, or had only told a part of the truth. Was there some even deeper mystery that surrounded my birth? Or were there clues to the mystery which he had deliberately withheld from me? And what reason could he have had for revealing something but not all? Was his consideration for his wife's honour or for his own? Or had he wished to spare me the knowledge of some degradation or disability?

So I thought and questioned myself vainly during the night, and the same thoughts and questions returned to me while I was shaving and dressing for breakfast on

43

the next day. Clearly I could ask no questions of my guardians when they were both together, but I determined that I would make, as tactfully as I could, further inquiries from each of them separately whenever an occasion presented itself.

I arrived somewhat late at the breakfast table and observed nothing remarkable in the bearing either of the Rector or of his wife. The Rector had finished his egg and was reading the morning paper. His wife, who as a rule ate little at this meal, was sitting with her hands folded in her lap. She did not turn her head as I entered the room, but smiled at me across the gleaming silver of the coffee pot and milk jug; then slowly extended one hand towards the cup which she would fill for me.

The Rector looked up from his newspaper. I noticed that this morning he was entirely himself; the pallor of the previous night had left his face, and his eyes were twinkling beneath his thick black eyebrows. So he would appear nearly always in the morning, fresh and energetic, though by the evening he would often be tired and dis-spirited, sitting for long periods, gazing into the fire, a pipe between his lips and an unopened book upon his knees. I understood him better now, and thought that every morning, perhaps, for more than twenty years he must have braced himself to carry through the day the consciousness of a crime. But, though I understood him better, I began to feel for the first time ill at ease in his company. This morning there was some embarrassment in my smile that answered his smile, and I began to wish that he would not speak to me.

He began speaking at once. 'Well, Roy,' he said,

'I'm afraid you had rather a distressing time of it last night.'

For a moment I thought that he was alluding to the scene in the study, and I stared at him blankly, determined not to give myself away or, if I was discovered, at least to put as good a face on the matter as I could. And I was suddenly shocked to find that my feelings towards my guardians were no longer frank and open as they had been; for now my first thought was to dissemble. The Rector went on speaking and I saw, with relief, that he was speaking not of his confession, but of the dinner party.

'Did you see your friend again?' he asked. 'He behaved abominably, I thought.'

'No,' I said, 'I didn't seem him again. I'm afraid I behaved pretty badly myself in not coming back again. I hope the others didn't mind. It was rather a surprise, you see.' I paused, and saw that the Rector was smiling at me. I rather disliked his smile, and was shocked to find it so. 'He suffers badly from nerves,' I added.

'Yes, yes,' said the Rector. 'No one is thinking of blaming you, my boy.'

He seemed embarrassed, I thought, and I was glad when his wife leaned towards me. 'Here is your coffee, Roy,' she said. 'Now let's talk about something else. Have you both forgotten the show?'

'No, no, my dear,' said the Rector. 'Most certainly not, my love. We shall enjoy ourselves no end.'

He looked at me as though expecting corroboration, but I was drinking my coffee and made no move. I was horrified with myself for so deliberately refusing to join in his gaiety. In a night my feelings towards him had

45

changed, and I asked myself whether this was due to the fact that he was not in reality my father or to the fact that he was a murderer.

There was a long pause and I thought of the Agricultural Show which was held every year in the meadows by the river about a mile away from our village. Last night at the pub there had been much talk of the show, of the likely winners in various classes and of the beer which could be drunk at any hour of the day, both at the canteens and, by those in the know, at the private bars at the back of the booths belonging to firms selling agricultural implements, poultry foods, dogs, rabbits, and other livestock. This year also the authorities of the aerodrome were giving an exhibition of stunt flying, and there would also be some demonstrations of the latest type of machine-guns. I wondered whether we would meet the Flight-Lieutenant and, if so, what account he would give of his behaviour on the previous night.

I thought, too, of the landlord's daughter who had promised to meet me that afternoon at twelve o'clock behind the big marquee in which the horticultural exhibits were shown. I thought of her long yellow hair which I had wound round the fingers of my hand; of her smooth throat that swelled out into an arch when she leant her head back, as she had done not long ago, sitting with me on a branch projecting over the swirling river, and I had kissed her mouth and eyes and ears over and over again, trembling, for it was my first experience of love, and still I could not think of her as of a person like myself, but rather as a sudden glow on water or something exquisite and airy and apt to move away, like a bird or a cloud's shadow sweeping across a wood. Thus there was fear and perturbation in my intense happiness. Every pleasure seemed unexpected, unlikely to be repeated, too good to be true. Yet the pleasure was real and now, at the breakfast table, when I thought of it even the disclosures of the previous night, my uncertainty, my changed attitude towards my guardians ceased to perplex me, so delicious and pervasive was my feeling of desire.

For days she had occupied the chief place in my thoughts and now it seemed strange to me to reflect that I had other things to think about, had indeed been thinking about them to the exclusion of all else since the dinner party. But now I could not pursue my inquiries, for from the time when breakfast was over until the time when we were due to start for the show I had no opportunity to speak in private either to the Rector or to his wife, and shortly after eleven o'clock we all three walked across the road to the Manor, for we had arranged to visit the show together with the Squire and his sister.

I began to feel somewhat ill at ease as we walked down the drive that was edged with neatly clipped cypresses, for I knew that my friends had every reason to be affronted by my behaviour of last night and yet, even now, I could not see how I could have acted differently. But the manners both of the Squire and of his sister very soon reassured me. They were waiting for us in the oak-panelled hall, the walls of which were hung with a variety of interesting objects—cutlasses, riding-whips, swords, guns, oars, cricket-bats, knobkerries, musical instruments, and miniature portraits. The Squire was sitting in a high-backed chair with a rug over his knees. He did not rise to greet us, for he was, so his sister informed us, indisposed, and would be unable to accompany us to the show. 'I wanted him to allow me to stay with him,' she said, 'but he won't hear of it.'

The Squire looked up at us with eyes that twinkled in his grey and sunken face. 'We old men,' he said 'mustn't be allowed to make ourselves a nuisance. Florence' (he turned to his sister) 'will be extremely happy in your company, if you are quite sure that you can make room for her in your car.'

'She will give us the greatest pleasure if she will come with us,' said the Rector. 'I am only sorry that you cannot come yourself,' and his wife added: 'Are you sure that there is nothing that we can do?'

'Nothing, thank you,' said the Squire, and his sister went upstairs to put on her coat and hat. While she was away the Squire tapped nervously with one finger on the arm of his chair, and seemed ill at ease now that the necessary courtesies had been exchanged. He was evidently relieved when his sister returned and waved to us as we went towards the door. 'I am afraid that my weak health always interferes with the pleasures of others,' he said. 'Please forgive me. I wish it could be avoided.'

The Rector's wife turned her head towards him and said brightly: 'You mustn't say things like that. You know how fond of you we all are,' and, as we left the hall, the Squire smiled at her as though he found her words incredible.

'In a way I hate to leave him,' said his sister, while we were walking up the drive, 'but he would never rest if he thought I were depriving myself of anything for his sake.'

'He is quite a saint,' the Rector said, but by now we had reached the end of the drive where we found our car which Joe, the gardener, had just brought round for us. Joe stood beside the car, his feet firmly placed apart and one hand raised in the air. He had recently taken the part of the Archangel Gabriel in a nativity play and still, on any ceremonial occasion, would adopt this stance which he had learnt to hold throughout the tableau of the Annunciation.

'A fine day, Joe,' said the Rector, and the Squire's sister inquired about his wife. To the statement and the question Joe replied appropriately, and then we all got into the car, with the Rector driving and myself sitting by his side.

We drove up the village street and, past the pub, turned to the right into the main road that ran alongside the aerodrome. As we passed one of the great gates flanked by high pylons from which flags were flying I heard the Squire's sister say: 'It seems difficult to imagine the village as it used to be, doesn't it?'

I had never been near the aerodrome in her company without hearing her make this remark, and was not surprised to hear from the Rector's wife the customary reply: 'Times certainly do change.'

I turned round in order to ask the ladies whether they would like the rug on which I was sitting, and observed on both their faces a look of wistfulness which I took to be a token of regret for the simpler days before the Air Force had established itself in this part of the country. But I did not ask them about the rug, for suddenly six or seven fighter aircraft swooped down on us from the clouds, deafening us with the roar of their engines. The ladies put their hands to their ears and opened their mouths. The Rector looked up apprehensively, for it seemed almost as though we were the object of a concerted attack, so near to us did the leading aircraft dive before it straightened out, followed by the others, and zoomed away from us over the extended airfield.

'Crazy monkeys!' said the Rector. 'One of these days they'll come to some harm.'

'There ought to be some sort of regulations,' the Squire's sister said, as I turned round again with the rug and noticed that the Rector's wife was staring after the vanishing planes with a look of something very like pride or pleasure in her eyes.

She caught my eye and smiled at me. I said: 'I wouldn't mind flying one of those things,' and as I said this she looked gravely at me and made an interrupted gesture with her hand.

The Rector had heard my remark and, slightly turning his head, shouted: 'We'll find something better for you to do than that, eh, Roy!'

He was alluding to what he regarded as my excellent chance of obtaining a high place in the examination for the Civil Service and, knowing his solicitude for me, I was again shocked with myself for finding something repellent in the jocosity of his voice. For half a second a rude reply was on the tip of my tongue. I repressed it, with something like horror, and then for a few moments began actually to envisage the possibility of my becoming associated in some capacity with the aerodrome, although I knew that the lives and manners of its inmates were quite unlike those which were regarded as estimable by my guardians and my friends.

So we sat silent until we turned again to the right and drove slowly downhill to the large meadow in which the Agricultural Show was held, and soon we saw over the tops of hedges the white sloping roofs of marquees, the flags flying, poles and pieces of machinery extending upwards into the air. We could hear the music that accompanied the roundabouts, the sound of shots from the shooting alleys, the shouts of men and the lowing of cattle. We parked the car and walked slowly to the turnstiles that had been installed at the entrance to the meadow. Around it was already collected a crowd of farmers and labourers with some county gentry. Fred was there, together with some other of my friends from our village. Some of them winked at me and pointed over their shoulders towards the beer tent, indicating that they would see me there later on; for they did not care to join me now that I was in the company of gentlefolk.

The Rector paid our entrance money, after some protests by the Squire's sister, and we began to walk over the marshy ground on a path constructed of planks. At each side of us was an impressive display of agricultural and horticultural implements. Some of the best known firms in the county had sent specimens of their latest mechanical devices, and around each huge toothed engine was gathered a small crowd of men estimating the merits of the new invention. A number of women were queued up outside a tent in which a butter-making competition was shortly to be held. Others surrounded a cow which was being milked mechanically. And between the larger tents were small booths, where rabbits, ferrets, and ducks were being sold; also some local products such as ash walking-sticks, rustic seats, wicker-work, and dog leashes of plaited reeds.

At the top of the meadow towards which this main avenue led were the ring and stands for the riding and jumping competitions which were now due to begin; and near here, too, were the long tents covered in with hessian canvas where bulls, sheep, and goats awaited the judges. At the suggestion of the Squire's sister, we approached one of these tents, for she was anxious to see her brother's prize bull, Slazenger, which was being shown once again this year.

We went in single file through the canvas curtain and along the narrow passage-way past the stalls where the great animals were tethered. There was a hot smell of straw, dung, and animal flesh, and we patted the moist flanks of the recumbent beasts as we went along the tent. The Squire's sister knew the names and the owners of many of the animals which were on show, and she was, I remember, pointing out to me a par-ticularly fine creature, beige-coloured, lying on his massive side and breathing heavily into the straw, when we heard an exclamation from in front of us, and turning in the direction from which the sound came, saw the Flight-Lieutenant coming towards us with out-stretched hand.

He was dressed in uniform and was smiling broadly as he approached us. On his handsome face was no sign of embarrassment, indeed this feeling was confined to our own party, who had perhaps secretly determined to take no notice of him, should they meet him again. But in the confined space in which we found ourselves it was impossible to pretend not to see a person who was blocking the whole passageway and who was also, it seemed, resolved to speak first. And any overt discourtesy might well have led to an altercation. So the ladies smiled in a distant manner, and the Rector, though he showed no pleasure at the sight of the young man, nevertheless appeared willing to listen to what he had to say.

The Flight-Lieutenant greeted us breezily. 'I was hoping I'd run up against you folks,' he said, 'because I'm afraid I rather broke up the party last night.' He paused and looked inquiringly from face to face. 'Oh yes, I did,' he continued, although no one had shown any disposition to contradict him. 'It was rather a bad show, in a way.'

The Rector cleared his throat as though he were about to speak, but before he could begin the Flight-Lieutenant stepped forward, forcing the Squire's sister almost against the nose of the bull which she had previously been inspecting, and gripped him by the arm. 'To tell the truth, Padre,' he said, 'I was a bit tight.' The Rector did not appear much mollified, so he continued: 'Oh come on, sir, you know what that's like, I bet. You were young once I dare say.'

He smiled confidently while the Squire's sister remarked: 'Excuse me, but you are pushing me against the bull.'

'Oh am I?' said the Flight-Lieutenant. 'Not really? Oh, I say!' And he stepped back, surveying us quizzically as though he had just acted in some particularly generous manner towards us all.

'Well, now that that's settled . . .' he began, but the

Rector interrupted him by saying: 'Some day I should like to have a word with you.'

'Yes,' said the Squire's sister firmly, as though the same idea had occurred to her independently as a good one; and the Flight-Lieutenant replied: 'Of course. Any time. I should be delighted. But now you must come and see this walloping great bull.' He seized the hand of the Rector's wife and dragged her after him along the tent, while the Rector and the Squire's sister followed as though perforce, and I came behind them.

We halted at the end of the tent where the Flight-Lieutenant stood gazing at Slazenger, the Squire's prize bull, who was standing up with his back to us, tossing his huge head from side to side, for he seemed restive and was tethered by a greater length of rope than most of the other animals in the tent. I remember how the muscles rippled over his black shoulders and flowed along his neck when he turned to us his dignified and stupid head surmounted by wide extended horns. He rolled his eyes and shook the ring and rope at the end of his nose.

'Good boy, Slazenger! Quiet boy! Good!' said the Squire's sister.

'It wouldn't be a bad idea,' said the Flight-Lieutenant, 'to let that fellow loose.'

The Squire's sister laughed nervously, and the Rector coughed. His wife, as though the remark had been an idle one, said meditatively: 'Yes, I do so love seeing him when he is really at liberty.'

I attempted to move forward from behind the others, so as to be in a position to restrain the Flight-Lieutenant from any hasty action which he might contemplate;

but I was too late for, almost before the Rector's wife had finished speaking, the expression on his face had changed. He smiled broadly and bowed to her. 'I act under instructions,' he said, and at once sprang on to the bull's back.

Slazenger stood quite still for a moment, and then it seemed that the whole of his body was quivering. He flung his head round towards the Flight-Lieutenant's knees and bellowed. The sound seemed one of pain. Meanwhile the Flight-Lieutenant had taken a knife from his pocket and was hacking away the canvas wall of the tent. Then he leant down, in great danger, I thought, from the bull's horns, and cut the rope by which the animal was fastened. He stood up on Slazenger's back and jumped over his head through the canvas wall into the open. Here he struck an attitude which was no doubt intended to resemble the pose of a Spanish matador; then, for the bull had lowered his head and was pawing the ground, turned and began to run away. The huge animal, breathing heavily, lumbered after him through the hole in the wall and seemed to have left an unreasonable gap in front of our eyes, as though he had been done away by magic.

We heard shouts and screams from outside, and hurried through the tent to a scene of the utmost confusion. Men, women, and children were falling over each other in their eagerness to be out of danger. The sheep on show in an adjoining tent suddenly lifted up their voices together in a sharp and humming mist of sound like a chorus of monstrous gnats. Two men, who had mounted their horses in readiness for the jumping competition, now found it impossible to control their mounts, who began to gallop madly down the main avenue of the show, where one of the horses slipped on the planks and threw his rider into the tent where the mechanical milking was in process. We could see nothing of either Slazenger or the Flight-Lieutenant, and so stood for some moments silent in the shouting and excited crowd.

CHAPTER IV

The Accident

NOT THAT THE incident was of any great importance. Neither the Flight-Lieutenant nor Slazenger, the bull, were injured. The rider who was hurled against the mechanically milked cow, a few children, a bookmaker, and an old woman sustained cuts and bruises, none of them of a serious character. The Flight-Lieutenant's action was only one of many actions performed by him or other members of the aerodrome staff in direct contravention of the rules that governed the life of villagers. Some indignation was expressed, but it was well known that the offender would not be brought to trial in any magistrate's court, and, since the bull was soon recaptured and no great damage done, before very long people began to laugh rather than grumble at what had happened.

But the incident for my story is not without significance. It shows that on this particular day the Flight-Lieutenant's habit of mind was perhaps even more than usually irresponsible, so that to the reader the far more serious event which followed may seem not natural nor inevitable, but not wholly unexpected. Also to my mind this cavalier treatment of a prize bull by a member of our powerful Air Force appears, in the light of what followed, almost as a text or symbol.

Certainly the effect of the incident on our party was most unfortunate, and had we met the Flight-Lieutenant again after his escapade there is no doubt that a serious quarrel would have ensued. The Squire's sister was, until the recapture of the bull, so upset that there was talk of going home immediately. The Rector proposed a scheme by which a letter signed by the most important of local residents should be dispatched to the Air Ministry; and his wife, a perplexed and harassed look upon her face, suggested a good talk and some rest in a tent near by where coffee and tea were being served.

Thither we went through the bustling or dawdling crowd, and when my friends were settled at their table I excused myself, saying that I wished to see the jumping and would meet them either in the ring or in this very place in two hours' time. They did not attempt to delay me, and I fancied that in their desire to discuss the conduct of the Flight-Lieutenant they might in any case have been embarrassed by my company. So I hurried off to the stall of our local seller of chicken food; for I knew that at the back of his stall there was a bar where I would find some of the men from our village, as I had still some time to wait before I was to meet the landlord's daughter.

Mr Crosby, the seller of poultry food, winked at me as I approached him. 'Hear your young friend's been stirring things up again,' he said. He looked at me with a doubtful and cunning expression in his small black eyes, and I felt a sudden flow of affection for the little man with his long drooping moustache, thin hands, and bowler hat tilted to the back of his head. I had no wish then to see the Flight-Lieutenant again, and thought with distaste of the aerodrome, its easy and inconsiderate manners.

'Mac here?' I said.

'Oh, yes,' Mr Crosby replied. 'They're all inside.

Can't you hear them singing? They're rare lads from your place. For the beer that is. So long as it does them good.'

I listened and heard a confused droning sound from behind the stall. 'Go right through,' said Mr Crosby, and following his invitation I went past him, lifted up a canvas curtain and entered the small and crowded bar. At the very entrance I stumbled against Fred who had, apparently, fallen to the ground. Mac was bending over him and as I came in looked up to me with his flushed face.

'God set fire!' he said. 'Look what's blown in! Thought you'd given up the beer after last night!'

'When I can't hold a dart straight,' I said, 'then sometimes you can give me a game.'

Mac bellowed with laughter at this, and Fred, struggling to his feet, said: 'Hare and dog; hare and dog!'

People began to say 'Sh!' and, looking across to the other side of the tent, we saw an old man with white hair, a retired grocer, who had risen from one of the benches and was swaying from side to side as he supported himself with his stick. His face was, through long drinking, as red as the wattles of a turkey-cock, and the extreme gravity and fixedness of his expression contrasted strangely with the swaying motion of his swollen body as he stood. When there was something like silence he removed his hat and, holding it in front of him, attempted a slow and dignified bow; but in so doing he had shifted from the centre of his gravity and fell to his knees. There was some laughter at this, but the old man, while two of his friends picked him up, preserved on his face the same expression of unbroken gravity that he had held throughout. A man whom I did not know whispered to me: 'Harry used to be good when he was young.'

The old grocer took a step forward and struck his stick upon the ground. An immensely strong and clear voice issued from his massive red jowl. 'Mother!' he shouted, and extending his hands, one of which still held the walking stick, he peered inquiringly and challengingly round the tent. 'Mother! Mother! Where is your baby boy?'

There was a long pause while the grocer, though still swaying slightly on his heels, held with set jaw his appealing posture. One man in the audience sniggered, but the others turned roughly to him while the grocer fixed him with his eye. Finally he dropped the walking-stick, and after a gesture of dismissal to a man who had offered to pick it up for him, he clasped his hands beneath his chin and, turning up his eyes so that only the bloodshot whites of them were visible, continued in a low and crooning voice: 'Mother, you held me on your knee. Mother, you worked for me. Mother, you taught me to toddle. Mother, you fed me at your dear old breast.'

His voice died away to a whisper and in the ensuing silence I looked round the tent at the dim, grave faces of the listeners. In some eyes there were tears already; others gazed abstractedly at or past the pipes or cigarettes which had been taken from their lips. But the eyes brightened as the grocer began to speak again, this time in a cracked but ringing voice signifying repentance and desperation.

'Where am I now, mother of mine? Where is the dandy suit I bought with the savings from the work of your old hands? Where are the cabs and horses that I would have?

Where is the book you gave me? Where is the little locket? Where is my honour? Where? Oh mother, I see you in your poor little cottage, poking the fire, thinking, ah, thinking of your wandering son. I thank God you cannot see him. Among the burning globes, in the din and degradation, mother, of a gin hell he is to be beheld. A gaol-bird, mother, a broken reed: and the woman at his side is not his wedded wife.'

The grocer's voice dropped for a moment; then flinging out his arms, he began to roar out the concluding passage of his recitation, although sobs at times interrupted his delivery.

'A monster of vice, mother, but with the soft heart of a little boy, he thinks of the cradle that night after night you rocked. Yes, he has lost his honour and his savings. Yes, he is soaked in alcohol's pernicious fumes. He has scoffed at religion. He brags and fights. But in spite of it all there is one clean spot in him, one corner of that rotten heart which the Devil cannot enter. Is it love, mother? Is it love? Love for the old place, for the days that are lost? That is what it is, I think. Don't you?'

With these words the grocer fell to the ground and I saw the tears pouring down his thick red face. Some of his friends assisted him to his feet; there was general applause, and several of the audience bought him half-pints of beer which were laid in a row along the bench where he was sitting. The old man drank two or three of the half-pints rapidly and then, pleased with the success of his performance, volunteered a comic song. But by this time no one was in a mood for listening and, though the grocer sang a few notes, shuffling his feet heavily upon the ground, while one or two of his immediate friends said: 'Listen to the old chap. This is a good one,' nearly all the men in the bar had turned their backs and become interested in other occupations.

In one corner of the tent a crowd of people was congregated around a man whom I had seen before, a rat-catcher who, I knew, always carried about with him in a small bag an old rat whose fangs had been drawn and with which he would, if a sufficient number of pints were offered, engage in fight. He would kneel down on the ground, his hands clasped behind his back, with the rat in front of him, and would slowly, while gnashing his teeth, force the animal into a corner. Then, after a great show of ferocity, he would seize the rat in his jaws, worry it like a dog, and finally rise to his feet, bow to the audience and replace the rat in the bag which, as a rule, he carried in his hand. This time, however, he was giving a different performance. Evidently he had been out rat-catching that day and, when I first noticed him, he had just taken a young live rat from his pocket and was holding it out, gripped in his fist, in front of him. He was a large red-faced man, with a pink and white skin, very smooth, so that one wondered whether he ever shaved. 'Half a pint, is it?' he was saying, and looked round him confidently as an auctioneer might look.

'Half a pint it is,' said one of the onlookers, and the rat-catcher immediately put his hand to his mouth, wrinkled back his lips, and with his long white teeth bit off the rat's head. A chorus of laughter and chuckling greeted this exploit, which the rat-catcher repeated twice more and then passed up his glass tankard to be filled.

But at the wooden counter behind which the drinks were served a quarrel seemed upon the point of breaking out. Two men were standing close together, their faces thrust forward, staring into each other's eyes. One was George Birkett, our chief bellringer. His big face was flushed with drink, but not a muscle upon it quivered as he stared before him. His jaw was thrust out, his eyes narrowed, and by his side I could see his fist clenched. Scarcely moving his lips, he pronounced the words 'Say that again, you bastard,' and people in the immediate vicinity stopped talking to look in an interested but somewhat embarrassed manner towards the scene of the dispute. The man facing George was a small man whom I had not seen before. Someone whispered that he was attached to the ground staff at the aerodrome. He was black-haired, pale-faced, and some dark stubble was clinging to his chin, although the sides of his face were cleanly shaved. He, too, had thrust his head forward, and was staring contemptuously at George, with a cigarette dangling from the corner of his mouth. 'All right,' he said slowly, 'I will say it again.'

I saw the muscles on George's arm tighten, but the little man, as he was speaking his last words, had dashed his glass tankard against the top of the counter; then, holding the broken mug by the bottom he had thrust the jagged glass into George's face. At once he ducked down and ran for the door which he reached before anyone had thought of stopping him. George wiped the back of his hand across his eyes. His face was running with blood, and he plunged forward with something in his demeanour that reminded me of Slazenger, the prize bull, at the moment when the Flight-Lieutenant had jumped upon his back.

Mac, who was standing near me, shouted: 'Stop him!'

63

and flung his arms round George's waist. I and one or two others joined in, but it was a difficult matter to keep George under restraint and finally to persuade him to sit down again and let his face be washed.

'We'll get that little swine,' we all said. 'Have a drink, George?' But it was some time before anything like quiet had been restored to the bar and, before this happened, Mr Crosby had entered from his shop and had threatened to call in the police. Mac talked more than anybody and seemed, in the course of this incident, to have won for himself a position of authority and general confidence when, just as he was opening his mouth to express some new view on the affair, he was, whether as a result of his exertions or of the quantity of beer which he had drunk, suddenly sick. A space was cleared round him, and two people held him by the shoulders. Then he was escorted to one of the benches at the side of the tent, where he sat down next to the retired grocer, holding his head in his hands. Mr Crosby's boy cleared up the mess.

I played a couple of games of darts and then, for it was time for me to meet the landlord's daughter, I left the tent and wandered through the increasing crowd towards the horticultural exhibition. I saw Bess when I was still a hundred yards from the big marquee, but did not hurry towards her, or only hurried for a few paces, and then would loiter. Though I knew that what I saw was she, still I hesitated and looked more closely, for to my eyes she seemed to throw off a kind of radiance, blurring the image; every time I saw her she appeared different, so that I could never convince myself that I was sure of recognizing her. There was something piercing and fragile in any picture that my mind's eye might form of her, for to me she was another world, as remote or more so than the aerodrome itself, though I had already kissed her on several occasions and fancied that she was by no means indifferent to me. So I lingered and looked at the figure that was waiting for me as though it were some bright ghost.

Not that there was anything fragile or ghostly in Bess's appearance. She was a well-made girl, slim certainly, but not weak. She would laugh and joke with the men in the bar, showing no embarrassment at what might be said, except for that embarrassment which is conventionally affected. Yet, at other times, and particularly when we were alone, she would adopt a different manner. Her head would be drooping, her eyes slide away from mine, or, when our eyes met, there would be a mistiness in her gaze, a withdrawal into some other world that attracted me, but attracted me to something other than herself. So that seeing her afterwards in the company of others she would appear to me for a moment as a stranger, and then in a moment or two it would be that other vision of her that would be strange to me. With uncertainty, then, as to what I should see when I saw her, I now loitered and from some distance admired the light green dress she was wearing and her yellow hair swinging about her neck.

She saw me and waved her hand. The gesture was both timid and inviting. Her face appeared flat to me, delicate as I knew her features to be, so that it was something tall and swaying that I saw, green growing out of the ground, then white, and then gold flowing into the air. I felt my heart beating quickly and a contraction of the muscles in my stomach. I smiled like a dog smiles and said: 'I hope I'm not late.'

She ran a few steps towards me and touched with her fingers the cuff of my jacket. 'No, no,' she said, 'it's me that's early.' Her face seemed to me as soft as petals, with the widely set and somewhat narrow eyes liquid and swimming and drowning me. I held her wrist gently and bent forward to kiss her, but she turned her head aside, looking suddenly like a small child, and said: 'Oh no, really. Look at all the people.' Then we both smiled. I was feeling slightly sick, and we began to walk together among the tents and booths. I felt that, as we walked, people turned their heads to look at us, although in point of fact this was not the case; my feeling of sickness passed and I was suffused with a sense of pride, but not of confidence.

By a coconut-shy Bess clapped her hands and jumped, tugging at my elbow. 'Oh let's have a throw!' she cried, and I paid sixpence for her and then watched her as with a kind of gracious clumsiness she attempted to aim at the coconuts. Even had she hit one, there was so little force behind her arm that she would not, I think, have dislodged it from its pedestal; but she threw so in-accurately that the wooden balls either hit the ground a few feet in front of her or else sailed far above the row of coconuts into the hands of a boy who was waiting at the back of the tent to collect them. 'Oh I did so want one,' she said, looking at me with an expression in which there was some real as well as some assumed dejection.

'It's easy,' I said, knowing that I was good at this kind of activity. I paid my money and had soon dislodged four coconuts, being so absorbed in this pursuit that I hardly noticed Bess's screams of delight as the brown hairy things toppled over or spun sideways across the tent.

'Would you like any more?' I said, when I had exhausted my ammunition and the stall-keeper had piled up the four prizes in front of me, congratulating me at the same time upon my marksmanship.

'Oh no, that's plenty,' Bess said. 'Besides we can't carry any more.' And they were, indeed, I found, somewhat difficult to carry.

We began to walk farther through the crowds. 'I think you're wonderful,' Bess said, and squeezed my arm. I, too, began to think that I had accomplished something remarkable, but as I looked down at her shoulder and her arm beside me I again began to feel sick and my knees trembled. I pressed the coconuts hard against my side, extending my fingers so as to cover as much as possible of their surfaces.

A voice on our left hailed me and, turning my head, I saw the Flight-Lieutenant bending over a machine-gun in a small tent from which the Aerodrome colours were flying. He was informing a considerable crowd of bystanders of the mechanism and working of the gun, but had broken off his lecture, and shouted to me: 'Be good, Roy! The bull's O.K.'

Bess smiled at him, and I nodded my head. Then we went out through the turnstile at the bottom of the field and, passing through the car park, entered another field in the corner of which were the remains of a haystack and, close to this, an old roofless mill with the river running smoothly past its grey stones. We sat down in the loose hay and looked towards the river and the meadows on the other side. Far away on the sunny grass

I saw a hare sitting up on his hind legs. From some trees behind us came the continual calling of rooks. The show, the tents, and the crowd seemed to have been removed from us much farther than we had come and, as I looked at Bess, we seemed like castaways, not knowing what to expect. Her eyes held that soft, serious, remote, and unnatural look which I had come to know, and, as I stared into her eyes, the river, the meadow, the hare, and the rooks seemed to recede from us as the whole Agricultural Show had already receded. There was nothing now but the small space between us, and as I leaned towards her, stumbling over some foolish words, she also leaned to me, saying: 'I love you, I love you,' and as we pressed against each other in each other's arms I was stiff and blinded for some moments by my desire.

Soon that wave of feeling receded and we lay more quietly, but soon it returned again, and we began fumbling with our clothes, reaching in an inexpert way for the satisfaction with which neither of us was perfectly acquainted. There were difficulties and dangers of which we had heard, expostulations and timidity. And there was something loose and scrambling in our love-making, nor was anything conspicuously beautiful or satisfactory achieved. Yet something had been done and, as I looked at Bess's flushed face, a new feeling of trust and of gratitude swelled up in my heart. 'I shall always love you,' I said, and was surprised to see her face not changed, but much more ordinary than it had been before. She rose to her feet, shaking the hay out of her hair. 'We must go back,' she said, and I saw that she was thinking already of the coconut shies, the roundabouts, the riding, and the jumping.

I tried to find words to express my sense of the reality of what had happened and of my love, but I saw that, as I was speaking, Bess was giving me only half of her attention, and I began to feel that, in spite of what I was impelled to say, nothing very remarkable had taken place. This feeling increased both my tenderness and my desire. Bess was setting her clothes to rights, but I clutched her to me and pressed my mouth into her mouth, holding her tightly and cruelly, since she was wriggling in my arms. I saw her eyes, filled with fear, look into my eyes, and I felt, together with a wave of tenderness, a sharp pang of exasperation and almost of contempt for her. My grip on her relaxed and I stood dejected, with tears, I remember, beginning to brim over my eyelids.

Just at this moment I heard someone call my name. We stepped apart from each other and saw the Flight-Lieutenant running towards us across the field. I seemed to detect what surprised me, a certain embarrassment in his manner, and he had ceased to run before he reached us. He spoke hesitatingly and said: 'I say, Roy, something rather rotten has happened. I'm afraid I've potted your old man.'

I knew immediately from these words, inadequate as they were, that the Rector had been either killed or seriously wounded in some accident for which the Flight-Lieutenant had been responsible. I listened as he continued: 'Of course, it was quite unintentional, but I can't help feeling a bit cut up about it.'

Bess was trembling as she stared from one to the other of us. She began to brush the hay off her dress and, as we walked away, the Flight-Lieutenant told us that he had accidentally used live instead of blank ammunition in the machine-gun whose performance he had been demonstrating. 'The old boy took it right in the face,' he said, 'and went over like a ninepin.' He smiled as he recalled the scene to his memory, then added, in a more serious voice: 'It was a really bad show.'

I could think of nothing but of the appearance of my guardian's face that morning at breakfast. Still the story that I had heard seemed unreal to me, but as we went through the turnstile I could see a large crowd around the tent where the machine-gun demonstration had been given. People made way for us as we approached and, without noticing whether the others were following, I went through the crowd to a space in the centre, where I saw the Rector's wife, the Squire's sister, and an officer from the Aerodrome standing above a body prostrate on the ground. A national flag had been thrown over the face and the upper part of the body, but I could easily recognize the watchchain, the trousers, and the boots of my guardian. I fell down on my knees, with the idea of removing the cloth from his face, but a Pilot Officer held me by the shoulders and pulled me to my feet. 'Steady, steady, old man,' he said. The Rector's wife put her arms round me, and I held her tight, fancying that it was Bess whom I was holding. I kissed her on the ear and then looked up and round at the circle of silent respectful faces that surrounded us. The Pilot Officer began talking to me. He gave further details of the accident and made suggestions as to the transport of the body.

CHAPTER V

The Squire

IN OUR HOUSE, as I should say in many others, death had not been in the past a frequent topic of conversation; but now, with a dead body in an upper room lying beneath a sheet, both the presence and the certainty of death were never, during the days that preceded the funeral, far from our minds. It was not only when at meals our eyes strayed to the Rector's chair and the polished surface of the table where in the past knives, spoons, and forks had been set; or when, passing through the hall, one observed walking-sticks with the handles worn smooth by the grip of a hand whose muscles had stiffened for the last time; indeed these accidental and sudden reminders were hardly necessary. Everywhere in the house, it seemed to me, could be felt the influence and the presence of the one cold upstairs room in which the Rector's remains lay extended on a bed. Nor did it seem to anyone that there was anything either noble or sanctified about that presence and that influence.

It would have been better, perhaps, if the Rector's features had been left intact. Some effect of dignity or of the statuesque might then have been achieved. As it was it was only the pulp of a man that lay under the white sheet, unrecognizable except to those who possessed special knowledge. And the presence in the house of this shattered body produced in us, I think, feelings rather of horror than of affection. We knew, of course, that any corpse, however dignified, would not remain for long a lovely sight; and yet we would have wished to be able to look once more and for a short time at features that would have seemed familiar to us, however unfamiliar, in real fact, their lifelessness would have been. But what we had was nothing beautiful; more a trophy of an abstract power than a reminder of the living.

So, though I now felt as much affection for the dead man as I had ever felt, I avoided the room where he lay. His wife and the Squire's sister would sometimes sing hymns there, but neither the Squire nor I joined them in these activities. The Squire, indeed, had never been inside the room at all. He had stood in the doorway, but when invited to enter had tapped with his stick upon the floor and, with a severe expression on his face, had appeared not to hear the invitation. He, I think, whether because of his intimacy with the dead man or because of his advancing years, had been more than any of us affected by the Rector's death. Now he would often begin, in a respectful voice, to tell stories of the Rector's schooldays; but frequently he broke off these stories in the middle or allowed them to ramble to an inconclusive end, pretending a lapse of memory, although it was clear that his mind moved far more easily among the events of his boyhood than in the present, and we all knew that it was strong emotion rather than forgetfulness that caused him on these occasions to stumble over his words.

I saw much of him in the days before the funeral, and I usually saw him alone, for his sister was, from early in the morning until late at night, in the company of the Rector's wife; the intimacy between the two ladies was so great that I could not but feel myself something of an intruder in their company. Moreover, at this time the

Rector's wife, though her manner was as affectionate as ever, seemed sometimes, I thought, anxious to avoid me. She was, I fancied, embarrassed by the fact that I shared with her the knowledge of her own infidelity and of the Rector's crime; and she may have feared, too, that I would seize the first opportunity to try to extract from her further information, if she possessed it, about my own birth.

This, indeed, I was determined some time to do; but I had decided to wait until after the funeral, although I had hoped, perhaps, that she might herself voluntarily have chosen to enlighten me. Her reluctance to speak on any subject even remotely connected with the confession which we had both heard in the study was, I thought, the result of what was evidently a sincere affection for the dead man. And, as for the story of my own birth, it was very likely that she knew nothing about it. It would have seemed indecent, when I remembered the body on the bed upstairs and its pervasive influence, to have pressed her at this time with questions which she might have no wish to answer. Had the Rector been not only her husband but my father, we might perhaps have more demonstratively shared the grief which we both felt. As it was, her main consolation came from the Squire's sister and I was, not by any means against my will, left very much to my own devices. Between them the two ladies made the necessary arrangements with the undertaker, and left me little or nothing to do, so that I spent much of my time at the Manor.

I was on the point of going there, I remember, on the day before the funeral, and had risen from the breakfast-table and said good-bye to the Rector's wife when the

Squire's sister entered the dining-room, carrying with her our letters which she had taken in the road outside from the postman. I noticed that there seemed to be a certain nervousness in her manner as she handed across the table a large envelope marked with the official stamp of the Air Ministry. The Rector's wife held the envelope out in front of her, as though deliberating whether or not she should open it, and looked inquiringly at the Squire's sister before she laid it face downwards on the table and slit the top of it with a paper-knife. The Squire's sister and I watched as though some conjuring trick were being performed. Indeed, it struck me at the time that the interest which we were showing was excessive.

The Rector's wife read and, as she read, I thought that her face showed an almost unnatural absence of expression. Then, with a smile, she passed the letter across the table to us and we read it together. It was a notice from the Ministry signed by the Air Vice-Marshal. Regret for the accident which had taken place was expressed in conventional terms. Finally it was suggested that, as a mark of respect for the dead man, the Vice-Marshal should himself attend the funeral. He would welcome, it was added, an opportunity to say a few words at some point during or after the funeral service.

Such were the contents of the letter and I, when I had heard them, felt at first nothing but distaste. No consideration had in the past ever, so far as I was aware, been shown by the Air Force either to our village or to ourselves. So what reason was there for gratification in this belated token of respect, these conventional amends for a disaster which had been caused in part by the general irresponsibility of the airmen towards anything

74

which was outside their own organization? So I thought, but it was evident that the two ladies thought differently. The Squire's sister received the news blushingly, as though some particular compliment had been paid to herself, and the Rector's wife, though her face was graver, was still, I could see, remarkably pleased with the letter which she watched meditatively with her eyes as her friend held it in her hand.

'We could offer the Air Vice-Marshal a room at the Manor,' said the Squire's sister. 'That is, if he wants to stay the night.' I thought that her face looked unnaturally, even pathetically, thin as she looked inquiringly at the Rector's wife who was now staring at the edge of the table with a slight frown on her face. She raised her eyes to me and smiled. 'What do you think, Roy?' she asked. 'Would it not be better if he stayed here?' And there was a kind of urgency in her question which surprised me.

'I really don't mind at all,' I said. 'Is it so important anyway? Probably he won't want to stay the night.'

Both ladies, I thought, seemed disappointed with my reply. There was a short pause, and then the Squire's sister, looking sharply at me, said: 'But the point is that we should decide what to do if he does want to stay.'

I said that it was better for them to decide the point between them, and that I was quite ready to fall in with any arrangement which they might care to make. Then I left the room and began to walk towards the Manor. As I went I thought with bitterness of the many humiliations and inconveniences which we in the village had already had to suffer from this Air Force whose belated expression of regret seemed so to please my two friends. There had been a time, I knew, when the authority of squire and parson in the village had been absolute, and had been wisely and tenderly exercised. That was before now; for now, although legally the position was just as it had always been, the very presence of the aerodrome on the hill, the very sound and sight of the machines crossing and recrossing our valley, seemed somehow to have dissipated the cohesion of our village and to have set up a standing threat to our régime.

The threat was even then nearer and more definite than I fancied. This I discovered very soon after I had entered the Manor, and had seen the Squire pacing up and down the hall, his hands clasped behind his back, and a look of intense concentration on his face. In front of him was standing at attention a man dressed in Air Force uniform. He was a small man, with red hair and moustache, and he was smiling as he watched the Squire who continued to turn back and forwards the length of the hearthrug as though he were confined in some invisible cage. Soon he looked towards me, and I offered to leave the room, but he raised his hand, stopping me.

'No, stay where you are, Roy,' he said. 'My business with this gentleman is just over.'

'I shall call again on you in a couple of days, then?' said the airman. He spoke, I thought, as though he were delivering an ultimatum and was enjoying his task.

The Squire looked at him sharply from beneath his thick white eyebrows. 'I can settle nothing before then,' he said.

The airman's eyes were going over the room. He seemed half amused by the wealth of mural decoration, and, without looking at the Squire, he said: 'It's a great pity, of course, but there it is.'

To this the Squire made no reply, but moved slowly in the direction of the door. The airman thrust one hand into a pocket, nodded towards me, and picked up his cap from the hall table. 'I'll be seeing you, then,' he said, and walked past the Squire without shaking hands. The old man just inclined his head and, after he had opened the hall door and closed it behind his visitor, turned back into the room towards me.

I had expected to see him smile and rub his hands together, and to hear him say, 'Well, now, my boy, what about a walk?' but he said nothing, and seemed to look right through me as though I were a ghost. I turned away from him and, looking through the window, saw the airman walking up the drive with short steps. He was swinging his cap by his side, and was constantly turning his head to look at the lawns, the cedar tree, the flower beds. Halfway up the drive he stopped to say a few words to the gardener who was standing beside a wheel-barrow.

I stepped away from the window and saw the Squire standing as he had been standing before. But my movement had caught his attention. He began to smile and took a few steps towards the high-backed chair by the fireplace, where he sat down.

'I'm sorry to have disturbed you,' I said. 'I hope you haven't had any bad news.'

He looked up at me sharply and said: 'Yes, my boy, I've had some very bad news.'

For some moments we remained silent. He was staring down between his knees at the carpet and I noticed his long eyebrows twitching as he concentrated his gaze. Then he began to speak very quietly, and without raising his head. 'The fact is,' he said, 'that the Government want my land.'

I spoke sympathetically, for I knew how he loved all the country that I loved. 'It's the fields up by the aerodrome, I suppose,' I said, and then, seeing that I had guessed wrongly, I added: 'Surely they can't want the land by the river.'

The Squire looked up at me quickly, and I saw his eyes flash. 'Lock, stock, and barrel,' he said. 'They want it all!'

I looked round the room, so familiar to me, and through the window at well-known trees. I was frightened by what I had heard and also by the look on the Squire's face. Pride stiffened and regulated his features, but for an instant I had fancied that I was looking at something dead.

'How can they do that?' I said. 'What possible reason could there be?'

He looked at me and, seeing my agitation, seemed about to smile. There was, I knew, an almost childlike modesty and kindness in his face; but now these qualities were frustrated and he spoke harshly and as though defeated. 'It seems,' he said, 'that some lawyer fellows have got some sort of a law passed. They are within their rights, they say; though I must say that it seems to me a queer sort of right if men are to be deprived of their land. It's quite well known that the Government understand nothing of these things. Things for some time have been going from bad to worse. Of course, we must obey the law.'

I saw that indeed he could do nothing else. There was something pathetic and out of place in the dignity of his remarks. He continued. 'It isn't simply a question of my land and my house. The Air Force want to occupy the whole village. The school, I understand, will be done away with and replaced by some sort of training establishment. What will happen to the church I hardly like to think. You know these fellows have hardly any regard for religion.'

He looked up at me again, and there was more of bewilderment than anything else in his face. I, too, was bewildered and, anxious as I was to express my sympathy in his misfortune, could think of nothing appropriate to say. Finally I said: 'I suppose there'll be no more cricket.'

The Squire nodded his head, and spoke at once. 'Not a doubt of it.' Then he seemed to sink into himself and remained for perhaps a minute relaxed in his chair, his shoulders hunched and his eyes fixed on the floor between his feet. I stood looking down at him, somewhat perturbed to find that I, in my youth, was stronger and more confident than this good man to whom I had always looked up as to a second father, and who now, in spite of and in a way because of his dignity, was suddenly so abject.

I leant forward and touched his sleeve with my hand. 'Even if this can't be avoided,' I said, 'you'll be able to think of all you've done here.'

He made no sign to show that he had heard me, and I continued in a somewhat awkward attitude, leaning forward and peering into his face. At length he began to speak, though rather to himself than as though he were addressing his words to me. 'You think much too kindly of me,' he said. 'I have begun to see recently how worthless and useless my life has been. I have never made anyone happy.' He went on quickly and added: 'No, never,' as though fearing contradiction; and indeed I was on the point of speaking to remind him of the successful tenants' parties which he had held, of the gifts of butter and eggs to expectant and nursing mothers, of his constant support to the cricket and football teams, the bellringers, the mummers, the boys' club and indeed to every village activity. All this, maybe, was in his mind, but he was unwilling to hear of it, and I listened respectfully, but ill at ease, as he continued.

'Some good,' he said, 'may have been done by accident; but that is not exactly what I mean. My position has made it possible for a little ordinary human kindness to pass through me as a medium; but as for myself I have been a constant charge upon and nuisance to others. Look at Florence.'

Here he paused, but I made no move, for it seemed to me almost indecent to remind him of the good feeling and gratitude of which I knew he was the object. He must have been suffering from something much deeper than a mere uncertainty as to how he was regarded by others. Though I was deeply sorry for him, I looked at him rather as at the victim of a disease than as a man whom I could help; for who was I, at my age, to supply wisdom and confidence to men much older and more experienced than myself? 'I wish I could help you,' I began, but he continued as though he had not heard me speak.

'Florence,' he said, 'has shared her life with me, and I have done nothing to deserve her devotion. She has never been happy, or only once, and for a short time. And at that time I did everything I could to deprive her of her happiness. I regret it now, although then I was convinced that I was acting for the best. Now it seems almost a retribution. Then I thought only of the scandal. Your guardian agreed with me.'

His words mystified me, but they seemed to hint at some secret which may have been shared between our two families, that is if I might be said to have a family at all. Though I felt sympathy for the old man, it was partly curiosity which prompted me to speak. 'I have heard her say so often,' I said, 'that her life with you has been the happiest one that she could have had.'

The Squire seemed suddenly to become aware of my presence. He sat up in his chair, almost as though he had awakened from a sleep. He would have wished, I think, to appear energetic, alert, and friendly; but though he looked straight at me his eyes still held that look of baffled bewilderment and of distress which I had observed when he was speaking of the loss of his land. 'Thank you for your sympathy, my boy,' he said. 'You are very good. You are young and must not allow an old man to take up your time.' He looked hurriedly round the room, at the pictures and extensive assortment of objects on the wall; and his look seemed to show a suspicion of danger. 'Youth!' he said. 'It's a great thing.'

I could see no appropriateness in this remark and for security went back to the beginning of the conversation. 'But what exactly is the position?' I asked. 'About the Government, I mean.'

The Squire, too, showed by his manner that he had observed how far we had strayed from the original subject. He now spoke precisely. 'They are giving me a week,' he said, 'in which to make an appeal; but as I have to appeal to the very batch of lawyers who have passed this law, obviously an appeal is not worth making. In short, I have a month before I am to clear out.'

I reflected that, except for a brief spell abroad, he had lived all his life in this house and among these surroundings. He had learnt as a child how to act when he was a man, and he had acted as he had learnt to do. The rest of the world, even the rest of his own country, was strange ground to him. It was nothing in himself, but something outside which had made him now so defenceless. I could think of no suitable comment to make and inquired merely whether he was being offered reasonable compensation. I knew that nothing could compensate him for what he was about to lose.

'Yes,' he said. 'They are offering me money.'

I thought suddenly of his sister and of the Rector's wife. I imagined how eagerly they would debate this situation as soon as they were informed of it. They would be genuinely concerned, and the Squire would listen gratefully to their discussions although he would know, as I knew now, that everything which they might say would be beside the point. What might be said was too cruel to say; and so I stood speechless until after a moment or two he rose from his chair and shook my hand. 'Forgive me,' he said, 'for having entertained you so badly. We all have our troubles, and I am to blame for inflicting mine on others.'

There was such sincerity in his words, he seemed so abject in his courtesy, that I longed for some power of speech or gesture that would enable me to show him affection that was more than pity. But this feeling, however warm, was momentary. I seemed to see in his sunken face and in the lines that constricted his temples something already dead which reminded me of the really dead body of the Rector lying still in the upper room. And against this I reacted with aversion so strong that I felt hypocritical as I pressed his hand and urged him to make use of me in any way that he could do so. I hope that he recognized the love and did not notice the aversion. Both feelings were genuine and both spontaneous.

I said good-bye and returned to the Rectory. When I arrived there I found the two ladies together in the hall. They were holding each other's hand and talking in hushed voices. On the stairs I could hear the tramp of feet. The undertaker's men were removing the body in its coffin, since for the night preceding the funeral it was to be placed in the church.

CHAPTER VI

The Funeral

TO BE THINKING of the pleasures of love while dressing for a funeral may seem an incongruous thing; but I remember clearly that on the morning of the day when the Rector was buried I had been dreaming of lying with Bess in the hay, and when I got out of bed I was still thinking of her. I went to the window of my room and looked out over the lawn towards the chestnut tree. The young green now sprouting from the buds was in shadow, but a long splinter of sunlight went past the black trunk over the grass where chaffinches and black-birds were picking their way among the heavy dew. From the laurustinus bush at the edge of the lawn a wren let go his startling effusion of song. I could see the tiny body shaking with his music. Farther off there were thrushes, blackbirds, and robins in the trees. Out of sight, past the corner of the house, I could hear the crunch of Joe's wheelbarrow on the gravel as he went towards the kitchen garden. From the road came the rattle of milk carts leaving or returning to the Manor farm. I was innocent enough then to think how sweet it would be to wake like this day after day with Bess at my side in the eager country air.

Then I thought of the funeral and of my black clothes. It was with a feeling of relief that I remembered that today we were finally to put out of sight the too solid reminder of death; and, whether as a result of an un-conscious shame for this feeling of relief or whether in

84

some way the disappearance of the decaying body could liberate some more generous feelings, I began to think with my old affection of the dead man. I remembered his innumerable small acts of kindness and saw vividly in my mind's eye the expression of severe strain which he would have on his face while delivering a sermon to his congregation. I realized how he, who had lied, deceived, and murdered, must in the end have come to shrink from the honour in which he was held and the reputation for sanctity which he had won.

I thought, too, of the Squire, of my recent interview with him and of his sense of guilt. Was no one confident, I wondered, except the young; and how long would that confidence remain? For myself I was confident enough, even though the mere imagination of Bess would throw me into a state of trepidation, even though I had seen already the weakness of the two men whom I had most respected, even though the Rector's speech on my twenty-first birthday had deprived me of both my parents. At this time I still felt that for me at least life must inevitably be good.

I was whistling as I went down the stairs to breakfast, and checked myself outside the door of the dining-room, remembering what day it was. But the Rector's wife also seemed unusually cheerful, and we talked more at this meal than we had done since her husband's death. She asked me questions about the clothes which she would wear at the funeral, and told me to make sure that we had whisky in the house, in case the Air Vice-Marshal should care to stay the night. She even began to discuss the future and to make suggestions about how I should now get the right kind of coaching for my Civil

Service examination. Indeed, she seemed wholly to have recovered from the depression and nervousness of the last few days, and I should perhaps have begun to ask her the questions which ever since the dinner party I had been wishing to ask, if we had not, before the end of the meal, been interrupted by the Squire's sister.

She came into the room unannounced and, I thought, in a state of some agitation. Her first questions were about the visit of the Air Vice-Marshal, and I was surprised that she who, in my experience of her, so far from showing any eagerness in social life had tended rather to avoid company should now be anxious about a person who was not even, except for his connection with the aerodrome, of any consequence in our neighbourhood. She asked us all, including the Air Vice-Marshal, to have lunch with her at the Manor after the funeral, and then, as though surprised at herself for not having spoken of this first, told us that her brother had been taken ill in the night, and for a day or two would be confined to his room. 'It is nothing serious,' she said. 'And in a way I am glad. You know how fond he was of the dear Rector. The funeral, I am afraid, would have been very upsetting for him.'

'I quite understand,' said the Rector's wife, and the two ladies looked gravely at each other, and then smiled.

It would have been to do them a great injustice to have supposed that now, when the preparations for the funeral had all been made and the ceremony itself was at hand, they were becoming indifferent to the dead man himself. I, too, had felt relief that morning when I realized that now at last the body was to be lowered into the ground. Yet what were, no doubt, the same feelings in others made me indignant. I thought with pity and a kind of anguish of the coffin lying beneath hot-house flowers in the centre of the cold aisle, and of how soon its contents would be forgotten or only remembered as a character out of a book. So I felt all through the day, and it was this feeling which made the Air Vice-Marshal's speech at the funeral particularly distasteful to me.

He had arrived only ten minutes before the service was due to begin, and until he arrived not only the Rector's wife and the Squire's sister but all the other relatives and friends who had gathered at our house seemed unable to conceal their impatience. They talked in low respectful voices, and those who had not met for many years showed on this occasion unusual affection towards each other. But after the normal courtesies had been exchanged they would one and all begin to speak of the Vice-Marshal's visit, interested, but as a rule not caring either to approve or disapprove of it. And as the time drew on towards eleven o'clock people would rise, as though aimlessly, from their chairs and look out through the window towards the road. At length the visiting clergyman, who was to conduct the ceremony, and who had been wandering nervously round the room with his eye never straying far from the window, re-marked in a low but clear voice: 'I believe that the representative of the Air Force is arriving.'

The considerable gathering of those who were assumed to be my aunts, uncles, and cousins rose all together from their chairs and in indecent haste struggled towards positions at the window. I remained standing by the fireplace and listened to their comments on the size and colour of the distinguished visitor's car. The Rector's wife, too, stood aloof, and I noticed that her face was pale, though whether this was due to the tense atmosphere which is nearly always generated by a gathering of relatives, or to embarrassment at the thought of entertaining the important officer, I did not know.

We heard the sound of the car's door being shut and the tinkling of the bell. A moment or two later the Air Vice-Marshal was shown into the room, a mark for the eyes of all the family and friends who had faced about from the window and now stood silent gazing at the man who paused at the threshold as though uncertain whether to enter the room or not. It seemed almost as though they were awaiting his orders or else that he had discovered them in some crime; for he looked boldly, almost insolently, along the row of mild inquisitive faces, until the Rector's wife stepped forward and advanced to meet him, holding out her hand. There was, I had to confess, something remarkably impressive about the man. He was not unusually tall, but had such an upright carriage that one fancied him to be taller than he was. Though he must have been, I supposed, at least as old as the Rector, his face was not deeply lined and it expressed both energy and resolution. The eyes below his high forehead were large, though now he narrowed them slightly in an expression of distaste as he looked round the room. I disliked the complete assurance of his look, but at the same time felt attracted to the apparent power and confidence of the man. He took one step forward to meet the Rector's wife, disregarded her outstretched hand, and saluted with a brisk and sudden gesture. His lips were tightly pressed together. All his movements seemed to be made unwillingly, and yet with perfect dignity and precision.

'It is very good of you,' the Rector's wife began, 'at this time . . .' He did not allow her to finish her sentence.

'Not at all,' he said. 'I am only doing my duty. The accident was unfortunate.'

There was a pause. The Air Vice-Marshal had no more to say, and the Rector's wife seemed to have forgotten the form of greeting which she had intended to use when he had interrupted her. Her eyes were straying round the room and finally became fixed on me. She beckoned me towards her and said: 'This is my son, Roy. I am sure he would like to join me in thanking you for coming.'

Actually I had no such wish and was indeed distressed at the disturbance and trepidation caused by this courtesy visit of an official. But I stepped forward and smiled as I was being presented. The Air Vice-Marshal looked at me sharply and I stared back at him, not, perhaps, too respectfully, for I thought continually of the dead body in the church and felt this ceremony to be unreal in comparison with it. Nor did I imagine, then, that I should ever see the Air Vice-Marshal again.

He turned quickly from me, without shaking hands, and said to the Rector's wife: 'What is the boy going to do?'

I saw her eyes waver as she looked at him, and in order to spare her the effort of answering his question I replied that I was shortly to sit for the Civil Service examination. The Air Vice-Marshal paid no attention to me at all while I was speaking, so that I wondered whether he had heard what I said; but when I had finished he turned his head to me abruptly and said: 'Why not the Air Force? Better pay, better conditions, more discipline.'

I was in doubt what to reply, for I did not wish to insult him by confessing my dislike for the organization in which he occupied so prominent a place, and at his mention of discipline I was inclined to smile, remembering the many outrageous and irresponsible acts that had been committed in our neighbourhood by the aerodrome staff. But, before I had time to answer at all, he smiled at me and shook my hand. I was surprised by both gestures. 'Write to me when you like,' he said, 'care of the Air Ministry.' Then he turned quickly to the Rector's wife. 'Where is the clergyman?' he asked. 'We must be getting a move on.'

The relatives and friends, who had listened intently to every word spoken, now made a way through their ranks for the visiting clergyman, who bustled forward, rubbing his hands together in front of him and smiling in a way that seemed to me indecent on such an occasion. The Air Vice-Marshal took no notice of the hand offered to him but turned on his heel, taking the clergyman by the elbow. 'We had better go straight to the church,' he said, and proceeded to march the perplexed gentleman out of the room.

But before they left the Rector's wife took two or three quick steps forward and, to attract his attention, touched the Vice-Marshal on the arm. It seemed to me, as I watched, that his whole body stiffened as though affected by an insult or the sting of some insect or snake. Yet he behaved with perfect correctness, stopping still, slightly inclining his head and looking with his large inquiring eyes at the lady who had touched him. The Rector's wife, however, must have received the same impression as I had done. She fell back a pace and spoke nervously. She was inviting him to lunch and indicating to him the Squire's sister who was responsible for the invitation. The Squire's sister stepped forward, and she, too, appeared to me unusually nervous. Her large eyes were staring as though she were walking in her sleep, and her thin peaked features were as though the skin had been drawn back over them by some force behind her head. It was a face almost indecently naked, and the smile upon it seemed out of place.

The Vice-Marshal bowed to her and said: 'I shall be delighted.' Then he turned round and escorted the clergyman towards the church.

As soon as he had left the room an excited buzz of conversation arose. Nothing very remarkable was said. Most of the ladies pronounced the Air Vice-Marshal handsome, distinguished, or impressive. One old gentleman, an uncle of the Rector's wife, said: 'I don't like his manners.' What surprised me was not so much the impression which the man had made, as the extraordinary and callous curiosity of these friends of the family who had become so interested in a stranger whom they would never see again that they seemed wholly to have forgotten the purpose for which they were assembled.

The bell in the church tower was now tolling, and people began to look hurriedly about them for gloves, handbags, and prayer-books. Inquisitive faces took on suddenly a look of conventional solemnity, and the whole scene began to appear to me as infinitely pathetic; for I kept always in my mind's eye the picture of the coffin beneath the flowers, and the man inside the coffin with all his lust and pride and his repentance quite extinguished. I could even think now without pain of the unsightliness of the corpse and of its inevitable decay. The disappearance of life itself had made a gulf too deep for any affection to reach the end of it.

I took the arm of the Rector's wife as we went through the churchyard to the church door. In the porch stood George Birkett, the chief bellringer, dressed in his dark suit, and with sticking plaster covering the wounds on his face. He bowed gravely to us and opened the door that separated the porch from the nave. I saw Bess standing behind him, frowning as she pulled on her black gloves. She looked up at me and smiled, and I, since I was close to her, touched her hand with my fingers. I should have liked her to have sympathized with me in some of the distress which I now felt; but she looked puzzled when I touched her and, leaning forward, whispered in my ear: 'I've broken one of the buttons on my gloves.' She smiled again, as she might smile across the counter of the bar, and I smiled back at her, feeling for some reason tears in my eyes.

Then we went into the church, which was fuller than I had ever seen it; for in addition to the villagers there was a contingent of perhaps some twenty men from the aerodrome sitting in the back pews. As I went past them I noticed that while they were all silent and most of them were staring in front of them with cool impassive faces, one or two were reading newspapers. Among these I noticed the Flight-Lieutenant, who turned his head and winked at me. I paid no attention to him and indeed hardly took in the details of the disrespect which the Air Force was showing now, as always, to what we in the village held sacred.

In front of the pews occupied by the contingent from

the aerodrome were the people whom I knew. Nearly all the men who worked on the Squire's estate (and they were most of the village) had been given a holiday so as to attend the funeral. Some of them would be, I knew, already drunk, and many of them had never entered the church since the days when they were married or confirmed. But for the duration of the service they would behave with the utmost scrupulous correctness, for they were united in their respect for the church itself and for the man who had been for more than twenty years a leading character among them. Wives, sisters, and mothers sat with the men. Some were endeavouring to make their children sit straight in the pews; some looked, as I did, reverently and with a sense of loss at the wood of the coffin shining between the wreaths. Some of the older women were already dabbing their eyes with pocket handkerchiefs.

We took our places in one of the front pews and soon the bell ceased to toll. The cessation of sound seemed to me like one of those strange silences that one notices in the summer, sitting in the woods, perhaps, when the birds suddenly stop singing and the sound of insects dies away and one strains one's ears after what is inaudible. I could think of nothing now but my grief for the dead man whose body, however unlike the living it might be, was soon to be taken wholly away from us. I turned my head involuntarily towards the Rector's wife and saw that she was looking at me. Her lips were tightly compressed. I had no idea of what thoughts were passing through her mind.

We heard the clergyman's voice raised in prayer. The organ began to play and the choir filed out of the vestry to their places in the choir stalls. At the end of the procession came the Air Vice-Marshal, walking slowly and deliberately as though he were unconscious of those who preceded him. He took the place that had been occupied by the Rector during his lifetime, while the officiating clergyman sat at the reading desk which faced him.

I listened intently to the words of the funeral service, for their beauty and even their harshness seemed to soothe; but from time to time I found my attention distracted by the straight figure of the man in uniform, standing where I had seen stand so often the man whom I had believed to be my father. His face was impassive, his attitude correct, and yet there was something in his bearing which showed a complete withdrawal from and rejection of the ceremony in which he was taking a part. I felt his very presence to be incongruous and almost threatening, and when I found myself watching him or thinking of him I turned my attention back indignantly to the words which the clergyman was pronouncing. When the time came for the address to be delivered, I felt no curiosity but some distaste, as I watched him proceed to the pulpit.

He stood there stiffly, most unlike any occupant of the position whom I had ever seen before. The congregation remained standing, waiting for the usual prayer and, after a pause of a moment or two, the Air Vice-Marshal made an impatient movement of his hand and said: 'Sit down, please.' There was something shocking in the peremptoriness of his manner, but the congregation sat down devoutly and turned up their faces to the pulpit as they had been accustomed to do when listening to a minister of religion. The Air Vice-Marshal spoke without any hesitation, and rather in the manner of one who was delivering important instructions to his subordinates.

'We are here to-day,' he said, 'to bury a man. His body is in that coffin, and his death was the result of an unfortunate accident. Death is often a matter of accident, and there is no reason to be particularly dismayed by the fact that your Rector's death was accidental. He might just as well have been run over by a passing car or fallen off a precipice as have died in the way in which he actually did die. We need, I think, feel no pity for him, as far as the manner of his death is concerned.

'As for his life, he himself best knew whether it was well or badly lived. If he has friends among you, let them reflect that the objects of this kind of affection are not immortal. If he has enemies, they would do well to remember that hatred of individuals is invariably a waste both of time and energy. The man is dead. His family is, I believe, well provided for. That, on this subject, is all, I think, which needs to be said.'

Here he paused and I felt, as I am sure the greater part of the congregation felt, a kind of impotent rage at the inhumanity of the words which we had heard. Yet far stronger than this rage was my consciousness of the body lying behind me, over my right shoulder, on the hearse in the centre of the aisle. The thought flashed through my mind of making some protest against what had been said; but to do any such thing would have seemed to disturb the peace and dignity of the dead which was wholly unaffected by our words and movements.

But the old gentleman, the uncle of the Rector's wife, who previously had commented adversely on the Vice-

Marshal's manners, evidently did not share my feelings. I heard a noise of coughing behind me and then a voice. Turning round, I saw that the old man had risen to his feet and was shaking his fist in the direction of the pulpit. He was breathing heavily, opening his mouth with labour like a fish, and struggling with his emotion to produce words. Before he had time to speak, however, I heard the Vice-Marshal's voice. It was as calm and deliberate as it had been throughout his address.

'Will someone kindly remove that man?' he said, and immediately two airmen rose from their places at the back of the church, stepped smartly down the aisle and, gripping the old gentleman firmly by the elbow, escorted him to the church door. The old man was still incapable of forming words, but emitted a kind of spluttering sound as he was being forced out of the building.

There were restless movements among the congregation, but no open demonstration was made. People were affected, I think, as much by surprise as by indignation, and this surprise took away from them the immediate impetus of anger which might otherwise have caused something like a riot. I glanced at the Rector's wife beside me, and saw that she was looking intently at the Air Vice-Marshal. Her eyes were narrowed, but there was something soft about her mouth. Had not the notion seemed so absurd, I should have thought that the expression on her face showed pity.

The rest of the congregation continued to stare at the figure in the pulpit. There seemed to me something dumb and ox-like in their attentive frowning faces. The Air Vice-Marshal went on speaking as though no interruption had occurred.

'I have made these preliminary remarks,' he said, 'because it is customary at a funeral to make some mention of the dead man. But I would have you know that what is customary among you—sentimentality, mawkishness, and extravagant praise of those who are already sufficiently well known—is considered amongst us of the Air Force neither customary nor proper. The fact of death itself is of such far-reaching significance that neither the manner of dying nor the person who dies can, at such times as this, be considered of much importance. Nor would I be among you to-day if it were simply a question of an old clergyman shot accidentally by one of my officers. As it happens I have much more important things of which to speak to you.'

Here he paused again, and now it was curiosity rather than anything else which kept his audience silent and attentive. What was perhaps most remarkable was not the outrageous manner in which the service was being conducted, but the complete self-assurance of the speaker. In no way whatever did he show any consciousness of offending almost every ear by the words he used.

'Whether any of you,' he said, 'is yet aware of what is shortly to happen in this village, I do not know. Briefly, it is to be taken over by the Air Force. The property of your leading landowner, who gives most of you work at very low rates of pay, will be bought up by the Government. We shall install an Air Force padre in the place of your deceased Rector. You will be given work to do which, in many cases, will be different from the work which you have been in the habit of doing. Your pay, as long as the work is done conscientiously, will be increased. All this will be explained to you later. Now I merely wish to point out to you that you would do well to prepare for a great change in your lives. We in the Air Force look upon things very differently from those who have been used to dictate your ideas to you. Muddle, inefficiency, any kind of slackness are things which we simply do not tolerate. You will be given your instructions later. At the moment I have done what I came here to do, namely to prepare you for considerable changes. That is enough for the present. Now we shall bury the dead body.'

He glanced towards the coffin in the aisle and descended the steps of the pulpit. If the first part of his speech had outraged the congregation, by the second part they were quite dumbfounded. Men stared at one another as though they had been listening to something incredible or mad. There was already some muttering to be heard, when the visiting clergyman, pronouncing in a loud voice the words 'Let us pray!', brought back an illusion of normality.

The service continued as though the Air Vice-Marshal's speech had not been made; but there was a weakness and faltering in the singing and an air of uncertainty and desperation among us all as we followed the body, borne by four aircraftsmen, to the grave in the churchyard.

Most conflicting feelings succeeded each other in my mind. At one moment I felt impelled to jostle one of the aircraftsmen out of the way and to take the handle of the bier upon my shoulder; for it seemed the last indignity that no friend should carry for the last time the man who had been to me as a father. But still his rest seemed to me more complete and solid than our agitation; and, as the coffin was lowered into the ground, and the earth scattered upon it, I seemed to see before my eyes the figure of the bearded man standing, as he had stood at the dinner party proposing my health. I could think of nothing then but of the finality of what was happening. I felt the Rector's wife grip my arm as we heard the earth falling upon the wood of the coffin.

We turned away from the grave together and were confronted by the Air Vice-Marshal, who was looking at us gravely. The Squire's sister was standing at his side. He turned to her and, addressing the Rector's wife and me together, said: 'I think we have accepted this lady's invitation to lunch.'

Both the ladies smiled, nervously, but almost as though they were discounting his behaviour at the funeral. 'I don't think that I shall come,' I said, and looked angrily at them from face to face.

The Rector's wife had an imploring look in her eyes. The Squire's sister was staring at the ground. 'No doubt I shall see you later,' the Vice-Marshal said, 'that is, if your mother will be good enough to put me up for the night.'

I could find nothing even approximately polite to say; so I turned away from them and walked quickly out of the churchyard.

CHAPTER VII

New Plans

I WALKED slowly up the hill to the pub and, when I had entered the door, found the bar more than usually full of men who were talking animatedly, still wearing the suits which they had worn at the funeral. Those who noticed me stopped talking and one or two came forward and shook hands with me. They looked hard into my eyes with set jaws, and I saw in their faces, even though some of them were already drunk, more affection and more respect for the dead man than anything else which I had seen that day. We said nothing; indeed I knew that my presence had momentarily constrained their conversation; and I went to the bar, behind which Bess was serving, to order myself a drink.

Bess, too, was wearing the dress which she had worn at the funeral, but her face was alive with a gaiety that rather surprised me. As she handed me my tankard she leant her head close to mine, so that the yellow hair brushed against my cheek, and whispered: 'I'm free at two o'clock.' She blushed as her eyes met mine, and I nodded my head. All the distress which I had felt that day, all the humiliations which I fancied I had suffered seemed to be lost in the concentration of my desire for her. I thought again, as I had thought that morning while watching the blackbirds on the lawn, of how it would be if she and I were always together, always eager for each other, and the thought made me feel faint. By now she had turned to another customer, and I took the cold handle of the tankard in my hand and turned back into the room.

The men around me were still silent, evidently at a loss as to how they should speak to me of the funeral. At last Mac placed his tankard on the bar and, looking round him as though he anticipated contradiction, said: 'Say what you like, the old Rector was a good man.'

There was a chorus of 'He was that', and only Tony, the village carpenter, a thin wizened man who rarely said anything at all at these gatherings, spoke up suddenly and said: 'More respect ought rightly to have been paid.'

'It's a fact,' came from some of the others. 'It's a bloody fact,' and now I noticed in their faces both bewilderment and anger.

'What do you think about the Air Force occupying the village?' I asked, and at once everybody started speaking.

George Birkett elbowed his way forward through the others until he faced me. He must have drunk much before the funeral, and now his face was oddly flushed in patches of red between the pieces of sticking plaster.

'What do you think, Mr Roy?' he asked. 'Was that chap mad? The old Squire wouldn't allow it, would he now?'

There was something pathetic in the tone of voice used by the big half-drunken man. The others clustered round waiting attentively for what I had to say, and I told them briefly what I knew, that the Squire, however he might wish to do so, could not resist the demands of the Government, and that in all probability everything which the Air Vice-Marshal had said was strictly true.

When I had finished there was a silence of consternation. Then nearly everyone started speaking at once in a hubbub of high and angry voices. Fred made himself heard above the rest. As I remember him he was young, slight, with a quizzical look in his eye. One had usually to strain one's ears to hear what he was saying, but now he was shouting at the top of his voice. 'I shall bloody well leave the bloody village,' he was saying. 'Work for a lot of soldiers! Not me!'

'That's right, that's quite right!' said the others, and most of them looked at Fred with admiration, though mingled with it was some regret, for those who had wives and children knew that it would be impossible for them to leave their houses, and the older men knew that the habits of their lifetimes could not be transplanted.

A general conversation, eager and bitter, took place, and the hard words used of the aerodrome seemed gradually to relieve the men's pent-up feelings. More and more beer was drunk, and soon some of those who had been standing close to each other in eager talk sat down separately and lit their pipes. First one group and then another would begin to talk of subjects other than the aerodrome, and from time to time short bursts of laughter would arise to mark the conclusion of some story. Mac strolled slowly towards the dartboard and Fred followed him. They tossed up and Mac, having won, took his stand on the rubber mat that marked the throw. Several others turned their heads to watch the players. "Cross-bred puppy!' Mac said, as his first dart missed the double. He took the second dart between his fingers, kissed it, and murmured, 'Come now, my little sucking-pig', but it too missed the mark. Then he shook his head and shouted out what we had come to regard

as his especial battle cry, 'Come, fever, from the South!'
His third dart fixed in the double twenty. There was
general laughter and Fred, taking his place on the mat,
swore as he spilt some beer over his trousers. Jollity was,
for the moment, restored.

The landlord came into the bar from an inner room.
He nodded towards me gravely and leant over the bar,
puffing at his pipe, surveying the dart-players with
satisfaction. He was a large man, kindly in his way, and
with determined views on politics. He had nothing in
him of his daughter's grace of manner. I inquired after
his wife, and learnt that she had been ill and was away,
staying with a friend.

That morning I could not join in the general merri-
ment. I ordered some bread and cheese and sat down in
a corner away from the dartboard, watching Bess as she
went to and fro filling and washing out the glass tankards.
From time to time she would look at me and smile with
her head twisted round, perhaps, while she measured out
whisky with her back to the room, or staring up at me
from beneath her eyebrows as she bent down to replace
glasses on the shelf below the bar. But I felt insecure and
her beauty only left me weak. Though I knew the people
here well, and loved them, I was disgusted and frightened
by the contrast between their quick anger, their sudden
levity, and the undeviating precision and resolution of the
Air Vice-Marshal. I longed for the time when the bar
would close and I could put my arms round Bess, for I
fancied that in her love there was some security, and I
wished to tell her of my feelings at the funeral and to
discuss with her plans for the future which I now began to
hope that we would share together.

It seemed long to wait before the landlord removed the pipe from his lips, stared solemnly at the clock, and in his ringing voice cried out: 'Time now, all you gentlemen, please.' There was a decent pause, and then the men, now mostly drunk, began to walk or stumble out into the road. Some shook my hand on their way out, and I could see that now, in their drunkenness, their original impressions of the dead Rector and of the funeral were returning to them.

I followed them out of the pub and walked up the hill to the stile leading into one of the fields below the aerodrome. The air was warm in spite of a light breeze that chased a few high clouds over the spring-clear sky. From the stile I could see a portion of one of the large hangars at the top of the hill curved in a way so like the natural roundness of this land, and yet in its perfect regularity so unlike. I looked back towards the white and empty village street and soon saw Bess coming up it to meet me. She had changed her dress for the one which she had worn at the Agricultural Show and, as I looked at her, I felt that all that had happened to me since then had in some way deepened my love for her and made it more vivid and exacting.

When she came to the stile I took her hands and kissed them. There was a more than usual gaiety and frankness in her eyes; and, though we were in full view of the road, she pressed her body against mine and kissed me lightly on the mouth. We turned round, crossed the stile, and began to walk over the field. Her first words to me were: 'Wasn't he marvellous?' and, when I inquired of whom she was speaking, she said it was the Air Vice-Marshal, and then paused, embarrassed perhaps because it had occurred to her that she had said something to offend me, as indeed she had.

I replied indignantly, asking what consideration the Air Force had ever shown for the village, and in particular what right had one of their officials to come down and speak with such inhumanity at a funeral; but as I spoke I saw that she was hardly listening, and the absence of her attention had the effect of confusing my own ideas, so I found myself saying the same things over and over again, amazed at her lack of comprehension, for at this time I fancied that her ideas and feelings must be, by some law of nature, not unlike my own.

'I see what you mean,' she said at last, in a slow voice, 'but all the same he was marvellous.' She turned to me quickly and gripped my arm. 'Oh, how wonderful it would be,' she said, 'if you were an airman.'

Her smiling face and the vivacity of her voice dissipated at once the feelings of dismay and indignation which had filled me a moment before. I laughed and, stopping in the middle of the field, held her in my arms and kissed her.

'Would you marry me, then?' I asked.

The idea seemed to her a new and exciting one. She clapped her hands and then laid them on my shoulders, looking into my eyes. 'Oh, yes!' she said. 'And live at the aerodrome.'

I remember now the delight that her face showed then, and I remember hearing a lark singing high up above us and above the dark stubble field where we stood. Bess's proposition was far from disgusting to me. There was a wild excitement in all my limbs, and I laughed upwards at the lark in the sky. It was not exactly that her freshness, her beauty, and her exuberance had charmed my wits away from thinking as I should have thought. I had changed none of my ideas and was still, in some part of my mind, bitter and indignant against her for her admiration of the part which the Air Vice-Marshal had taken at the funeral. I was not even at that time blind enough to believe that love in itself was a sufficient diet for two people to live upon, and yet something in me impelled me to act as though this were precisely what I believed. Now the sweetest and most desirable of all things seemed to me to throw down before her feet all my ideas, all my plans, all my hopes, and to act exactly as she would have me act; nor was I wholly conscious of this impulsion, but felt simply as I looked at her that, whatever might be done, our complete happiness was already assured.

I squeezed her arms, and said: 'But in the Air Force they are not allowed to be married until after several years' service.'

Bess shook her head. Her face was very serious as she looked at me with an expression of tenderness that I had not seen there before. She was like a child waiting in a shop patiently for some present to be delivered to her. 'No,' she said, 'that's not true. It's just that only the wives of officers are allowed to live in the aerodrome. Even if you sign on for training you can get married by a special chaplain with a special licence, without banns or anything. Oh, Roy, we could be married secretly. Wouldn't it be fun?'

Her face lit up again with anticipation and delight. As I looked at her I thought calmly of my long preparation for the Civil service, and of the assurances which I had received that I was likely to receive good marks in the examination. I remembered how often I had envisaged life in one of the big cities where I should probably have to work. This was what the Rector had planned for me, and what he would still have advised, had he been alive. I hardly know now why it was that the prospect of such a life suddenly seemed unattractive to me. It was certainly not that I shared any of Bess's ideas of the glory of flying in the sky or of the dignity of an officer's uniform. I had little respect and no liking for the organization which she was urging me to join. Nor was I by any means in the position of one who is inclined to make a conscious sacrifice for another person.

I began to think, almost automatically, that her plan was by no means so mad as it might seem at first sight. My qualifications for the Civil Service examination would stand me in good stead in another profession. I had already received what amounted to an offer of assistance from the Air Vice-Marshal. Nor, indeed, if I signed on for training, was I even then irrevocably committed. As a rule several months elapsed before those who had signed on were even called up. In those months I could be married to Bess, and when they were over there would be more time still before finally adopting the Air Force as a profession. I was young, and there was time enough for us to decide what life was best suited to us. So I thought in my vanity, my wish to please, and the abandonment of my desire. The Rector's speech at the dinner party, the Squire's confession of failure, the indignity of the funeral, the cordiality shown by the Rector's wife to the Air Vice-Marshal, the irresolution of my friends in the pub—all this, too, may have contributed to the complete and joyful recklessness with which I now faced the future. Having lost the security in which I had been bred, I now looked at Bess, weak and childish as she was, as at a new and certain world. I fancied that my own love was strong enough to withstand all the shocks that time and circumstance could bring; and here, perhaps, I was not wholly wrong, although at this time I did not imagine it to be possible that I would have to face any very serious setbacks.

I looked deep into Bess's eager waiting eyes. 'Why not?' I said, and we remained silent for some moments, our eyes drawn together, each knowing that already the resolution had been made. The lark still sang above our heads, and I looked deep into the face in front of me, seeking there, perhaps, some of the strength and certainty of which I stood in need and with which, in my mood of recklessness, I already imagined myself to be filled. The face was soft and timid in its relaxation. The beginnings of a smile flickered at the corners of her mouth. As I bent forward to kiss her, her eyes grew wet with tears and her arms were loose about my neck. She pressed her face into my shoulder and said: 'We shall be like this for ever. For ever and ever.'

My arms tightened round her, and I felt a lump rise in my throat. My thoughts about the aerodrome, about the funeral, and about my parentage seemed suddenly unconnected with me, and yet menacing. 'For ever,' I said, and so we stood for some time.

Bess drew away from me and shook my arm. Her face was alight again with animation. 'Let's talk about it,' she said, and half dragged me towards the hedge, in the shadow of which we sat down and began to plan with laughter and excitement our future, breaking off the talk every now and then to kiss each other's hands and faces or to look long and with astonishment into each other's eyes.

It was clear to us that the marriage would have to be a secret one. The Rector's wife would undoubtedly be opposed to it, I thought, since she had always agreed with the Rector as to the advantages for me of a Civil Service career. Bess's father and mother, though I fancied that they would not object to me as a son-in-law, would shrink from offending the Rector's wife and her friends, the Squire and his sister. Yet every objection that could be made to the marriage by our friends or our relatives seemed to me selfish, merely conventional, lacking in understanding, or short-sighted. I felt fully able to take on myself the responsibility for any step which we might take together, since the responsibility was presented to my mind in the form of extreme and confident delight, in the face of which both the village and the aerodrome itself seemed hardly stable things, but malleable to my own desires. I began to be infected with Bess's positive enthusiasm for the secrecy of the thing, not so much because I believed that there was romance in secrecy, but rather because I saw a kind of liberation in avoiding the obligations, the conventions, the manners in which I had been brought up and which now for me, perhaps owing to my present lack of security, seemed buried in the ground with the body of the man whom I had thought to be my father.

So we talked and talked, and finally lay still in each other's arms, exhausted not by passion but by the resolution we had taken and the novelties which we anticipated. There seemed no more to be said, and I was listening to the larks in the air and watching the head of a bluebell nodding above Bess's head when we heard the sound of steps and whistling approaching us along the hedge. We sat up quickly, smiling, as we brushed down our clothes and, looking to the left, saw the Flight-Lieutenant walking slowly towards us, with his eyes fixed on the ground. He was carrying a small cane with which from time to time he switched off the heads of bluebells in the hedge. His lips were pursed together as he whistled a dance tune, and the sunlight striking him in the face flashed back from his tight yellow curls. I had not spoken to the man since the Rector's death, and had seldom thought kindly of him; but now, knowing that he could help us, and watching the grace and beauty of his bearing which in the past I had so admired, I began to feel for him some of the affection which I had felt before the dinner party.

Bess squeezed my arm. 'Ask him now,' she whispered, and I shouted out to him.

He raised his head, looked at us calmly, and gave an ironical salute. 'Beg pardon,' he said, 'if I'm intruding.'

I laughed, and replied: 'Not at all. We want you to help us.'

He walked forward slowly and sat down next to Bess. 'Anything within reason,' he said, patting her on the arm. 'What is it? Advice on birth control? Or what?'

Bess giggled, and I said 'No'. The Flight-Lieutenant was looking at me coolly, as though this were the most ordinary conversation. 'The fact is,' I said, and for a moment felt an unreasonable embarrassment, 'the fact is that we want to get married.'

There was no change whatever in the expression of his face. 'What on earth for?' he said.

Bess looked at him quickly and, I thought, with distaste. I laughed again and said: 'Never mind what for.
We do. That's all, and we want you to help us.'

'But it's absurd,' he said, turning his head slowly
towards Bess. 'Why, you could have lots of men.' He
glanced at me and, for the first time, smiled. 'You could
do all right, too.' Then he turned back to Bess. 'Do you
really want to?' he asked.

Bess spoke timidly. 'Of course I do,' she said. 'We've
just decided.'

The Flight-Lieutenant unclasped his hands from his
knees and lay back on the ground. He held his cane to
his shoulder and, pointing it upwards, squinted along
it as though it were a gun which he was aiming at the
sky. There was a long silence until I said: 'Well, what
about it?'

He did not change his attitude, and I began to tell
him our plan and to ask whether it would indeed be
possible to get married without the usual formalities if
I were to sign on for training at the aerodrome. At this
he sat up and began speaking as though the subject had
for the first time become interesting to him.

'Joining us,' he said, 'isn't at all a bad idea. You'd
pass the medical exam all right, and it would be a pretty
good show to get away from the old women in the village
while the going's good. As for the marriage business, if
you really think that sort of thing important, I can fix
it up for you in no time.'

Bess and I looked at each other, and I fancied that I
saw a trace of timidity or hesitation in her eyes. This I
attributed to her modesty. We both smiled.

The Flight-Lieutenant was staring down at his boots

from which he was removing mud with the point of his cane.

'As a matter of fact,' he said, 'I could do the whole thing for you myself. Meet your new vicar.'

He looked towards me and winked one eye. I had no idea about what he was speaking, and listened with increasing surprise as he continued. 'I've just been transferred to the religious department,' he said, 'and when we occupy the village I'm going to be the padre. It's a funny sort of idea, but someone's got to do the job and, apart from the office work, it only means getting on my hind legs every now and then and making a kind of speech. In a way it'll be rather fun. As far as your business is concerned it fits in very well. I've got all the qualifications, and could marry you tonight if you like. Though I still think you're fools.'

At first I could hardly believe my ears and, when it became apparent that he was speaking the truth, my first feeling was one of horror at what I could only regard as the desecration of the church in which I had so often heard the Rector speak. I can hardly tell now how it was that this feeling of horror so soon passed away and I began to think of the Flight-Lieutenant's appointment as slightly amusing and certainly convenient. The disclosure at the dinner party had seemed to sever some of the ties that had connected me with my childhood. Subsequent events had continued the work, and now the resolution which I had made had cut me off, or so I thought, completely from the past in which I had grown up. I laughed, and looked at Bess.

'Why not tonight?' I said.

The Flight-Lieutenant continued to stare at his boots.

A quick expression of irresolution passed over Bess's face. She looked at me coaxingly and said: 'Let's wait till tomorrow.'

She blushed as she spoke and, although if we had been alone I should have begun to argue with her, I found the look in her eyes infinitely appealing and was suffused with a kind of tenderness that slowed up the rapidity and damped down the ardour of my desire to have everything settled at once and, as I imagined, for ever. I nodded and said, 'All right, tomorrow then', and the Flight-Lieutenant said: 'I'll bring the papers that you'll have to sign.'

We all rose to our feet as though we had reached a decision to conclude some long and difficult debate. I should like to have had some more words with Bess alone, but the Flight-Lieutenant seemed wholly unaware of my state of mind and was evidently determined to accompany us wherever we went. We walked through a couple of fields and then back to the pub by the main road. None of us said much, and only the Flight-Lieutenant appeared wholly at his ease. I thought of mentioning the funeral and the Air-Marshal's speech, but said nothing either. From time to time I thought with delight and trepidation of the decision which we had taken. Then the presence of a third person seemed hardly to matter, and I looked urgently and inquiringly at Bess to see whether she was feeling as I felt. As usual on these occasions she was staring at the ground, with a remote and almost secretive smile upon her face. I thought of my love surrounding her like a cloak and of her walking forward sweet and unconscious of it.

We arrived at the pub and found the landlord outside,

dressed in his best suit, and smoking a pipe. He raised one hand to greet us, wholly unaware of the subject of our recent discussions, and began to speak slowly and ponderously of the regulations governing the marketing of pigs. He spoke at length, ending most of his sentences with the words 'There's not a question of it', and taking little or no notice of his auditors.

The Flight-Lieutenant made no attempt to pretend that he was paying attention to the landlord's words. He scratched with the point of his cane on the top of the low wall in front of the pub. I looked over his shoulder and saw that he was inscribing the first words of an obscene song. Finally he turned abruptly and walked away up the hill towards the aerodrome. The speaker paused and removed his pipe from his mouth. 'Seems he knows nothing about pigs,' he said, and was prepared to resume when I took advantage of the interruption to press Bess's hand and to move away myself. 'See you tomorrow,' I said, and she smiled at me quickly, and then looked down at the wall where the Flight-Lieutenant had been writing.

I walked towards the Rectory, feeling now that the house was entirely strange to me. My head was full of plans, and I hardly thought of the discourtesy I had shown to the Air Vice-Marshal and to the Rector's wife.

CHAPTER VIII

The Impulse

NOT LONG AFTERWARDS I was sitting before a large
fire in an upper room of the Manor. At my elbow was a
small table covered with bottles, glasses, and spoons;
and in the hot heavy air, thick with the smell of medicine
and of disinfectant, nothing moved except the long
flames flickering in the grate. From time to time I stared
across the table to the big bed with its spotless white
sheets and pillows which I had just seen smoothed by
the Squire's sister.

Lying in the bed on his back, with his knees tucked
up, was the unconscious Squire, breathing slowly and
heavily. His face appeared curiously small and pale, with
the skin dragged back from the bones; and his body, too,
under the bedclothes, seemed to have lost importance.
I was reminded of a skinned rabbit as I watched him
anxiously to see if he would wake, and I counted his deep
breaths, not certain whether or not they were becoming
less regular. I felt pity for the unconscious figure, and at
the same time less noble feelings—a certain fear that he
would die and that it would be discovered afterwards that
I, while left on watch, had neglected some elementary
precaution; a certain exasperation at the fact that now,
when my mind was so busy on other things, I should be
hurried from a funeral to a deathbed.

For after leaving Bess I had got no farther than the
Rectory gate before seeing the Squire's butler, Wilkinson,
running up the drive, his head bare of the bowler hat

which as a rule distinguished him from everyone else in the village. The carefully oiled lock of hair which usually lay stuck above his left eyebrow was falling over his nose, and he looked ridiculous as he came puffing and blowing (for he was a big man) towards me. While still some distance away he had managed to call out to me: 'The old Squire, Mr Roy, the old Squire, he's failing fast'; and then, after just turning his large soft eyes on me, he had trotted on cumbrously up the village street. I had wondered what his errand had been, and I reflected now with some shame that my first feeling, after the initial surprise, had been one of exasperation.

As I thought of this I looked quickly across at the body on the bed as if its unconsciousness could pardon me my lack of consideration and my preoccupation with my own affairs. The great eyebrows jutted into the air. The breathing was still thick and heavy, and this was the one sign of animation. I wished now that after meeting the butler I had come straight to the Manor instead of going on to the Rectory partly to obtain further information and partly, I was compelled to admit, to avoid for the moment the distress and the disturbance which I imagined that I would find in the Squire's home. I had entered the Rectory quietly and had stood uncertain, as though waiting for something, on the stone flags of the hall. What with the information which I had just received and the decision which I had reached that afternoon, I had forgotten that the Air Vice-Marshal would still be at our house, and had not immediately recognized his voice when I heard the sound of conversation in the sitting-room to the left of the front door.

The door had been slightly ajar and I had paused

with my hand outstretched to open it, for I had been surprised at a note of anger in the voice of the Rector's wife. 'Surely,' she was saying, 'it is shameful to gloat over it. What harm could he possibly have done you?'

The voice of the Air Vice-Marshal was cool and precise as he replied. 'You are doing me an injustice. We do not gloat over things. I was merely observing that those who have been my enemies tend to die out, usually as a result of their own weakness or incompetence, while *I* survive them. You can hardly expect me to feel distressed.'

Then there had been a pause, and again I had been on the point of opening the door when I was arrested by a new note, almost of tenderness, in the voice of the Rector's wife. 'You do not speak much,' she was saying, 'of your friends.'

The reply came immediately on the conclusion of her sentence. 'They have had a way of either denying or avoiding their obligations.'

The Rector's wife had spoken again. It was as though she were meditating aloud. 'And if one of them,' she said, 'should attempt to make up for the past . . .'

Although I had no idea of what was the subject of their conversation, I was repelled by the coldness in the Air Vice-Marshal's voice as he replied: 'It is a thing which I have never seen done.'

I had pushed open the door then, and had seen him standing with his back to the window, almost at attention and yet in appearance so sure of himself that there seemed to be nothing stiff in his attitude. He made no sign of recognition as I entered the room, and I looked from him to the Rector's wife who was leaning from her chair towards the fire, stretching out, as I had so often seen her do, one hand towards the red coals. She had smiled, and then her face had taken on a look of gravity. 'You had better go to the Manor at once, Roy,' she said. 'Florence has just been in. He's very ill. Hardly likely to get through the night. He's been asking for you.'

I had made as though to leave the room, but before I did so the Air Vice-Marshal had taken two or three steps towards me. I was, for some reason, surprised to see him smiling. 'Good-bye, my boy,' he said. 'I may not see you again. I've just rung for my car and shall leave tonight. Remember that if I can do anything to help you, I shall be glad to do so.'

I had stumbled over my words of thanks. Though previously I had been repelled by almost everything which the man had done and said, now I felt myself attracted to what appeared to be his power and the small amount of cordiality in his voice. Or perhaps my feelings were the result of a sudden realization of how useful to me, in the plans which I had just made, this offer of assistance might be. We shook hands and I had felt, I remember, unaccountably elated as I went down the drive to the Manor; though as soon as I had entered the hall I found myself caught up into an atmosphere in which it was impossible to think of myself. A maid and a nurse were crossing each other as one walked to the kitchen, the other to the foot of the stairs. Tears were streaming down the maid's face; her back was a little bent, and there was something furtive in the way she walked. The nurse's manner was firm, determined, and spiritual. Evidently, I had thought, the Squire is very ill.

His sister had stood facing me, very erect, very pale, and with a look in her eyes which had rather surprised me. It was as though the approach of death had exalted her with feelings more active than resignation, almost as though she were welcoming this occasion as one for which she had herself fully prepared. She had advanced to meet me with outstretched hand, and it was only the low tone of her voice that made her appear different in manner from a hostess welcoming an expected guest. Her voice was very quiet. 'Come upstairs, Roy,' she had said. 'Perhaps he will recognize you', and she had taken me by the hand and led me to the old man's room where, after she had smoothed the pillows and poked the fire, she had left me alone, instructing me to ring the bell if the Squire should regain consciousness or if there should be any marked change in the regularity of his breathing.

As I sat there now before the fire, waiting for the old man to wake or else to die, I thought often of his sister and of how his death would be to her what the loss of his land had been to the Squire himself. Except for the short period of time in which the Squire had been on military service abroad, the two had spent their lives together, and though the old man, in his illness, had blamed himself for having so attached her to him and had hinted at some happenings in the past in which he imagined himself to have acted unkindly towards her, I had seen in the relations between the two nothing but mutual gratitude and the most devoted friendship.

But, though I thought of the loss which she would have

to undergo, I was not greatly moved by the thought. I was chiefly sorry, I think, to be reminded of death, and was not much grieved at the knowledge that it was the Squire who was dying. I admired him, but he seemed to have little now for which to live. I remembered, not without satisfaction, that he would not be there to oppose, as he would certainly have done, my entry into the Air Force and my hurried marriage; nor was I at this time ashamed, as I should certainly have been a day or two before, by the selfishness and inhumanity of my way of thinking. Indeed, I began to feel constrained and irritated in the hot still air, and wished that the body on the bed would do something else than breathe so loudly and unnaturally. Occasionally a kind of choking stop, succeeded by a snore, would come in the monotonous sound; then I would turn, almost with relief, to the bell, ready to ring it. There would be a short pause and the heavy breathing would be renewed. I stretched my legs out in front of me, and sat with closed eyes, counting the breaths.

Suddenly I heard the bed creak and the breathing stop. I turned round and saw that the Squire had moved, and that he was lying on his side facing me, his mouth wide open and in his eyes a look of distress which was caused, perhaps, by the effort which he had made to shift his position. I rang the bell immediately, and went over to the bed relieved that something was happening, but frightened, too; for, if the breathing had been unnatural, the appearance of the dying man's face was more unnatural still. The eyes glared at me hopelessly; the mouth kept opening and shutting, in an effort to breathe or to articulate words; and when the mouth was shut the lips quivered in a way that I found not pathetic but horrible. I noticed particularly three white hairs on his imperfectly shaven chin. He at length gasped out some word which may have been my name, attempting at the same time to move his hand beneath the bedclothes; and there was something in this gesture which immediately dissolved in me those feelings of repulsion and exasperation which only just before I had felt and had hardly noticed that I was feeling. I knelt down on the floor and, folding back the bedclothes, took his thin hand in mine. His twitching mouth seemed to be attempting a smile, and for a short moment the look of horror and dismay passed from his eyes. He spoke in a deep guttural voice, most unlike himself: 'I have something to tell you', and I remained kneeling on the floor, looking into his tortured eyes and his writhing mouth; for he seemed dreadfully harassed by the thought that he would not have the time or else the strength to say what he wished.

He suddenly pronounced the words 'Your father', and then fell silent again with a look of concentration on his face and the breath pouting his lips. It at once occurred to me that he was not speaking of the Rector, but was about to reveal to me something connected with my real father, whose name he might even know. I listened eagerly, but was aware at the same time that my eagerness was by no means so intense as it would have been only a few days before. Was this the effect just of the tired and dying face in front of me, or had I become, I wondered, habituated to a kind of isolation from the roots of my childhood? Was I prepared even to enjoy this isolation?

The Squire spoke again, this time in a much softer

voice. He said the one word 'Florence', and then looked at me gravely as though either expecting an answer or else watching the effect of some important announcement.

I began to think now that his mind must be wandering, and that no disclosure was to be made. I looked at him with rather less sympathy though I pressed his hand and smiled into his unresponsive face. His eyes were watching me closely while his mouth, over which he had no control, pitiably writhed and pouted.

I heard the door open and, looking round, saw his sister enter the room. She came quickly to the bedside, stood beside me and gently laid one hand on the forehead of the dying man. I saw him turn his eyes upward and fancied that, though he could see and feel his sister's hand, he could not, having focused his eyes on me, make out her face which was farther away from him. She began to move her hand, stroking him over his eyes and nose; and suddenly I felt the grip of the old man's fingers tighten on mine, and saw that he had kicked out his legs convulsively. There was a sharp cry of pain, and I observed with horror that he had fixed his teeth in his sister's hand. For a short moment she turned towards me with an appealing and frightened look, and then began to pull at her arm in an effort to release herself; I saw the muscles on the old man's jaws bulge as he tightened his grip. His last strength seemed to be put into this horrible and insane action; but what was more horrible was what happened next. The expression on his sister's face suddenly changed so that her first look of terror and pain was replaced by one of frantic anger. Her lips hardened, and she bent right over the body, hissing into its ear: 'You would, would you?' Then, with her disengaged hand, she began to slap the Squire's face. For one moment, I think, he may have recognized his sister, for across his eyes there seemed to pass a sudden look of surprise. Then both his legs were drawn up and, as he released his grip on the hand, his breath came in a long rattle through his throat. His head lolled back and, though I had never seen this happen before, I had no doubt that he was dead.

I turned towards his sister, and my face must have expressed both shame and indignation. She was looking at me oddly, but soon put her hands in front of her face, and began to make a soft sound that might have been sobbing or else the beginnings of hysterical laughter. I led her to the chair in which I had been sitting, and then stood back from her; for, after what I had seen her do, I shrank from touching her and had nothing in me with which I could comfort her. One action had revealed what I could never have suspected, a deep hatred for the man to whom she had, to all appearances, sacrificed her life; and, though I felt some pity for her in her present distress, I could not help feeling horror also and bewilderment. I looked at the body on the bed and looked away again quickly. For relief my mind turned fully to my own plans for finally separating myself from the influences and characters which had surrounded me up to now, and which I saw now to have been quite other from what I had imagined them to be. They had been symbols to me of security and peace; but I had learnt that they could represent neither of these qualities. What I had thought to be solid, rounded, and entire, now seemed to melt into frightful shapes of mist, to dissolve into intricacies wherein I was lost as though I had never been. At this intricacy I felt no wonder, but only bewilderment; and so I looked indifferently at the Squire's sister and at her brother's body.

In a few moments the lady ceased to sob. She was wringing her hands and staring at me with large inquiring eyes. 'How could I have done it?' she asked. 'How could I?' She spoke as though I were likely to know the answer to her question.

'One gets overwrought,' I said, conscious of the feebleness of my reply and irritated with her for requiring from me assurance in such a situation. 'He was trying to tell me,' I added, 'something about my father.'

She looked at me as though my words had startled her, and then, turning away from me, rose from her chair and stumbled towards the bed. Here she fell on her knees and, burying her head in the pillow by the dead man's head, began to weep unconstrainedly. Her body was relaxed, and her neck and head, with some locks of hair loose, looked beautiful, I thought, as I watched her sorrow and the relief which evidently it was bringing her. Over her shoulder I could see the Squire's nose and sunken chin. I thought of him as I had seen him often—in his regular pew in church, standing at the door of the pavilion to pat on the shoulder a village batsman who had distinguished himself, saying grace at a tenants' party, digging in his garden or, as he had sometimes done, playing charades in our house. Now he and all these scenes, although I felt some tenderness at the memory of them, appeared to me as wholly dead.

I went on tiptoe to the door and, opening it, saw the butler, his wife, the cook, and several maids standing huddled in the passage-way. Closing the door, I began to walk past them, and as I went Mrs Wainwright, the cook, touched my elbow and whispered in my ear, 'Has he passed beyond, sir?' I nodded my head, and proceeded down the stairs, having no comment to make. Behind me I heard the butler reassuring in a low voice some of the servants who had begun to weep.

In the hall I paused for a moment to look at the empty oak chair by the fireside and the gleaming ornaments and oddments on the walls. I remembered that only a day ago I had seen the official from the aerodrome glance just so around the room, and I reflected that the house itself now was, with its owner, a thing of the past. This reflection actually elated me, for I could see here no longer the certain innocence and stability that I had always imagined. The outrageous outbreak of the Squire's sister which had preceded and perhaps caused her brother's death was clearer in my mind than was the sight of common sorrow and of the collapse of a house which had been, together with the church, for generations the centre of a village's life. Yet against the Squire's sister I felt no animosity, as for the Squire himself I felt little pity. Even the curiosity with which his last words had filled me began now to grow faint and to disappear.

I walked quickly towards the Rectory and at the gate saw the erect figure of the Air Vice-Marshal standing by the running board of his large grey car. He was looking down to the ground while pulling the tight gloves on to his hands, but before I reached him he raised his head and noticed me. Somewhat to my surprise he lifted up one hand in a gesture of greeting and smiled at me as I approached.

'Is he dead?' he asked and, as he spoke, I seemed to see again most vividly the distorted face and to hear the frantic inhuman breathing of the dying Squire. The very ordinariness of the Air Vice-Marshal's voice, contrasted in my mind with what I had just seen and heard, frightened me, and I paused for a moment or two, unable to frame a reply. I felt the man's keen eyes on my face. 'It's not a pleasant sight,' he said. 'One gets used to it.'

I looked at him with, for the first time, a kind of admiration, for his words had seemed certain and had certainly charmed away my fear. The chauffeur had now left the driving seat and was standing at attention, ready, when needed, to open the door of the car. The Air Vice-Marshal himself was buttoning up one of his gloves and, as he looked down at his hand, continued to speak to me. 'In the case of this gentleman,' he said, 'death was probably a great relief. So it is for anybody who has not a purpose in life.'

'Yes,' I said, 'I suppose so', and without much reflection I added: 'I am thinking of joining the Air Force.'

He raised his eyes quickly and looked at me, I thought, with satisfaction. 'Then we shall most probably meet again,' he said, and nodded quickly to his chauffeur who stepped forward smartly, a rug over one arm. The car's door was opened and shut. I caught a glimpse of the Air Vice-Marshal's face as he leant back against the cushions and took from his pocket some papers which he proceeded to study. I followed the car with my eyes all the way up the village street and, when it was out of sight, stood for some moments looking after it before going into the Rectory to acquaint the Rector's wife of her friend's loss.

CHAPTER IX

The Honeymoon

ONE MIGHT DESCRIBE, I suppose, as a honeymoon that state of existence between two worlds in which I lived for the three months after my marriage and before my entry into the Air Force. If unreflecting happiness, indifference to the outside world, a sudden and prolonged delight in the pleasures of the senses are characteristic of honeymoons, then certainly this period of time in my life deserves the title. When I held Bess in my arms, naked or clothed, I felt assured that I was laying hold of a brilliant, a better, an unexpected world, never thinking that I was doing only what every other man had done and what had finally satisfied nobody.

With the Rector and the Squire all my upbringing seemed to have been dead and buried. Though I still lived, and often slept, at the Rectory, I made no effort to speak or behave with any intimacy towards the Rector's wife or the Squire's sister. They noticed, as they were bound to do, the elation in which I lived, but, if they questioned me about this or about my frequent absences from the house, I would put them off with some light-hearted reply, and would be amused to find that, although they may have suspected something which was not far from the truth, they seemed to shrink in timidity from pressing their inquiries too far. And this reluctance of theirs to attempt to force my secret from me, whether it came from a refinement of feeling or from fear, gave me pleasure and caused me to believe myself independent, strong, and progressive, although in reality I had no title to these qualities except my pride in the sudden and unrestrained exercise of my sexual powers. Of the future I hardly thought at all, although before my marriage I had signed on for training in the Air Force and Bess would speak often of what she imagined to be the delights of living at the aerodrome.

For me the delights of each day were enough and plenty. Every afternoon and many nights of the week I would meet Bess in a corrugated iron shed at the bottom of one of the fields below the aerodrome. It was on Government property but was, so the Flight-Lieutenant had informed us, quite safe for our purpose. Thither he and two friends of his who had acted as witnesses at the wedding had escorted us when the ceremony was over. They had brought some old sacks with them, and these had been our first wedding bed, though later we had added to our comfort and convenience in various ways. Even now, when I think of that shed and of the times we spent together there, I feel an excitement rising in my blood—that and different feelings, too.

I remember the night after the wedding when we stood in the light of a candle which one of the Flight-Lieutenant's friends had brought with him, saying good night gladly and nervously to the airmen. Huge shadows swung and flickered on the walls of the shed, and through the creaking door, above the round heads of the Flight-Lieutenant and his friends, I could see two or three stars. We had shaken hands and 'Sleep well' one of the men had said, to which the Flight-Lieutenant added, 'I shouldn't bother', and I had laughed and observed Bess looking at him as though his words had pleased her, for she was smiling slowly. Then they had gone away and I had secured the door and turned round to see Bess watching me. And so we stood for some moments listening to the retreating footsteps until their sound had died away and nothing was to be heard but the light swishing of the breeze against the iron roof. Then I stepped forward and Bess did too, so that we fell into each other's arms, and I covered with kisses her mouth and eyes and neck, and finding her body soft and yielding, I pressed my fingers into it, my muscles hard and angry with desire, but with my soul, as I know now, more soft and yielding than her body, crying out for the warmth and succour which I believed that she could give to me and I to her.

I remember how, when my lust was spent (and this time more successfully than had been the case on the day of the Rector's death), I lay relaxed with my arms about her, and felt the tips of her fingers on my forehead and shoulders, entranced and as it were listening to something very far away, though I was conscious of the fusion of our flesh and the warmth about me; and then her voice with something of triumph in it, 'You do love me, don't you?' and this seemed to drag me back into the nerves of my body and, unaccountably, to make me sad, while it accentuated my desire; and I held her tighter, muttering incoherent words, as people at such moments do, words that seemed to hurt my body as they were dragged through it, words that mean much, but not always what one thinks they mean.

But in these weeks I was in no mood to reflect upon the meaning of what we said or did. I went eagerly from one delight to another and she followed me, always gentle, usually calm. Often I would gaze at her for minutes on end while she sat staring out of the door of our shed, until she would turn her head and smile as she saw me as though she were seeing me for the first time. Then the blood would race to my heart and at the same time I would feel my limbs weakened by an overwhelming tenderness for her, a wish to please, a sad sense of the weakness of all my passion before her sweetness and her calm. At such moments she would often begin to speak of our future life together at the aerodrome, when I should become fully qualified as an officer, and somehow this topic of conversation always seemed to me most inapt, so pressing and inexhaustible was the present time, so much I wished her to see not the possibilities of a future career but the depth and severity of what I now felt; and as I stared into her calm or slightly puzzled eyes I would be hopelessly at a loss for words with which to tell her how gladly I would give her my life, how wholly I trusted in her goodness or adored her beauty.

She would look at me then with a small smile on her mouth and her eyebrows raised a little incredulously, as one might look perhaps from the shore at a child who believes that he is venturing in the sea beyond his depth. And I would feel a growing despair with words, as though it were they that were to blame, and would go again to the body, concentrating it in a moment's flame or stretching it out in the broad splendour of desire, and fancying that what I found there, because it was new, was indeed what I was forced to seek. And when I left her, returning in the late evening or early morning to the pub or Rectory, I would be sure that I was leaving what was the most precious thing of all to me, what made my life at the moment and would form it for the future. Away from her I could still feel her flesh against my flesh, hear the sound of her voice, imagine the shapes of shadows that our candle would throw over her face; and when I thought of these things, I would know my love and be proud of it and cherish within me the melting tenderness I felt for her softness, her delicacy, her mild and gentle ways.

So day after day passed, and in the midst of this novelty and delight I hardly noticed the events that were taking place around me, although I heard them frequently discussed and although they were of great importance both to myself and others.

The promise or threat made by the Air Vice-Marshal at the Rector's funeral was strictly fulfilled, and it so happened that it was the day on which the Squire was buried that was chosen for the formal occupation by the authorities of the aerodrome of his land and the village which it surrounded. This particular choice of dates might well have been regarded as one more deliberate insult offered by the Air Force to the feelings of the villagers, although it was maintained that the order had come direct from the government who could not, of course, have been informed of how exactly things stood with us.

At all events the Squire's sister was determined that her brother should not be buried in the village, since this would mean a service conducted entirely by an officer from the aerodrome; and when it became known that it was the Flight-Lieutenant who had been appointed to

132

take the church services amongst us, the lady's indignation knew no bounds. Indeed, this appointment created
an unpleasant effect everywhere. Even those who in the
pub had liked and respected the young man (and they
were not very many) were horrified at the thought that
one so young and one who, moreover, had been, however
indirectly, responsible for the late Rector's death should
now take the dead man's place among them. 'Why, he's
not a clergyman at all,' they would say and, though the
Flight-Lieutenant himself would occasionally remark that
he did not pretend to be much interested in religion, and
regarded his new post merely as a 'job of work', these
remarks were considered by most people to be improper
or scandalous. People even resented the fact that the
Flight-Lieutenant refused the title of Rector or 'your
reverence' and demanded to be known simply as 'padre'
or 'skypilot'; although, if he had chosen the former title,
his choice would have been, no doubt, equally unpopular
and, in point of fact, he had no right to claim them since
his appointment had nothing to do with the bishop of the
diocese but was entirely the business of the administration at the aerodrome. His duty was not to live in the
village, but merely to read the appropriate services on
Sundays and, in his sermon, to pass on to the villagers
any instructions which his superiors considered could be
best given in this way. On these occasions he wore neither
surplice nor cassock, I was told (for I did not attend
church myself), but appeared always in his Air Force
uniform. He read the prayers distinctly but in a voice
that was generally agreed to be lacking in reverence; and
though on the Sunday of his appointment a considerable
congregation had been brought together out of curiosity,

for some time after this fewer and fewer people attended the services which he conducted.

I met him often in the days after my marriage and was, as a rule, glad to see him, for above everything else I remembered that it was he who had, in a way, brought Bess and me together. With this in my mind I hardly remembered his conduct at the dinner party or even his negligence at the Agricultural Show. When I thought, which was not often, of the fact that I had signed the papers applying for work at the aerodrome and that in the course of time I should no doubt be called up, I was glad to think that I had a friend there who would help me with his advice at the beginning of my new venture. In particular I enjoyed talking to him of Bess, and this even although his attitude to the subject was seldom serious and often somewhat embarrassing; for he spoke of her, and indeed of all women, in a way which, at this time, I imagined to be peculiar to himself.

It was not merely that he regarded marriage in itself as being a kind of lunacy; this opinion would have been shared by Fred and Mac and others of the young men in the village who would spend the long summer nights, after the pubs were shut, in roaming the fields on the look-out for easy and almost indiscriminate love. They would afterwards roar with laughter as they told of their adventures, and yet in their laughter there was always something of affection. 'She was a prettily marked child,' one might say when he reached the end of a story. 'I wouldn't mind seeing her again some day.' The Flight-Lieutenant, on the other hand, never laughed about this subject, though he took at least as great an interest in it as did any of the men from the village. He would speak coolly, dispassionately, and at some length about the physical details of making love; but if I mentioned any of the feelings which I had in my heart, he would cut the conversation short, sometimes smiling condescendingly at me as if I were a child, sometimes appearing almost indignant, as though I were speaking of something boring or disgusting. 'You'll get over that sort of thing,' he would say, and I would smile to myself, though I felt sorry for him, fancying that perhaps at some earlier period of his life he had suffered a disappointment which had warped his nature. But, so great still was his ascendancy over me, that I did not question him about himself; once indeed, long before, I had asked him about his parents, and he had replied: 'What on earth do they matter?' Since then I had made no effort to discover anything about the life he had led before he had joined the Air Force.

Of the Air Force itself he was now much more willing to talk than he had been previously, and it was on this subject alone that he seemed to me to speak seriously. Indeed, he often showed annoyance at my own attitude, which was simply that I had signed on for training so as the more easily to be able to marry Bess and for no other reason. I could see that to him it was really shocking that I should think in this way, and this was the more remarkable because he never told me anything about the aerodrome which could account for his devotion to the life there. He would describe cocktail parties, love affairs with some of the officers' wives, new buildings, improvements made in the construction of the planes or of their instruments; but he never seemed to me to have any clear idea of the purpose or of the future of the organization to which he belonged. He carried out his duties in the village with perfect regularity, although they would have seemed to be wholly unsuited to a person of his character, and this contrast between his complete irresponsibility in ordinary life and his perfect efficiency when it came to carrying out an order was a thing which surprised not only me but everyone else in the village; for we had become accustomed to considering the officers of the aerodrome as characters from a different world whose conduct was incalculable; now, however, we found them in our midst and discovered that, though their way of life was indeed different from our own, their official actions were precise and certain.

After an initial period of bewilderment when no one knew what to make of the changes which were coming so rapidly, two fairly distinct parties formed themselves among us. On one side were the older men and women, who grumbled at every step taken by the aerodrome authorities and would speak with tears in their eyes of the time when Rector and Squire had been alive; and on the other hand were many of the young men who, apart from their interest in mechanical devices such as aeroplanes, were attracted to the new order of things by the higher rates of pay which were now offered for their work and by the opportunities which might come in time of wearing uniforms; for they were encouraged by the Flight-Lieutenant and others to believe that there might be room for the more intelligent and ambitious among them on the ground staff of the aerodrome itself. They had merely to give up their old way of life (the Squire's farms had been liquidated and agriculture in our village had now come to an end) and to attend punctually the classes which were arranged for them in building and mechanical engineering. So a great many of the young men, while not exactly welcoming the occupation of the village, were at least prepared at first to adapt themselves as well as possible to the new conditions; and very soon a clear-cut division might be noticed between them and their elders whose whole life had been spent under a quite different régime and whose minds and bodies were alike unfitted for the learning of new kinds of work. In the pub the two groups, of the young and of the old, were more separated than they ever had been, and what was more remarkable was that the old men were no longer treated with any respect at all by the young, so that soon they were reduced to whispering together in corners, for no one would pay the slightest attention to them if they were ever to raise their voices.

Between the two parties the landlord occupied a central position. He would speak gravely and respectfully of the past, but would at the same time encourage the young men in their schemes for their own advancement. 'Progress,' he would often declare, 'is the law of life,' and the young would agree enthusiastically with this sentiment. Though he would criticize some of the many new regulations which were coming into force amongst us—such as the one which forbade the sale of drinks during the hours when classes for men were in progress in the village schoolroom—on the whole he would assert his belief in discipline and obedience, qualities which, he informed us, had stood him in good stead during his military service in his youth. The young men, though these ideals were strange to them, would listen to him with respect: but among the old a comment frequently made was that the landlord knew which side his bread was buttered.

In many of these discussions Bess, when she was serving in the bar, would join eagerly, and I would support her in everything that she said, although I believe now that I was at that time quite indifferent to the arguments on one side or the other, and only wished to further anything which gave her pleasure. Occasionally I would feel a twinge of something like conscience when I thought of how completely I had deserted the whole world of my upbringing, and I was sometimes almost offended by the indifference with which Bess would speak of the dead Squire and Rector, especially since I knew that she had been with the Rector a particular favourite among the village girls. But these impressions on my mind were most transitory; a smile or her next words would do away with them, and I would see in her beauty, her gentleness, and her ambition something infinitely fresher and more desirable than the world which I believed that both she and I had left behind. I would even begin myself to employ arguments which I had heard from her and in which I hardly believed, and would speak as she might speak even in front of the Squire's sister and the Rector's wife although I knew that my words must distress at least the former and probably both of these ladies.

I say 'probably' because at this time, though the Squire's sister was without doubt most bitterly opposed to the new order of things, it was hard to say what exactly was the attitude of the Rector's wife. She had been informed that she could remain in the Rectory for another month at the end of which time the building was to be converted into a gymnasium; and now the Squire's sister was staying there with her, for work on the Manor had begun almost immediately after the occupation of the village. The exterior was being camouflaged and the interior redecorated so as to serve as an officers' club house.

I had imagined at first that the two ladies, after what had taken place amongst us, would wish to live in some other part of the country, and was surprised to find that they were now planning to take a house together just outside the limit of Government property. The Squire's sister would declare that she would never leave the scenes in which she and her brother had grown up, and that she even cherished hopes that at some future time the conditions of the past might be re-established. Meanwhile she regarded the present with anger and with scorn. She would stop in the street for long conversations with those of the villagers who shared her views. She ceased to attend church from the time when the Flight-Lieutenant was appointed to its care, and she encouraged others to boycott the services. Indeed, I was surprised at the resolution and pertinacity which she now showed. It was almost as though her brother's death had given her fresh strength which she had decided to use, by what means she could, in attacking the organization which could be held, with some reason, responsible for that death; and her influence with the older men and women of the village might well make her, I feared, not a menace but a decided nuisance to the aerodrome authorities. Both the Rector's wife and I advised her on several occasions to be less outspoken in her opinions; but our advice had no effect on her whatever, and the bitterness of her feelings was such that she became,

139

what she had never been in the past, somewhat eccentric in her manners. She had been seen to twirl her walking-stick round her head and even to spit in the gutter when the Flight-Lieutenant had passed her in the street; and altogether, though her character seemed to have gained surprisingly in resolution, one could not help observing in her face and gestures a kind of constraint and tenseness that was also new to her.

The Rector's wife, on the other hand, was to all appearance quite unchanged by all the events which had certainly changed her way of living. While she would not often object verbally to the frequent strictures made by the Squire's sister against the aerodrome and its management, she would still make it clear that she was not greatly impressed by them. She attended church as regularly as before, and continued for the time being to organize the Sunday school, although it was clear that in the end this, together with all the other activities of the church, would be denied any kind of official existence by the authorities of the aerodrome.

'One must resign oneself' was one of her favourite expressions at this time, and she succeeded so well in this plan that her very presence in the house acted as a kind of balm for the agitated spirit of her friend who, somewhat surprisingly, was never offended when her tirades were met only by a gentle smile and even when in the course of an argument the Rector's wife would seem to incline rather to my side than to hers. But what had surprised me most of all was that, on one occasion not long after my marriage, she had taken me aside and actually recommended me to consider seriously the offer of help which had been made me by the Air Vice-

Marshal. She had spoken uncertainly and almost apologetically.

'I know,' she had said, 'that my husband would not have approved; but jobs are difficult to get nowadays, and it seems to me that the thing is worth thinking over.' Then she had laid her hand against my cheek and patted it. 'You would be nearer home, too,' she said, and I remember feeling surprise at the fact that she still regarded me, even after the disclosure at the dinner party and the Rector's confession, as having any longer a home in which she was the central figure; for when I thought of home now, I thought of the shed where I had spent nights and afternoons with Bess. I had come gradually, perhaps almost insensibly, but quite finally to regard myself as cut off from the Rectory and all that it had once meant to me. What seemed to me stranger still was the fact that I felt no longer any curiosity about the early life of the Rector or about my true parents. If a secret existed I was prepared to allow it to remain a secret, indeed, I preferred it to be so and now, so far from wishing to question the Rector's wife about the confession which we had heard, I was actually relieved that she showed no signs of referring to the subject. My life in future was to be, so I told myself, my own, and if it were not that I had promised Bess that our marriage was to remain clandestine, I should probably have revealed it, so careless was I of what my old friends might think of what I had determined to do.

I think that my surprise at the Rector's wife's unexpected attitude towards the Air Force was chiefly responsible for my not telling her that I had already applied to join it. Instead, I promised her that I would think the matter over, a course which I did not pursue, and never had done, for my constant preoccupation was with Bess, and in competition with my thoughts of her no career in the world would have occupied my attention for long. So I attended only half-heartedly to what I saw and heard in the village during these months; I thought little, if at all, of the two dead men who had exercised such an influence over my childhood. But I noticed the flowers beginning to blossom below the hedges and the dew which I kicked away from the grass in the early mornings. I listened to the birds and imagined that they and all the sky was friendly to me, thinking of my love which I found so full of joy and believed to be so strong.

CHAPTER X

A Disclosure

SO PASSED THREE months in which I thought seriously of no single object, although I would pause now and then to admire and to reflect upon the novelty of my situation and what I imagined to be my freedom from all the associations of my childhood. Even when this period of time was almost over I had hardly begun to envisage the sort of life to which I had pledged myself when I had signed the papers applying for training at the aerodrome, although Bess would be constantly talking of the possibilities of my quick promotion, of the uniforms which I would wear, and of the probable date at which we should be able to afford a car.

To all this I was wholly indifferent, and was indeed somewhat irritated by her apparent conviction that the future could hold for us anything more splendid than the present. Not that I was at all averse from joining the Air Force; but what to Bess seemed glamorous—the concealed houses of the officers' wives, the powerful organization, the very thought of flying in the air—appeared to me as trivial and easy things compared with the opening out to each other of our minds and bodies in love. I can remember often holding her in my arms and wishing, as people do, that this would last for ever; but if I said so she would wriggle away from me and say: 'Oh yes, it would be nice. But think of all the places we've never been to!' And to me there was something infinitely endearing in her dismay at the thought of never going abroad or never flying in the air; for though these experiences attracted me too, their attraction was nothing at all like the force which she exercised over me. I would reassure her and say yes, we would go abroad, yes, we would fly, if need be, to the North Pole; and she would come close to me again and whisper into my ear or gently touch my eyes with her lips; and I would feel that between us we possessed a secret and an understanding certain to assure us both of happiness and success.

Her occasional abstractions from me when she would sit in the doorway of our hut gazing, as though she were sleep-walking, over the shadows lengthening at sunset across the fields were, I thought at first, due to her preoccupation with the future and her reflections on our way of life that must soon come to an end; for when I questioned her as to what she was thinking, she would say it was either nothing, or else, with a smile, the aerodrome and what I should look like as an officer. But once I remember, almost at the end of our three months' honeymoon, when I asked my usual question as I watched her face in profile, moody and with a frown just weighing down the eyebrows, she turned to me without changing her expression, and said: 'It's Mother, Roy. She seems to be against you for some reason.'

I laughed, and asked what did it matter, having no idea at this time of whither the conversation would lead me. I had noticed myself that Bess's mother, who had only returned to the village a week ago, had not been in these last few days as cordial to me as she had always been in the past. I had observed her looking at me in a manner that seemed to show hesitation as well as disapproval when I was sitting in the pub; and, though there were other times when she looked kindly at me, I had thought that even in her kindness there was something of constraint, and I had been puzzled to account for this change in her attitude, since always in the past I had been a favourite of hers, more at ease with her, indeed, than I ever was with her husband. Did she suspect, I wondered, the actual relationship between Bess and me? If so, her doubts could easily be set at rest. She had been at one time a maid in the service of the Rector's wife and had often looked after me in my childhood. The Rector himself had had, I knew, a high opinion of her. I imagined that she at least, whatever her husband might think, would be glad to have me as a son-in-law; and so I had been surprised by her attitude to me since her return to the village, and I was surprised by what Bess said now.

'I'll go and see her,' I said, 'and ask what the trouble is. I don't know what I've done wrong. Certainly it wasn't marrying you.'

Bess's eyes were narrowed as she looked at me. It seemed that she had been struck by a new idea. 'It is all right, isn't it?' she said. 'I mean, we really are married, aren't we?'

I came towards her and knelt down at her side; but she drew away from me, putting up her hand between us, not in anger or in playfulness, but with a kind of aversion, so that I too drew back from her. I felt unreasonably angry with her as I watched her looking away from me down the hill, and noticed the quick shadow of a cloud running towards us across the fields. When I saw that there were tears in her eyes I could see no reason for them and, though I was sorry for her, I was, in a way, indignant. 'Of course we're married,' I said. 'And even if we weren't, we could be, and it wouldn't make any difference.'

She put her head in her hands and began to cry. When I touched her she shook her head without looking up, and I sat back on the ground, perplexed, and feeling for the first time remote from her. Soon she stopped crying and began to wipe her eyes with the corner of her dress. She looked at me and smiled, and began speaking; but, though I listened to her words, I thought still with amazement of how she had withdrawn herself from me, shaking off from her what comfort I had to give her; for this seemed to me then unnatural.

'Mother worries me so much,' she was saying. 'She keeps telling me not to have anything to do with you, and she won't tell me why. Of course I haven't told her anything. But it makes me so sad. Because we haven't done anything really wrong, have we?'

She was smiling now in a way that showed that she knew that her suggestion to be a foolish one, and I looked at the skin of her face, flushed and wet in patches, but so smooth and tender an envelope for the flesh beneath. My anger with her had wholly disappeared, or rather had been transferred to her mother as it would have been transferred to any other person or object that could cause us unhappiness.

'I'll go and see her,' I said. 'I'll go now. It's absurd for you to be worried like this. I won't tell her that we're married, but I'll make her see that I can't do you any harm if that's what she thinks I'm doing.'

As I spoke I felt, for some reason, peculiarly elated as though I were championing successfully some mis-

146

understood but splendid cause. I was surprised that Bess did not seem to share my enthusiasm; for the expression of her face did not alter and, when I rose to my feet, she stretched out a hand as though to detain me. Then she smiled, but rather as if she were thinking of something else. 'Go along, then,' she said, 'if you like. But you won't be able to see me again today. I'm going out to tea.'

She looked up at me from below her eyebrows in a way that I found particularly appealing, for there was a kind of secretiveness, even a kind of guiltiness in her expression. I said: 'Never mind. We'll be here tomorrow'; and I looked into her eyes and saw them looking away from me down the path that led to the bottom of the field. I asked her whether she would come with me, but she said no, she would prefer to wait in the hut for a little and think. She was not feeling very well, she said, and I thought there was something pathetic in the look of her eyes when I kissed her before I went away. At the bottom of the field I turned round to wave to her, and I remember now, when I saw her raise her hand in reply to me, how I thought that the two gestures were a kind of pledge between us of the certainty of our love and, in spite of the distance, of our closeness.

I walked quickly across another field, hot in the summer sun, and looked away to my right at the fields where three months ago we had heard the larks singing, and I had decided to do what I had done and what filled me with pride. Soon I reached the pub and saw over the low wall, among the masses of bright flowers that filled the beds at each side of the door, Bess's mother sitting on a hard chair with some knitting in her lap;

and as I looked at her I no longer felt the anger that I had felt, for there was something in the woman before me that reminded me of Bess, and I remembered, too, her kindness to me when I had been a child. I was more bewildered now than indignant as I watched her with her head bent down over her knitting. I saw now what I had hardly noticed before, that she was exceptionally handsome. From her Bess must have inherited that charm that comes from a certain remoteness, a quality which caused the Squire's sister often to describe the landlord's wife as a 'superior' woman. Her hair, though it was growing white at the sides, was light yellow on top, and though her face and body were plump, one could still imagine her as being in her youth lithe, active, and lovable as Bess was now. But her face was deeply lined and, as she knitted, there was an expression of worry and exasperation on her mouth. I opened the gate and she raised her eyes somewhat wearily, as though in dislike of the thought of visitors; but when she recognized me I fancied that I saw in her eyes a look of fear, and this look surprised me, although it soon passed away and she smiled in greeting.

I went through the gate and sat down at her side on the bricks that bordered the flower-bed. There were red-hot pokers, delphiniums, and lupins behind me, and all around us the noise of insects buzzing in the air. I leant my head back towards the flowers, where there was some shade, straightened my shoulders, and pressed the palms of my hands into the friable earth of the flower-bed. Bess's mother was looking at me sharply. The sun was behind her, so that light gleamed from the top of her head, while her face, except for the eyes, was indistinct.

'Listen, Eva,' I said (for I had been taught to call her by her Christian name when she had been my nurse), 'what's the matter?'

For a moment her face seemed to soften towards me, but almost at once the look of affection was replaced by something which might have been pity or might have been distaste. 'Has Bess been talking to you?' she asked.

'Yes,' I said, 'she has. She tells me that you're always running me down.'

I paused and looked up at the landlord's wife, expecting an answer, but for some moments she did not speak. She was staring at the ground, her lips pursed together and a frown on her face; and in this posture she so reminded me of Bess that I almost laughed; for I was fond of her and was certain that she could have no serious objection to what had taken place between her daughter and me. When she looked at me she was smiling. I smiled back, fancying that we were on the verge of some scene of reconciliation.

'I like you, my dear,' she said. 'You know I do. You mustn't think I'm against you. But I don't want you to go making love to my Bess. It wouldn't be right.'

'But I wouldn't make love to her,' I said, 'unless I was serious about it.'

She still smiled at me, but now I felt sure that there was something hidden behind her smiling. She began to speak to me as she would do when I was a child, and pointed out gently the obstacles that would prevent me from ever marrying Bess—my youth and Bess's youth, our different upbringings, what the Rector would have thought, how the Rector's wife would disapprove, my approaching examination. 'It would never do,' she said,

149

'and I want you to promise me that you will never think of it.'

The expression on her face changed almost to one of desperation when she realized that her words were having little or no effect. For I was becoming indignant with what I regarded as an unwarrantable interference with something that I knew to be good. 'Suppose I were to tell you,' I said, 'that I'd already asked her to marry me and that she's accepted?'

I had spoken light-heartedly, but my words seemed to have startled her as though they had been the confession of some crime. She turned to me quickly and spoke with a kind of exasperation. 'It's not true!' she said. 'Tell me it's not true.' Then she stretched out her hands to me, and I saw that she was almost in tears.

'It is true,' I said. 'And why shouldn't we be married?'

She made no reply to this but, after a pause, asked in a low and strangely businesslike voice, 'When did you decide you wanted to do this?'

I was on the point of telling her the whole story, but remembering my promise to Bess I decided to tell a lie. 'We've only just been talking about it,' I said, and I thought that the landlord's wife appeared relieved, though she smiled at me as one might smile at a child whom one has regretfully to disappoint. Then her mouth hardened and she rose suddenly from her chair. 'Come with me,' she said, and I followed her into the house.

We went past the bar, in a corner of which the landlord was asleep in his shirtsleeves, with his pipe lying precariously on a barrel behind his neck, and we climbed the stairs to the bedroom next to Bess's room, where her parents slept. The windows were tightly closed and, as the full heat of the afternoon sun beat upon them, the room was stiflingly hot; but for the moment I hardly noticed the discomfort of the place, so surprised was I to be brought here at all, and I followed the landlord's wife as sheepishly as I might have done in my childhood, though previously I had been so full of confidence.

I sat down beside her on the patchwork quilt which covered the bed and waited for her to speak. She was looking at me strangely and with an evident affection which somehow reassured me. There was a long pause as we sat staring at each other. Then she said: 'I see that I shall have to tell you why I don't want you to marry Bess.'

I smiled, since on this subject I felt sure of myself.

'Wait until I've opened the window, then,' I said, and she waited while I did so and until I had come back and had sat down again by her side.

She took one of my hands in her two hands and said: 'Bess is your sister.' Then she pressed my hand and looked hard into my eyes, as though estimating the effect of her words, and I remained as I was with my eyes not leaving her face.

I felt dully the shock of the meaning of her words, as I had felt what I had now almost forgotten, the disclosure made to me by the Rector at the dinner party which had been supposed to celebrate my twenty-first birthday. Then in a moment all the strength in me seemed to flow back into my heart to repudiate what I had heard. This was something which I would not believe. My face must have hardened and in this hardening perhaps the landlord's wife fancied that there was expressed either disappointment or despair. 'Never mind, Roy dear,' she said. 'You'll get over it.'

I thought suddenly of the mystery surrounding my birth, and was at once bewildered. Could it be that the woman beside me was my mother, or was it that the man in the bar below was my father? Had the landlord's wife known all the time of my parentage when she had brought me as a baby to the Rectory? Had the Rector known, too, and was this the 'whole truth' which he had mentioned in his confession and, if so, why had he kept it back from me? With all this in my mind, so incapable was I of connecting ideas together that I still refused to believe what I had heard. But I looked at the landlord's wife tenderly as though she were indeed my mother, and asked, 'Who am I, then? Who are my parents?' I noticed that I was trembling as I waited for her reply, but my question seemed to have surprised her. She looked at me as though I were speaking wildly.

'You know who your parents are,' she said, 'but you don't know about me. Your father was Bess's father, too.'

I saw at once that by my 'father' she meant the Rector, and my surprise at this revelation of the Rector's infidelity and of Bess's true parentage flashed through and out of my mind in an instant. Relief and joy took its place; for had not the Rector himself told me that my parents were unknown? And though he had hinted at some other secret which had not been disclosed, this secret certainly could not have been that he was himself what he had just denied himself to be. I felt at once that my own diffi-culties were settled, and looked with a new interest and affection at the landlord's wife. There must have been one thing more, I saw, beside the murder, to disturb the

Rector's conscience; but I thought kindly of him as I remembered how like Bess this old woman must have been in her youth. It seemed to be my part now to press her hand. 'It's all right,' I said. 'The Rector and his wife aren't my parents.'

She smiled at me, and I could see from her smile that she was quite incredulous of what I said, and surprised that I was saying it. I quickly told her of what had happened at the dinner party and of how the Rector had expressly mentioned her as the woman who had brought me as an infant to the house. While I was speaking I watched her face closely and eagerly for any sign that my story was convincing her; but, although I could see that she was surprised by some of my words, the expression on her face hardly altered. She still looked at me with commiseration, and still evidently adhered to her former opinion about my parentage.

I began to feel a growing sense of doubt as to the truth of what I was myself saying, a horrible suspicion that all the time I might have misunderstood something which the Rector had said, or that I had suffered a lapse of memory so that some explanation which he had given me later had passed completely from my mind. I began to fear that it might be found that what the landlord's wife believed was strictly true, and at the same time everything in me rebelled against accepting either that truth or its consequences. I knew that nothing would make me give Bess up, for apart from her, I thought, I had nowhere to stand, and for her I would break every law of man or nature. I listened sullenly and with a feeling of arrested fear as Bess's mother spoke.

'My dear,' she said, 'your father was very wrong to

tell you that story, even though he may have done it for the sake of his wife. He ought to have thought of what might happen.'

I broke in and said: 'But he wouldn't have said he was not my father if he really was.'

The landlord's wife continued as though she had not heard me. 'He was a strange man. He would do anything to shield his wife from any blame.' She smiled as though recalling to her mind some incident from the past, and then, turning to me, began to speak more quickly. 'He was right,' she said, 'when he told you that it was I who brought you to the Rectory. I came with your mother and I had been looking after you for nearly a year. I was the only one in the secret, because I was useful and your parents trusted me. And I'd never have told even you if it hadn't been for Bess. Don't you see? You were born only five months after the marriage?'

There was in her voice a gentle confidence which enraged me. 'What do you mean?' I said. 'What marriage? I don't understand.'

She laid one hand on mine as though to reassure me, and went on speaking. As she spoke I began to pull at the loose threads on the patchwork quilt. The squares were red and yellow and blue.

'Your father was a terrible man,' she said, 'when once he was fixed on a woman's love. I know that. It must have been like that with your mother. They couldn't get married for some time, not till your father got his post here; and he wasn't the man to stand a long courtship. So you came into the world too soon. Of course, your mother and father went away for their honeymoon and after that he came back to the village alone and sent me to look after his wife. I didn't think then that I should bear his child.'

She paused and laughed. I saw that the past had taken such a hold upon her mind that she was forgetting the present. She jerked back her neck as a girl might do to throw back into place a lock of hair; but her hair was thin and neatly compacted to the top and sides of her head. She looked at me sharply and almost as though in apology for having strayed from the purpose of her story.

'I looked after your mother,' she said, 'while she was carrying you, and I was present when you were born. Poor dear, she was upset and ill most of the time, and saw no one except your father who could only visit us from time to time. She was very fond of him and she was a handsome woman, too. I used to wonder sometimes what he saw in me. But even in those days he used to like me. He paid me well and used to say how he'd never forget the way I'd helped him and his wife. And, of course, if the true story had got out I suppose it would have been the end of him in this village. He used to say that it would be awkward if at any time you wanted a birth certificate because, you see, you were registered under your mother's maiden name. "Later on," I can remember him saying, "I may have to disown him." He was very serious about it.'

She paused again, and I began to be overwhelmed with a dreadful conviction that she was telling the truth. What reason indeed could she have for doing otherwise? I could see clearly that if, as she said, I had been conceived before the marriage of my parents this fact, considering the Rector's position, would have had to be concealed, and indeed it could only have been con-

cealed in the manner of which Bess's mother had just
told me. But still I was at a loss to account for the
Rector's speech at the dinner party. He had throughout
my life carried off successfully a deception that was only
in one small respect a deception. Why should he finally
replace this by a pure fabrication? I remembered that
some time previously I had indeed asked him for my birth
certificate, since I knew that this would be required at
the time when I was to apply for an entrance into the
Civil Service; but still it seemed to me absurd that so
small a thing as this could be responsible for so large a
falsehood. And yet it remained true, I saw, that it was
impossible for me to secure a birth certificate that would
have carried the name by which I had always been called.
I began to feel lost in the intricacies of deception which
seemed now always to have surrounded me, and I found
my mind wandering to inessential questions, such as
whether the Squire and his sister had known the truth
or whether they had been as misguided as myself.

Meanwhile the landlord's wife continued her story,
but I gave only half my attention to her account of how
within two months of my birth, the Rector had begun to
court her; of how she had felt herself to be acting dis-
loyally towards her mistress; how the Rector, 'a great
talker', as she called him, had set her doubts at rest, so
that they had become lovers. Bess had been the result of
this, and to conceal the true facts of her conception there
had been a hurried marriage to the man who was now
landlord of the pub. 'And I've been very happy,' she
concluded, 'though I didn't like giving up your father,
and I'm sure he didn't like giving me up. He was a real
man, my dear, and there's never been anyone like him.

He'd say terrible things, too. Often in the night he'd turn and cross himself and pray. I believe that he had something on his conscience, and never told me what it was.'

'Yes,' I said. 'He'd murdered a man.' The words came from me without my having willed to speak, and at once I realized that I should not have spoken them. Yet I hardly regretted them; for I felt no tenderness for the reputation of the man who was, if this story were to be believed, the father both of Bess and of myself. Respect I did feel for him and a kind of admiration and pity for his passionate, self-reproachful, and tortured nature. I was glad, too, that he had both won and kept this woman's love; nor did I feel any bitterness against him for his part in the situation where I was now placed. But I knew already that, just as he had disowned me, so I would disown him. In my mind were horror and fear and hesitation, but behind them and stronger than them all was my resolve by some means or other to surmount this obstacle to my independence and my delight.

I looked at Bess's mother and saw that the words which I had just spoken had had very little effect on her. She was holding her head between her hands and smiling to herself secretively, as I had so often seen Bess smile. I rose from the bed and took a step towards the door, but she quickly put out a hand to stop me and, rising to her feet, too, stood facing me, looking at me in an appealing way and with the affection which I had known from her always in my childhood. But this affection, simple and profound as it was, seemed to me to have lost its solidity, and I was quite unwilling to resign myself to it. I looked at her now with more understanding but with much less faith. Here, I thought, was another of those who had guided my childhood and whose life I had imagined incorrectly to be simply as it had appeared to be, firmly based on the easy generalizations that a code of rules will supply. She felt certainly none of the agony of self-reproach with which both the Rector and the Squire had been afflicted, but she was no less than they bound up in secrecies and in dissembling. Now, when she held my hands and looked deeply into my eyes, I was both fond of her and sorry for her distress, but I felt her gesture to be a trifle foolish.

'My dear,' she was saying, 'I know that this will have been a shock to you, but you do see, don't you, why I had to tell you. And I am so sorry for you. I'm sure you'll get over it in time, though.'

She paused, expecting me to reply. I looked at her in some surprise, for it seemed to me that she was expecting from me altogether too much. I realized fully that it would be impossible for me to tell her what was in my mind and I smiled, as though this fact were amusing.

'One thing more,' she said. 'Would you like me to tell Bess, or not? I've promised never to tell her, but it may be the only way.'

I said: 'No, don't tell her. You'd better leave it to me.' Then I kissed her on the forehead and left the room.

CHAPTER XI

Change of Plan

As I WALKED away my mind raced from argument to argument and from plan to plan as to how I could escape from the dilemma in which I was placed. Yet, feverish and rapid as my thinking was, there was something behind the mind that was disconnected from it all, something that had already made its decision and was fixed and certain there, that was even calm, although so great was the overlying agitation of thought and feeling that the sky, I remember, and the bright light seemed to me, as I walked away from the pub, as unreal as a kind of scenery that might at any moment be removed or replaced by something else. I can say confidently that I felt no horror and no disgust at what I had done by accident. Whether, if it had to be done again and I had possessed full knowledge, I should still have done it is another question. No doubt I should have found myself restrained. As it was I knew that my feelings for Bess had not altered in any way, and I busied my mind with arguments to show that they should not alter, that they need not alter, or that the story which I had heard was false.

One obvious course of action was to go at once to the Rector's wife, tell her what I had heard, and seek from her an explanation or a confirmation. Yet I shrank from doing this; because if, as I feared would be the case, the story of the Rector's wife should tally with the story of Bess's mother, then I should be in no further doubt, and should have to face the full implications of my position. As it was I could still, in some part of my mind, fall back upon the Rector's express declaration that he was not my father and though, to be candid, I no longer believed in this, there was still a certain number of difficulties in accounting for the speech which he had made at the dinner party, and these difficulties my mind began to make the most of, but was unable by any means to make much of them.

I found that my steps had carried me back on the way which I had come, and I paused at the bottom of the fields below the aerodrome, looking uphill to the tin hut, some quarter of a mile distant, in which I had said good-bye to Bess. The late afternoon sun glistened from its roof, so that in the landscape it appeared an object of special importance as to me it was certainly more important than any other building; and as I noted its distance it seemed to me a jewel, minute and inestimable, of which my possession was already threatened, and to retain which I would use up all the energies that I had. I knew that by this time Bess would have left it and the thought of the empty tin walls between which she had lately been filled me with a certain unreasonable tender-ness for the vacant space and the rough furniture that I know so well. My mind still was turning over the advantages and disadvantages of seeking an interview with the Rector's wife and still I was so busy with my thoughts that I hardly noticed the shadows that were beginning to close upon the valley or the ground upon which I trod. I walked towards the tin hut with no definite object in view, but rather as though I were attracted thither by some force outside myself.

On reaching it I turned round and looked back over the village and the river beyond it winding through the fields, letting my thoughts relax. There were some duck flying high in the air above the river, and I watched them till their stiff formation was lost in the shadow of the farther hill. I noted the Air Force flag flying from the church, the school, and the Manor, and a detachment of aircraftsmen marching past the pub which I had just left. These visible signs of the subjection of our village to a different organization would, not long ago, have angered me. Now I smiled to think that they left me wholly indifferent, and that the sight of the airmen was, if anything, slightly stimulating to me. I began to consider my approaching entry into the Air Force and to reflect that if I were moved to some distant station I could go there with Bess and no one need know, as some did here, the truth of our relationship. The very necessity to defy or to deceive the whole opinion of the world had both strengthened my love and made it more tender. Now, I thought, I should have not only to enjoy but to defend.

While I was thinking in this way I became conscious of a noise behind me and had turned round to look at the hut with no definite intention or even any curiosity as to whether the noise were that of the wind against the tin walls or whether it proceeded from some other source; but as I turned I heard another sound, a low and delighted laughter, and I knew that it was Bess laughing. Immediately my body stiffened and a kind of pain seemed to freeze me and stagger me where I stood. I put out one hand against the wall of the hut, and was at a loss to know how or why this flood of feeling had come over me, for my mind had formed no precise conjecture and it was something quite different from my conscious thought which had so sharply and suddenly threatened me with distress. Indeed, my thoughts came immediately to my rescue and forced a smile upon my face. Again I heard the low laughter, and I shook my head as though to deny the sound or else innocently to explain it. I walked towards the door of the hut and, as I walked, I remember noticing and being surprised at the heaviness of my feet.

At the door I paused again, shrinking from putting my hand to the latch, and it was no conscious thought that determined my hesitation. Now I heard words murmured indistinctly in another voice, which I did not recognize, and there flashed into my mind the memory of how words spoken are indistinct when the mouth that speaks them is pressed into the flesh of breast or shoulder or neck. I thrust this thought from me, and indeed it was still unconnected with any idea which I had as yet formed of the present situation. I began to feel weak at the knees and raised my hand to the latch.

Now I heard Bess's voice again, a few words spoken rapidly and a low murmur, which I knew well and knew well when it was uttered. I was suddenly convinced of what I would find and, with no more deliberation, flung back the door with a crash against the iron wall. I stopped on the threshold with the sun behind my back pouring its light into the hut and radiating back golden from the two heads close together.

My attention was concentrated first on Bess who had been lying with her back to me, naked on the bed.

When the door had opened she had twisted round her flushed face, frowning in the sunlight, and there was a look of uncertainty and of surprise about her which I had seen often myself when some sudden noise of the wind or of an owl hooting had startled her in my embrace. I knew how her body would stiffen at such moments, and I noticed the hair damp about her forehead. In a moment she had recognized me and the surprise in her face was quickly chased away by a look of fear. She put her hands over her eyes and turned as though to seek protection from the man beside her. But he (it was the Flight-Lieutenant) had already left the bed and was hurriedly putting on his clothes. So she turned back to me, sat up, and pulled some of her own clothes around her. She looked as though she might either smile or cry and were trying to decide which it was that she would do.

The Flight-Lieutenant was buttoning up his jacket. His head was bent forward a little and his lips compressed as he closely watched my face. Perhaps he feared that I would attack him and, as I was taller and stronger than he was, he had some reason, perhaps, to be afraid. Indeed, had the mass of ill-defined feeling which now overwhelmed me been, by some accident, concentrated into anger, I might well have killed him; as it was I thought of no such thing, but was puzzled as I looked at him, for previously, I had admired his beauty, his experience, and his skill; I had looked up to him as at a superior being; but now I saw nothing superior in him, and was somewhat shocked to find it so. He took some papers from his pocket and held them out towards me. 'Here are your calling-up papers, Roy,' he said. 'I brought them along. They want you to report for duty tomorrow.'

He advanced towards me and made as though to put the papers in my pocket; but as he extended his hand I turned upon him quickly, for I could not bear to feel his touch. I felt a kind of weight upon my shoulders, and my arms lengthening towards him. He dropped the papers on the floor and sprang past me into the open air and, as I turned my head, I noticed a look of relief upon his face, though I did not know why he was relieved and was quite unconscious of how I was myself behaving. I turned back towards Bess and saw her staring past me with wide eyes towards the door. Behind me now the Flight-Lieutenant was speaking. 'Sorry about this,' he said. 'But all's fair, you know.'

Then I noticed the beginnings of a smile on Bess's face, and I put one hand in front of my eyes and the other hand against the wall to steady me. Soon I turned and looked out through the door and saw the Flight-Lieutenant walking quickly away across the fields. For a few moments I watched him and then, coming back into the shed, sat down on an empty packing case that faced the bed where Bess was lying. The clothes were huddled up round her, and in her eyes was again a look of fear, as though I were likely to be dangerous to her. There seemed to me something pathetic both in her look and in her posture. With no clear idea of what I was doing, I stretched out one hand towards her, and her eyes followed my hand as though fearing it and wishing it away, so that soon I removed it from the space between us and, looking across the space, began to see that now it was most difficult to cross, though all the more I wished to cross it and to hold her in my arms to find comfort there and a kind of explanation for this event that, in reality, held no comfort for me and could never be explained in any way that could cause me any satisfaction.

'When did this start?' I said, as though that mattered, and was surprised to find my voice trembling as I spoke.

Bess's eyes were wide open as she looked at me. Her voice was low, but expressed no hesitation. Rather there was a note of certainty and of defiance in it as she asked: 'Why do you want to know?'

I looked in her face before I answered, but I looked in vain for any expression there that would allow me to declare my love, to tell her that my whole life was bound up in her and to plead with her not to exercise against me that cruelty which those who are soft-hearted and weak and indifferent are alone capable of exercising.

'I just want to know,' I said. 'That's all.'

She smiled before replying, but smiled wryly, as though the information which she was giving was neither very important nor much to her taste. 'It started the day before we were married,' she said, and then, misinterpreting my look of surprise, she added quickly: 'It's all right. I know I've done wrong, but I couldn't help it. And I don't mind.'

I got up and walked to the door of the shed. The sun had set behind the farther hills, but I hardly noticed the cool and dampness of the evening air. A dog was barking in the garden behind the pub, and I could hear, too, the raised voices of men shouting at the animal, though the men themselves were out of sight. The dull pain which had settled on my mind was like the feeling which I had had months ago, at the time when I lay drunk in the meadow after the dinner party, so strangely disturbed by what I had imagined to be the loss of my parents whom now, it seemed, I had found again and in the meantime lost much more. I watched the smoke curling up from the cottage chimneys, heard a whistle blow from the village schoolroom, now occupied by the aerodrome authorities, and was conscious that behind me Bess was putting on her clothes.

I turned round and saw her sitting on the bed, pulling a stocking on to one leg and frowning as she wriggled her foot to make it fit the artificial silk. 'So you never loved me at all,' I said, and she looked up at me, smiling gratefully as though I had introduced a subject on which she wished to speak. Her tone was no longer defiant as she said brightly: 'Oh yes, I did love you. I loved you a lot. I still do. But with him it's so different. I wish I could explain. He says that it's because we're physically better adapted to each other.'

She paused and looked up at me shyly, as though to estimate the effect of the long words. I nodded my head and, having nothing to say, waited for her to continue.

'I'm sorry,' she said, 'if this has upset you', and then, since I still made no reply, she added: 'I never meant to do anybody any harm.' She looked hard into my face, as though claiming my sympathy, but I had none to spare, and so, after a moment or two, she turned away from me and began to comb her hair in front of the small mirror that hung from a nail in one of the walls. I watched her as she stood with her back to me, and found it painful to see the delicate carriage of her hips and the dress creased below the armpits as she raised her hands to her head. Still I had nothing to say, and yet felt strongly that it was time for me to speak, so that my own silence became embarrassing to me.

At last I said: 'Why was it that you married me when all the time you were in love with someone else?'

She turned round from the mirror and, though there was a puzzled look in her eyes, I could see that what was puzzling her was not the difficulty of answering my question, but merely the choice of the words which she would use. She looked at me as though I had spoken stupidly, as a child might speak on some subject of which he has not yet grasped the rudiments.

'It's not like that at all,' she said. 'I did love you. I've told you I loved you. But I loved him, too, and I didn't know which I loved best then, or I don't think I did. You see I hadn't had enough experience. I thought I was being nice to both of you. After all, we've only got one life to live.'

I smiled, for she was not speaking like herself, as I knew her, but was using the phrases which the Flight-Lieutenant would use, though without the logical coherence of his conversation. Then I began to wonder whether the part of her which I thought I knew had ever existed or whether it existed still.

'You bitch!' I said, and was startled by the violence in my voice. Bess began to cry, standing up straight and putting her hand before her face. I sat and watched her shoulders heaving and was glad to see her so, though I knew that if by any word or gesture she had expressed any need or affection for me that I could have understood I should have been at her side in an instant to soothe her trouble and to assure her of the strength and depth of my love for her. She made no such sign, but stood there tall and solitary, remote and, it seemed, out of place in these surroundings.

At length she took her hands away from her face and looked at me reproachfully, as though expecting me to take back the words which I had just used. I had no disposition to do so, and said: 'I suppose you've decided by this time which one it is that you really love.'

Again she looked at me as though I had insulted her, as indeed with a great part of my mind I wished to do. 'Please be kind to me, Roy,' she said. 'I never meant to do you any harm.'

She was going to say more, but I rose quickly from the packing case and came towards her as though to take her in my arms. Suddenly I could no longer bear the sight of her distress, and was impelled to show her that I asked for nothing better than to be kind to her, if she would but regard my kindness as a thing worth having. For an instant I was filled with a conviction that all that had happened in the last few hours was unreal, would somehow be miraculously annihilated and explained away, leaving us as I had imagined that we had been or else in an even better state. But as I stepped towards her she stepped back and raised her hand to part us. I saw then how things stood, and went back to the door where I remained, leaning against the doorpost, for I seemed to need some support, and noticed that my heart was beating unusually fast. 'Well, then,' I said, 'which one is it?'

Bess took the place which I had left on the packing case. She stretched out her feet in front of her, turning the toes inwards as she looked down at them. She spoke slowly: 'It's him, of course, though I know that in lots of ways he's not as good as you are. But he's so much more exciting, and he's done such a lot of unusual things. It may be silly of me, but I can't help being attracted to a man who's travelled a lot. And he says such funny things, too.' Here she paused and looked at me with a smile as though half expecting me to share in some joke. 'The first time,' she went on, 'I really don't know how it happened. He just managed to persuade me somehow and he said that if I didn't mean to do anyone any harm then I couldn't be doing them any. And he's really very fond of you. Somehow I'm more at ease with him than I am with you, because he's so sure of himself. And we're certainly just right for each other, physically, I mean. I'm quite different when I'm with him. Really I am.'

She smiled again, as though certain that this information would please me, and I reflected that the girl in front of me was, if her mother was to be believed, my sister, and I knew that, if she was aware of this fact, she would be much less well pleased with herself than she was at present. I began to smile as she continued speaking. 'But I really don't want to hurt you, Roy,' she was saying. 'You've been so good to me, and if I hadn't met him perhaps things would have been all right between us. I've felt that I ought to have told you this before, but really I wasn't sure quite what I wanted. But I do know now, and it's best to say so honestly, isn't it? Please don't be angry with me, because it just makes me cry.'

I saw how little sure of herself she was and yet how resolved she was against me. I began to reflect on the many advantages which the Flight-Lieutenant had had over me in this competition of love. It was not only that he had travelled extensively, was better-looking and had a wider experience of people and things; more important had been the fact that all the time he had had a complete knowledge of the situation, while all my knowledge had been partial. The very completeness of my love had caused me, most unreasonably, to imagine that Bess must feel as I did. In point of fact her feelings had been entirely different and the very thing which I had taken most for granted, a devotion to myself, was something which she had never felt at all. The Flight-Lieutenant had known all this, had made his dispositions accordingly, and with complete success. That he loved Bess in the same way and with the same strength as I loved her, I did not believe for a moment; but I began to see that this comparative indifference might well have been an advantage to him; for while I had been only too anxious to reveal my feelings and declare my devotion, he by exercising restraint had increased his own value.

But I knew that Bess was unlike him here and was giving or wishing to give him something of the same affection which I had given to her. She would certainly be disappointed, but I was convinced that no words of mine could help her, and I felt a new feeling of pity and of sadness as I watched her stretching out her feet in front of her and frowning at her shoes. I saw a small smile flicker at the corners of her mouth and the thought suddenly struck me that in this pity as in all my other views of her I might be wholly mistaken; for maybe she was content with what I knew to be the insincerity of her lover, and I began to suspect that in a love affair sincerity is not of much value, indeed a cumbrous and unexciting quality; that it was I myself who was in the wrong and who, in my desire to give away fully my love and to receive fully the love of another person, must be by nature both awkward and repulsive. To throw myself upon her mercy was what I had done long ago, and with no success whatever. I began now to shrink from her as she previously had shrunk from me. About the nature of the pleasures which she had shared with her lover and which had easily outweighed my love I was not curious. They seemed to me secret things of which I was afraid; and yet still, when I looked at her, my heart seemed to reach towards her, though my mind was clouding over in bitterness and a kind of helpless rage; for I had started to think of what next would happen and of what I had before me.

'Perhaps it's just as well,' I said, 'because it seems that I'm your brother.' I knew that the words would startle her and that the fact would pain her.

As she let her feet fall to the floor and looked up at me with an expression of horror on her face, I was suddenly glad to note the effect of what I had said. What complacency she had shown before had now fallen away from her. Her face was very pale, the corners of her mouth were now pitifully trembling and, as I looked down on her, I was filled again with a tenderness that prompted me to kneel by her side as I had done in the past, to reassure her and to comfort her. But now some overmastering force that was beyond my inclinations, strong as these were, restrained me. I felt that it was impossible for me to move as much as a foot in her direction, and I spoke coolly and distinctly as I leaned against the door and told her briefly what I had heard from her mother, but not the conclusion which I had afterwards reached.

All the time that I was speaking she stared at me with wide open eyes. Her chin had dropped helplessly and all intelligence seemed to have been drained away from her face, leaving an expression of mere terror and perplexity that was almost idiotic. When I had finished she let her head fall forward, covering her eyes with the palms of her hands, and I, remembering how different had been my own feelings when I had heard the same news, looked with a kind of contempt at her slight body, huddled up as it was on the packing case. I felt inclined to kick it or to push it over, but I stood still where I was, knowing well how superficial these feelings were, and that behind them there was no condemnation and no distaste, but merely pain. I waited for her to speak, and after a little time she sat up and turned her eyes full on me. Her face had changed so that she was looking at me with friendliness and with confidence; and I found myself surprisingly resenting this altered expression.

'How dreadful!' she said. 'We must never let anybody know. But in a way it makes it easier, doesn't it?' She smiled and was, I think, a little proud of herself for being able to adopt so sensible an attitude. 'I was terrified,' she said, 'when you came in just now. And I needn't have been, of course; but you were acting so strangely. Oh, Roy, what shall we do now?'

And as she spoke I saw suddenly, or thought I saw, how meaningless to her had been my extravagant devotion and how repulsive to her would seem the resolution which I had so quickly come to—never to leave her, in spite of what reason and opinion might demand. She stretched out a hand to me in an appealing and a friendly gesture, but I looked at the hand as though it were the hand of a ghost or else a snake.

'Do what you like,' I said, and walked out of the hut into the darkening air.

My first few steps were slow, I remember, and stumbling, for still I felt drawn to return and seemed to be wrenching myself away from some force that pulled upon me like a magnet; but after I had gone a few yards I began to walk more quickly and soon to run. I turned to the left, away from the road and the village, and ran downhill from field to field, scrambling over hedges and under wire as though my life depended on my speed, and did not stop till I reached the river, where I stood still, quite out of breath, and watched the moon rising above the willows on the other side and just streaking the dark water with its feeble light. Soon I took off my clothes and dived in. I remember swimming under the water and groping along the bottom with my fingers at the mud and the roots of weeds with a strange feeling of exhilaration, and on the surface lying on my back, staring at the moon and the long leaves between it and me, until the cold began to affect me and I scrambled up the bank, put on my clothes, and began to walk back to the village. I wished to examine as soon as possible the calling-up notice which the Flight-Lieutenant had handed me in the hut.

CHAPTER XII

The Air Vice-Marshal

SOME WEEKS AFTER the events narrated in the last chapter I was sitting together with some fifty or sixty other recruits in the aerodrome chapel, listening to an address that was being given to us by the Air Vice-Marshal himself, who had visited us expressly for this purpose. I call the building a chapel, since this was its name among us; but its appearance was quite unlike any other place of worship which I had known. It was indeed more like a cinema or a theatre than a religious building, for the seats were arranged in tiers facing a small stage or platform on which the Air Vice-Marshal was now standing. The chapel was, like much of the accommodation at the aerodrome, constructed beneath the earth and was reached by an underground railway which connected it with our sleeping quarters. By this railway we had come immediately after breakfast, accompanied by the three or four officers who were responsible for our training, and, since the early days after we had been called up had been rigorous enough, we had been surprised to find this place so luxuriously furnished and so unlike the severity of the quarters in which we had so far lived.

Indeed, if I had attached much importance to the stories which I had heard previously of the ease and richness of life in the Air Force, I should by this time have been, as many of my companions were, exceedingly disappointed. We had had to rise early and go to bed

174

late. Our beds were hard and crowded close together in underground dormitories. The food was neither plentiful nor particularly appetizing, and most of our days had been spent in the performance of arduous and, to our minds, unnecessary exercises. None of us had so far received any instruction in flying or, indeed, been anywhere near an aeroplane. Reading of any kind, card playing, and the writing of letters were prohibited, and although our instructors had told us that this period of preliminary training would soon be over, no definite time limit was mentioned to us, and before long it became clear that many of those who had been called up at the same time as myself were beginning to regret ever having volunteered for such a service. We were informed that the least word of complaint about our conditions would result in immediate dismissal, and as the days went by more and more recruits were in fact dismissed. Out of a hundred who had been called up together at least thirty were sent back to their homes because of making some remark that was held by our officers to constitute a complaint or to have been made in a tone of voice expressive either of self-pity or of lack of fortitude. A dozen or so more had found their health unable to bear the strain of the prolonged exercises, and I have no doubt that if this period had lasted much longer many others would have succumbed in the same way.

I myself had found the training easily endurable. My body was strong enough and my mind in such a state that the hard continuous work was more of a relief to me than a hardship. Though previously, in the days when I had fancied myself happy with Bess, I had thought very little of this profession, now I had become unthinkingly, savagely and, with no conscious effort of the will, determined to succeed and to excel in an Air Force of which I still understood neither the purpose nor the organization. I smiled now when I remembered that in the past the Flight-Lieutenant with his easy and inconsiderate manners had seemed to me to represent the splendid and mysterious life of which we in the village used to talk, although we had never shared in it. I thought of him now with some aversion and with no respect. In his place, if I wished to imagine a person in whose footsteps I would be proud to tread, I would set the figure of the Air Vice-Marshal, a figure of greater strength, more solid purpose, and more extensive power. Often I would think of him as I had seen him in the Rectory, by his mere presence intimidating a room full of my relations; and when I saw him standing, erect as he had been then, in the chapel to which we had been brought, I was glad to listen to him, and stared hard at his face as though there were some kinship between us or as though I might with my eyes attract to myself something of his concentration, his certainty, and his control.

We had stood at attention for some moments after reaching the chapel and were then told by our officers to sit down in the luxuriously upholstered chairs with which the building was equipped. As in a cinema there were ashtrays fastened to the backs of the seats and by the ashtrays packets of Turkish and Virginian cigarettes to which we were invited to help ourselves, while orderlies went along the rows serving sherry, whisky, or cocktails to those of us who wished to drink. There was a low murmur of conversation as we expressed to each other our relief at this improvement in our conditions or commented on the decoration of the building in which we found ourselves but, while we spoke to each other, we never lost sight of the figure on the stage, anticipating some sign or word of command from him.

For some time he gave us neither, but stood still with a few sheets of paper in one hand and the other hand just resting in the side pocket of his uniform. He looked coolly and slowly along the rows of seats as though searching with his eyes for someone in particular, but no change in his expression revealed whether or not he had discovered that for which he had been looking. Then, as the drinks were being poured out, he let his eyes wander over the roof and walls of the chapel and many of us followed his gaze round the rough grey stone (for the chapel had been hollowed out of solid rock) and the arrangement of lights, shaded with the Air Force colours, that brilliantly illuminated the whole space.

So for some time we waited until the lights began gradually to grow dimmer while at the same time small bulbs by the ashtrays in front of us were illuminated so that, when all the lights in the roof were out, we could still see our cigarettes, our knees, and the tables by our knees on which we had set our drinks. Two converging spotlights made a brilliant pool upon the stage. Into this pool the Air Vice-Marshal stepped and began at once to speak. He spoke somewhat quickly and without raising his voice, but with such evident command over himself and over his words that what he said seemed to need no tricks of oratory to make it emphatic. We had expected by way of introduction some explanation of why we had been brought to this place, or at least a summary of what the speaker was about to say to us. But there was no such preamble, and indeed the first few sentences rather surprised us.

'Some of you,' said the Air Vice-Marshal, 'are still thinking about your parents and your homes. You may be considering who or what your parents are, what are the sources of their incomes, the situations and dimensions of their houses. Please put all that out of your minds directly. For good or evil you are yourselves, poised for a brief and dazzling flash of time between two annihilations. Reflect, please, that "parenthood", "ownership", "locality" are the words of those who stick in the mud of the past to form the fresh deposit of the future. And so is "marriage". Those words are without wings. I do not care to hear an airman use them.

'Think, too, that even if you are certain of the identity of either one or both of your parents, the continued existence of these individuals can make very little difference to you, while your association with them is bound to do more harm than good. Your personalities, even so far as they are developed at present, owe very little to the man and woman whose pleasure resulted in your birth. That you are still tied to the immense and dreary procession of past time is true; it is the business of a man, and particularly of an airman, to rid himself, so far as he can, of this bond. And the first step to take towards this end is to shut out entirely from your lives your parents, people who are unimportant in themselves, but who have served in most cases as channels or conduits through which you have all in varying degrees been infected with the stupidity, the ugliness, and the servility of historical tradition.

'On the desirability of freeing oneself wholly from this tradition I need hardly speak. You have only to use your own eyes. You will have seen, for example, in this village before it was taken over by the Air Force, conditions approximating to those of the age of feudalism; a government that was ignorant in spite of its complacency, inefficient, though well-meaning, based on a faith that nobody perfectly understood, and that most people, in all practical affairs, disregarded entirely. Those who exist under such a régime must be slaves, incapable of clarity and consistency either in thought or action, drunk or hopelessly in love when they are not touching their caps to an employer or performing in accordance with some outworn system some mechanical and often unnecessary task. And in the cities you will see even worse things. There you will find people whose preoccupation is not even with an out-of-date machine, but whose lives are devoted to the lowest and meanest of all aims, the acquisition by cunning and hypocrisy of large or small sums of money. This is the type of man which our historical tradition has produced in our age, a monster, whether he be sensualist or ascetic, a man whose power, if he is successful, is accidental and not deliberate, a slave in himself to the most commonplace modes of thought and action, a creature whom you will agree with me, I hope, to treat with undeviating contempt.

'Such, then, gentlemen, is the civilization into which history has brought us and which, wholly indefensible as it is, it is yet part of our duty to defend. You will discover in course of time that we aim not entirely to defend it, but also to transform it. Now I wish merely to be sure that you realize one and all the importance of freeing yourselves, in what measure you can, from the stupefying influences of that immense period of time that went by before your birth. As one of many means towards this end we have laid down certain rules which forbid you in the future to address your parents by name, to hold any written communication with them, or to accept invitations to their houses.

'In this way we hope to help you to free yourselves from the bondage of the past. But there is another bondage, equally to be rejected. It is the bondage of the future. From this, too, you must be freed, if you are to be what you wish, conscious and deliberate shapers of your own destinies and of those of others. Irrational fear for the future can prove just as dangerous a drug, just as hampering a clog upon thought and action as is the fear of or subservience to the traditions of the past. Let me remind you once more that you are yourselves and only so for a short time. Nothing will matter to you when you are dead, and you cannot reasonably expect to be alive for much more than forty years from now. In this space of time there is much to be done, very much by you who have chosen by our course of discipline to obtain and secure freedom for yourselves and others.

'Now people become slavishly attached to the future in two ways, either through the acquisition of buildings, land, or money, or else by bearing or begetting children. I have received reports on each one of you individually from your officers, and I am sure that none of you is so unfortunate and so contemptible as to attach importance to the accumulation of material objects during life, let alone to identify himself with these pieces of material after his death. None of us, however, is averse from physical and emotional pleasure. Consequently the rules which we have had to lay down on this subject are clear and distinct. No airman is to be the father of a child. Failure to comply with this regulation will be punished with the utmost severity.'

Here the Air Vice-Marshal paused for a moment and stood as though recollecting his thoughts,' not looking at us, who must indeed have been almost invisible to him, but staring up at the ceiling. I glanced along the rows of seats and noticed that every face which I could see was intent upon the stage. Surprising as had been much that we had heard, no one, it seemed, had for that reason allowed his attention to wander; and this fact seemed to me a tribute to the personal force of the man before us who, without any obvious effort or deliberate style of oratory, still compelled us to hang upon his words and to remember them, as I knew that we should do, long after his speech was finished. Even now, though we as yet did not perfectly understand the creed and faith which was being put before us, and though there was more of severity than of comfort in what was being said, nevertheless we listened to him with a kind of joy, for it seemed that his own confidence was infused into us so that we believed that any conclusion which he had reached must be accurate, necessary, and inspiring.

'Sexual intercouse,' the Air Vice-Marshal continued, 'is, of course, not forbidden to you. In many ways it is even encouraged. But it must not result in the bearing of children who can possibly own any of you as father. And in connection with this subject it may be helpful perhaps if I give you a little advice which should regulate your conduct with women. The need for what, in a broad sense, may be called love is as powerful an instinctive urge as any, with the exception of the need to supply the body with nourishment. An organization outside yourselves will meet the needs of hunger. With love each of you has to deal more or less unaided; and for that reason I have a responsibility to declare to you what we regard as conduct worthy of an airman.

'In the first place you would do well to realize that in a love affair between a man and woman it is inevitable that in the end one of the two will suffer. You must be perfectly determined to see to it that that one is not yourself. It is, is it not, somewhat humiliating for a man to grow sleepless, to lose his peace of mind and his resolution because of the faithlessness, the stupidity, or the selfishness of a woman. And yet we have all seen this happen. Why does it seem humiliating? For it is only slightly humiliating for a man to be ill, and the distress of body and mind that comes from a necessary failure in a great undertaking is rather a matter for pride than for shame. The distress of lovers, however, must appear at first sight to everyone as weak, egotistic, infantile, and unnecessary. Reason will confirm our first impressions. For what sort of a man is he who cannot regulate and control his simplest desires so as to secure pleasure for himself and not pain?

'Unfortunately, however, we cannot help observing that in many cases pleasure is about the last thing that men seek or find in their relations with women. There are many men who having incompletely escaped from the traditions of the home seek in a woman's arms, not pleasure and the increased awareness of themselves, but merely oblivion and a delusive sort of comfort. This attitude in its simplest forms of expression is easily recognizable and can be treated with a proper contempt. For however much a man may wish that he had never been born, it is impossible for him to repeat the experience or to enjoy a second time what he imagines or remembers to have been the luxury of being wholly incorporated in a woman's body. None of you, I feel sure, is capable of making so elementary a mistake. Yet the complete self-mastery and independence at which we aim can be endangered in more subtle ways than this. In the process of falling in love you will often find that one of the two persons concerned will, as it is usually expressed, "give" himself or herself to the other. He or she will find a perverse pleasure in resigning force of impulse, will, and judgment to the caprice, the passion or the deliberate calculation of the partner. This is, in fact, the normal thing; and you must be certain that you are never the "giver" but always the receiver, though you may often pretend to "give yourself" and will derive an additional pleasure very often from the pretence.

'What you have to do is in reality quite simple. You must see women as they are and envisage clearly what it is that you want from them. You must distinguish carefully between a woman as a personality like yourself, and a woman who may be a source of pleasure to you. In so far as a woman is an individual she is bound, as you are, to the future and the past. Indeed the construction of her body must inevitably make her much more of a prisoner of time than you are yourselves. And yet there have been many women whose personalities have deserved both the friendship and the admiration of men, at least in many respects. Such women, rare as they are, may be and indeed should be treated as you would treat your own comrades amongst whom you will of course find, as a rule, much truer and more valuable friendship than you can look for in the opposite sex.

'But if love, not friendship, is your aim, your conduct must be entirely different. In this matter all women, even the best, are irrational and must be treated as such. If you attempt to secure love as you would secure friendship, by honesty, sincerity, openness, you are courting disaster. Believe me, the rules are wholly different and are perfectly well known. Indeed they were summarized by the Roman poet Ovid in the first century of our era, and his prescriptions, with certain modifications, are true today. It is necessary to remember that women's vanity, timidity, and capacity for self-deception are almost illimitable. You must recognize these qualities, try to overcome your disgust for them, and make of them the best use that you can. Flattery, so long as it is used with a certain air of independence, can be carried to almost any length of absurdity.

'If a woman were to inform any of you that you were in almost all respects the most wonderful person in the world, you would be justly incredulous of such a statement; but you may use the same words to any woman you like and be certain that they will be welcomed with gratitude and even with belief. It is advisable also to pretend that you can observe a great difference between the woman you love and all other women. Assure her of this and you will increase both her self-esteem and her reliance on you; for most women have, when they care to use their minds, a fairly shrewd idea of the defects of their own sex and are inexpressibly delighted if you can persuade them (as it is very easy to do) that they are for some reason entirely immune from the vices which they notice every day in others. A solicitude for her health, a claim for her sympathy, particularly in cases where you can pretend that you have been treated harshly by another woman, a care to arrange cushions in a certain way, a willingness to listen with respect to any kind of stupidity that masquerades either as independent thought or as deep feeling —all this will have the effect of adding to her self-esteem and of making her ready to fall in love with you who have succeeded in convincing her that she is right in looking upon herself as more exceptional than in reality she is. Indeed you now become more and more necessary; for if you were to drop from your hand the mirror which you hold up to her, she would have nowhere to look. By this time she will be speaking of "giving" herself or her love to you. The expression is not unjustified, for, by providing her with a wholly false sense of her own importance both to yourself and others, you have made her dependent on you for the satisfaction of her own vanity, and vanity, with women, is the key to desire. She will like to believe that she exercises over you an exceptional power, and will not realize immediately that the situation is exactly the reverse of this. Nor need you press the point or allow yourself or her to see too clearly the extent of her dependence; for in these matters the knowledge of complete power is the beginning of the end of love. For some time you can enjoy a delicious period of uncertainty during which she will become more and more fanatically and unreasonably devoted to you. You will find her, so long as you keep your head, extraordinarily easy to deal with. You may drop many of your pretences and, so long as she is normally efficient in body and mind, you will enjoy a very agreeable companionship.

'Soon, however, whether in order to test her power, or to secure herself for the future, she will begin to make unreasonable claims on you. Then you would do well to withdraw yourself from her very gradually and almost insensibly, and you will be pleased to find, as you do so, her passion for you increase, her reticence and modesty entirely disappear; a great part even of her vanity will go and, as she sheds the affectations and incrustations of her sex and of its history, she will even attain to a certain nobility in the process, although when the process ends, nothing very remarkable will be left behind, and the very abjectness of her self-surrender will, I think, disgust you. Remember, however, that this is the course of love and that if you had put into her hands the power which you hold yourself you would be now almost as abject as she is. Think of yourself as now perhaps you think of her, lying abandoned and unconstrained, in spite of her efforts uninteresting, in spite of her desires unwanted. You may be certain that if you were in such a position you would receive no mercy from the woman into whose power you had allowed yourself to come. For, in these affairs, though the gradual acquisition of power is pleasurable, exciting, and instructive, when once the power is fully attained, it will be observed that a domination of this sort is not worth preserving. No one loves or is greatly stimulated by the attentions of a slave. And so be as kind as you can, although it is difficult to be altogether kind to a creature whom, when at last you see her as she is, you will find to be wholly lacking in honour, generosity, or self-respect. These, however, are qualities which you should never have looked for in a sex that is emotionally so fettered to the functions of the body and to the automatic processes of time. Pity, certainly, you may feel for her. I should not care to have it thought that I spoke cynically of any human being. But let your pity be of that general and philosophical kind with which you might watch the inevitable sufferings of an animal or a child. Do not let pity or any other feeling drag you away from the certainty of your own integrity and the knowledge that in the last resort we love only ourselves.

'Your business as members of the Air Force is first and foremost to obtain freedom through the recognition of necessity; and necessity is no soft and feeble thing. It is not your business to attach yourself in any permanent sense to a woman. The thing is neither possible nor desirable. And I have spoken at some length on this subject because experience has taught me that many a promising airman is in danger of losing his confidence, his self-control, and his purposefulness simply through a failure to understand the facts of sex. Yet, like everything else, when once understood they can be dealt with easily, naturally, and satisfactorily.

'Remember that we expect from you conduct of a quite different order from that of the mass of mankind. Your actions, when off duty, may appear and indeed should appear wholly irresponsible. Your purpose—to escape the bondage of time, to obtain mastery over yourselves, and thus over your environment—must never waver. You will discover, if you do not know already, from the courses which have been arranged for you, the necessity for what we in this Force are in process of becoming, a new and a more adequate race of men.

'Please do not imagine, gentlemen, that I am speaking wildly. I mean precisely what I say and in course of time you will come to understand me more clearly than perhaps you do at present. Let me remind you finally of the pseudo-suchians, reptiles of an exceedingly remote period whose clumsy efforts resulted in the course of ages in that incredibly finely organized and adjusted thing, the first flyers, the race of birds. Science will show you that in our species the period of physical evolution is over. There remains the evolution, or rather the transformation, of consciousness and will, the escape from time, the mastery of the self, a task which has in fact been attempted with some success by individuals at various periods, but which is now to be attempted by us all. Your preliminary training has been exhausting, your discipline will continue to be exact, though the period of your hardships is over. But this discipline has one aim, the acquisition of power, and by power—freedom.'

With these words the Air Vice-Marshal concluded his speech. The lights in the roof were re-illumined and, by a single impulse, we rose to our feet. The Air Vice-Marshal stood still on the stage watching us gravely as we filed out of the chapel.

CHAPTER XIII

Alterations

THIS WAS BUT one of many lectures which we heard on a variety of subjects; for in additition to instruction in flying, engineering, and aerodynamics we were given classes in natural history, mathematics, economics, history, and philosophy. We studied the whole theory of flight in very great detail, spending, I remember, more than a month in an examination of the wing of an albatross, and many days in learning about bats, flying squirrels, and other animals whose destiny it had been to attempt, however feebly, some mastery over the air. And this part of our training was to me at least as interesting and exciting as was the actual flying, although I was myself a better pilot than a philosopher, and became indeed for some time rather ridiculously proud of my ability in this respect.

I had done my first solo some days before anyone else in my class, and I remember now the thrill of it as being no anticipation of danger but rather a delicious sense of confidence. At the moments of taking off and of landing I had felt much the same feeling as a footballer has from time to time, when he sees instantaneously a gap in the defence and his own ability to break through it. Indeed the footballer's confidence and exhilaration is, I believe, more intense, for in an open field where thirty players are competing there are more possible permutations, and much more of the surprising and the accidental than there is about the controls of an aircraft. Yet at the time when

I was learning to fly there was still a certain romance attached to the handling of these machines, a relic perhaps from the past when the ground staffs of aerodromes were less perfectly organized, and when many of the instruments which we now use had not even been thought of.

I used to listen with a kind of regret to the stories told to us by our instructor, a one-eyed sergeant-pilot, who was old enough to be the father of any of us, and who had been flying since he was sixteen. He would tell us of crashes caused by faulty construction that today would be impossible; of fights with storm and snow of which the pilot had not been forewarned; of how it had even been necessary to employ strength in handling the controls. He would look at us somewhat sadly from his one eye and say: 'A kite used to take some flying in those days', and then appear the slightest bit embarrassed by what he had said, as though his remark might be misconstrued into a criticism of modern flying. And indeed, although no one voluntarily rushes into danger, we would still envy him for the hazards through which he had successfully come and of which we would have little or no experience. For whatever we attempted in the air we could be certain at all times that our machines would respond with absolute accuracy to the controls, and there was consequently no danger whatever except for those who were either physically or mentally in any case unfit for flying.

I personally was at the right age and had the right habits of nerve to be rather exceptionally proficient, and before long was enrolled along with two others of my class in a special formation whose work it was to give, from time to time, displays of aerobatics in various parts of the country.

I was proud of this job and unduly proud of my ability to perform it satisfactorily; what gave me, most unreasonably, a special pleasure was that in this work I was already very much the superior of the Flight-Lieutenant whom for so long I had imagined to be as an airman in a class very much higher than any to which I could aspire; and I remember the feeling of consternation which I had when our instructor laughed at the mention of his name.

It appeared that he had shown very little aptitude for flying and indeed for some time had never been in the air at all, but, previously to his appointment to the Rectory, had merely been in charge of some of the stores. No one, certainly, questioned his loyalty and devotion to the Air Force; neither was he regarded by anyone as in any way remarkable, but rather as a useful and painstaking officer with no very special qualifications for any one branch of the service. It was some time before I could get used to the fact that I was regarded as a much more promising airman than he, and that while I was admired and envied, he was on the whole disregarded. I began to see now that his frequent visits to the village had been rather the result of incomplete satisfaction with the aerodrome, than of exuberance, and I began to feel pity for him where previously I had felt only admiration. Not that I thought of him very much; for when I thought of him I was reminded of Bess, and could still feel the pain of the wounds which I had received that evening in the hut, though, when busied with my work or in the company of other airmen, I scarcely remembered her, for I fancied that there was something final in my breakaway down the fields and in the alteration of my life.

I found now for the first time since my early boyhood

that I was eager to do something outside myself and not obviously connected with my emotions, something that won for me respect from others and something which I was naturally proficient in doing. For a long time my ambition was simply to excel, and in this I was successful so far as the piloting of an aircraft for trick flying is concerned. I won special commendation from the Air Vice-Marshal himself and remember how, just after he had congratulated me personally for my performance at one of the displays in which I took part, he contrived to show me and my friends how unimportant we really were in comparison with other branches of our personnel.

It was at the end of the display and the crowd which had attended had dispersed. We had changed into our uniforms and been introduced to the Air Vice-Marshal who, together with a few senior officers, remained on the flying field. I remember noticing in particular a tall elderly man with a small straggling beard who had previously been pointed out to me as one of the mathematicians engaged on research. He had a wife, I knew, called Eustasia, in whom the Flight-Lieutenant was believed to be interested, but I had forgotten his name. I remember wondering from the first what sort of a woman his wife was. The Air Vice-Marshal was talking earnestly to him as we approached, but smiled when he saw us, and congratulated us on our work. He spoke gravely and, though he said little, showed by what he said that he was perfectly acquainted not only with our machines but with the difficulties which we had surmounted and with each trifling irregularity in the display which had occurred, as such small irregularities must occur, from minute errors in timing or from mechanical reasons. Finally he turned to me, looking at me, I remember, very hard as though I were someone whom he found difficulty in recognizing. 'You have done particularly well,' he said. 'We are pleased with your work.'

Then he turned with a laugh to the mathematician at his side. 'Could you do it as well?' he asked, and to our surprise the mathematician nodded his head and mumbled indistinctly the words, 'I think so, don't you?', a remark which to most of us seemed to have been made in somewhat bad taste, though the Air Vice-Marshal smiled first at the speaker and then at us, as though enjoying the dubious expressions on our faces. 'Just let's watch these two fellows,' he said, and pointed to two aircraft of the latest type which were taxi-ing towards us across the flying field.

We watched, not at first with much interest, for we knew the performances of these machines which were not unlike those which we had flown ourselves that afternoon. But as the aircraft took off and turned to climb, we began to look more closely, for it was clear that the machines were being flown either very skilfully or very recklessly. The ailerons of the two planes were almost interlocked as they climbed together to a great height. Then they separated, turned, and proceeded to give a display of aerobatics which held us spellbound, for we could hardly believe in the reality of what we saw. Not that the machines accomplished anything in the air which most of us could not have done singly, but the co-ordinance between the pilots and their confidence in each other were things which seemed to us incredible. For they would climb together, loop, go into a spin, and all the time the undercarriage of one aircraft would appear to be only a few inches from the cockpit of another. In short, it was something impossible that we saw, so that we rubbed our eyes as we watched, and when the display was over could hardly have described what it was that we had seen. In all of our minds must have been the thoughts, 'Who are these pilots? What sort of pilots are we?' I remember noticing how pale were the faces of my friends, and have no doubt that my own face was equally pale.

The Air Vice-Marshal appeared delighted with the display and amused by our evident feelings. 'Pretty good,' he said, as he looked quizzically from one to another of us. 'I think you will agree, gentlemen.'

I was watching the two aircraft which had landed together and had come to a standstill some fifty yard away. Most of my friends were watching, too, since we wished to see and perhaps recognize the pilots. The Air Vice-Marshal spoke again. 'What would you think,' he said, 'if I told you that we can now put two thousand of those aircraft into the sky at once and see them fly as we have seen those two fly?'

We looked at him with a kind of consternation, for it seemed that he was speaking seriously.

'It is no use waiting to see the pilots,' he added, 'because there are none.' There was a long pause while he stood looking across the airfield, a slight smile as it were carved upon his face. Then he looked at his wristwatch and turned to go. 'You had better explain,' he said to the mathematician, 'it is time for me to be off. You fellows gave a good display.'

We saluted and watched him walk slowly towards his car; then we turned to the mathematician who at once began to speak, as though for a long time he had been repressing his longing to instruct us. As a dog wags his tail, so his beard seemed to wag with the enthusiasm that he felt for his invention. 'You know, of course,' he was saying, spluttering as he spoke, 'of the ordinary methods of remote control by wireless. This is a bit different, isn't it? Oh yes, this is another thing', and he launched into an explanation of the exact mechanism which had been used and the means by which it had been discovered.

We listened attentively, but with more interest than understanding, for he seemed to be giving us credit for a much greater knowledge of mathematics and electrical engineering than any of us, in fact, possessed, so that almost the whole of his speech was unintelligible to us. He concluded with the words: 'Two thousand! Yes, or three or four! The chief was right. We soon shan't be wanting any of you boys.' And he put back his head, staring up to the sky with his beard jutting out from his lean face, quivering as he laughed. We laughed, too, for we were proud of his achievement, however conscious we might be of our inability to understand it and of the fact that metal and electricity and one directing brain could so easily surpass the performances of our own eyes and nerves and muscles. Indeed, we felt somewhat foolish for, while we had never imagined ourselves to be people of the utmost importance, we had still been convinced that we could do things that others could not do. That night we talked much of what we had seen, realizing more than previously our ignorance of all but a very small part of the organization to which we belonged.

It was not only that we, as pilots, were ignorant of everything except the rudiments in such subjects as mathematics, electricity, magnetism, and aerodynamics, so that we were hardly able to understand the work of the research departments. There were other departments of the aerodrome also of which we had little or no knowledge. The political propaganda department, for example, employing as it did almost a third of the entire personnel and amongst them some of the best brains, was an institution of extraordinary complexity with branches covering religion, literature, morals, education, journalism, psychology, and medicine. Like everything else at the aerodrome it was under the constant supervision of the Air Vice-Marshal himself, and we saw, whenever we went to the village, evidences of its work; for it was thought desirable for the Air Force not only to occupy but also to transform any part of the country that fell within its sphere of interest. Of the grandiose extent of the transformation at which we aimed I was to be informed later. At this time I merely watched with admiration, with amusement, or with pity what was happening in the village which I used to know.

Indeed, had I by some chance gone away on the night of the dinner party and now returned, I should have been unable to believe my eyes, so rapidly and extensively had the place altered. In the white street that I remembered as empty except for a dog, some straying children, or a milk cart, and all these either stationary or slowly moving, were now always to be seen large or small bodies of men in uniform or overalls, marching in order or going rapidly from one business to another. And by the Manor, near the huge cedar just inside the wall, were parked large numbers of gaily painted sports cars belonging to those of us who used the place as our club house. The building itself and its grounds were almost unrecognizable. The exterior had been camouflaged, and alterations had been made to the roof so as to make room on top of it for an extensive ball-room and restaurant with glass walls and a sliding glass roof where dances were held every week-end. Most of the cypresses in the sunken garden had been cut down, for here a swimming bath was in process of construction. The rock garden had been levelled, beech hedges, herbaceous borders, and many rare shrubs removed to make way for squash courts, tennis lawns, and rifle ranges.

Changes of the same character had been made in the interior of the house. The walls were now bare of those interesting objects, each with its own history, which in the Squire's day had adorned the hall. In their place were gilt mirrors with ash-trays beneath them and heavy leather armchairs. What used to be a sitting-room had now been connected with the hall by a narrow archway in the Arab style, and inside this room was a bar over which the Squire's butler presided, a heavy and somewhat mournful figure, whose slowness of hand with a cocktail shaker made him really quite unsuited to this post. Sometimes when I was in the bar he would smile sadly at me, as though we shared in some secret, and I could see from his expression that he regretted the old days when he had had less work to do and had been a person of much greater consequence than he was now. As it was he was in constant danger of being sacked, and was regarded by most of the airmen as a mere half-wit who found it impossible to understand the simplest remark made to him. The deference with which he would listen both to their jokes and their instructions made him simply ridiculous. Nor did he receive much support from Mrs Wainwright, the cook, who was the only other member of the old staff who still worked at the Manor; for she was continually busy in the kitchen, and had so far adapted herself to the new conditions as to be delighted with the attentions which some of the older officers would occasionally pay her. She, too, if she passed me in the hall or in the billiard-room, would smile and perhaps say how times had changed, and other officers would ask me about the old appearance of the house, and laugh when I told them of the uses to which each room had been put, and of the articles of furniture which had now one and all been taken away.

I spent most of my leisure time here, only rarely visiting the pub, which indeed began to appear to me as a somewhat sordid and uninteresting place, though I would stop there occasionally on my way to the clubhouse for a game of darts with Fred or Mac or one of the others of my old friends. Yet I knew that their attitude had altered towards me since I began to wear the Air Force uniform and I was surprised to find that I, too, was beginning to look differently upon them. I could feel that, though they expressed little resentment against the aerodrome, they still felt it; and it was a new thing in them so to conceal their thoughts. They had both failed in the preliminary examination for aircraftsmen and were now engaged in navvying work with a gang of men brought from another part of the country. The pay was good, they said, but they lost much of it through arriving late for work in the morning or by being, through drunkenness, sometimes quite unfit for duty at all.

I could see that already they regretted the old régime, and noticed with some distaste the glee of the older men in the pub who now observed that their predictions were coming true; yet the old men could infuse no life themselves into these gatherings. Their remarks were either melancholy reflections or mere spitefulness. So that there was a feeling of constraint about the place which in the past had been so unconstrained, and though I felt my power as an officer among these people, and even some remains of our mutual affection, I began to see that this power and this affection were, as things stood, incompatible, that against my success they would set their own failure, against their old feelings of reckless friendship their new feelings of weakness and of dependence. And when I thought of the Air Vice-Marshal and of my own friends at the aerodrome, I wondered what these villagers could do except the most unskilled labour or what they could enjoy except the crudest pleasures. They had no sense of direction, I saw, no confidence, no initiative, and yet I was myself still wholly unaware of the real purpose of the organization to which I belonged and on which I was in reality just as dependent as was everyone else in the village.

I saw Bess sometimes in the pub, but rarely spoke to her, nor did she, after a time, show any desire to speak to me, and we avoided each other's eyes. At first she had attempted to adopt a manner of easy friendliness towards me, had congratulated me on what she had heard of my successes at the aerodrome, and had shown by the look in her eyes that she was often momentarily depressed by the thought of the pain which she had caused me and would wish that pain forgotten so that her own mind might be carefree. But I, when I saw this look, was stung into a kind of anger, and I spoke to her as though we were complete strangers; for I dreaded the thought of any softening in my feelings, knowing that I could not treat her as a friend, and that if I were to allow my imagination to go further than that then my misery and insecurity would return to leave me without ambition and make me uncertain of myself and unfitted for my work. So I forced myself to appear indifferent to her, and fancied myself really to be so, and did not notice at the time symptoms in my behaviour which indicated that this was not my real feeling.

I was displeased, for example, when I saw her looking happy; and when, after a little time, I noticed that she was often pale and dispirited, although there was a part of me that felt sorry, there was another part which caused me to look closely at her, estimating her distress and in a way pleased to see it. I could easily guess at its cause; for it appeared that the Flight-Lieutenant was showing much less interest in her than before and indeed was probably on the point of deserting her altogether. We all knew that he had become attached to Eustasia, the wife of the mathe-matician, and frequent strictures were passed upon his conduct in this connection. He was, it was said, quite ridiculously infatuated with the lady who, for her part, showed very little interest in him, and this was behaviour which, it was generally agreed, was both weak in itself and unworthy in particular of an airman. I remember wondering, when I first heard of this new intrigue, what kind of a woman this Eustasia was, and there even crossed my mind the thought that it might be interesting if I were able to supplant the Flight-Lieutenant in her affections.

But it was not only in regard to Bess that the Flight-Lieutenant had changed. What surprised us all was that he began to speak seriously of his work in the village as

though it had some importance of its own apart altogether from the aerodrome. He had, we were told, read
in the church a longer form of service than that which
was strictly necessary; he had reorganized the bellringers,
who, since the occupation of the village, had given up
their work; and he had made a nuisance of himself to the
supply department by asking for work to be done in the
strengthening of the church tower. Most surprising of all
to me was the fact that he was now a frequent visitor at
the house shared together by the Squire's sister and the
Rector's wife, for with neither of these ladies had he been
in the past at all popular. Indeed to the former of the two
he had been, since his appointment, an object of actual
aversion.

I went very seldom to the house myself, but I remember my astonishment when, having had to go there to
collect some clothes, I opened the door of the sitting-
room and saw the Flight-Lieutenant sitting on the floor
in front of the fire with his head resting against the arm
of the chair in which the Squire's sister was sitting. There
was, I observed with amazement, an expression of extraordinary tenderness on the lady's face. She was stroking
with the tips of her fingers the young man's yellow hair,
and opposite her on a divan was sitting the Rector's wife,
smiling as though this was a scene that both pleased and
interested her. When I entered the room both she and
her friend looked at me with an equal kindness, as though
this were some sort of family reunion. For myself I could
not see it as such, having taken to heart what the Air
Vice-Marshal had told us in the chapel; so I simply asked
for the clothes which I had come to fetch. The Flight-
Lieutenant, I observed, was somewhat embarrassed by

my presence. He rose to his feet and, when I left, said that he would accompany me.

As we walked away from the house towards the club I watched him closely, for I could not tell whether his evident embarrassment was due to his thoughts about Bess or about the scene which I had just witnessed. It was with some surprise that I realized that I was on the whole indifferent both to his feelings and to their source, that I was more assured of myself than he was, so that for a moment it seemed almost that we had changed characters; for he appeared anxious now to explain himself to me and to seek my advice, while I felt it to be probable that he had nothing very important to say. I remembered days in the past when we had walked together along this very road, and when our relation to each other had been the exact opposite of this.

'It's a funny thing,' he said. 'I really like those two old women very much.'

I made no reply, and after a short pause he continued.

'Particularly the old Squire's sister. You know the way she used to behave. I thought she loathed me like poison.'

'She isn't too fond of the aerodrome, is she?' I said.

He stopped still and looked straight at me, almost, I thought, as though he were seeking to find a kind of sympathy in my face. 'No,' he said, 'she isn't.' He looked at me again anxiously as if waiting for a reply. Finally he said in a low voice: 'I'm not so sure that I am either.'

I stared at him in consternation, but he was looking away from me. We had reached the top of the hill, and I followed his gaze over the whole valley with the straight stripped alders marking the river channel as though for navigation, the dark woods and curving pastures beyond.

A heron rose flapping from the river. It was a midwinter windless day. I thought suddenly of how this valley would appear to me from the air and, looking at it again, felt a kind of distaste for its proximity, for its mud and reeds and the stifling nature of its life. A squadron of heavy bombers was coming towards us high overhead. I looked up at them, and heard the Flight-Lieutenant say in a somewhat apologetic tone of voice: 'I sometimes wonder what it's all for.'

I kept my eyes on the bombers and smiled, as though he had spoken foolishly. We went on together to the club.

CHAPTER XIV

Eustasia

It WAS NOT long after this that I met Eustasia and, oddly enough, it was the Flight-Lieutenant who introduced us to each other. During my early days at the aerodrome I had tended to avoid his company, and he had shown little readiness to seek mine; but now, whether because he had finally deserted Bess or because he was not himself much sought after by the other officers, he seemed almost to be pursuing me in my leisure hours, so that I became somewhat bored with him and with his conversation, although the changes which were evidently taking place in his character and his aims both interested and surprised me. He very seldom ventured upon any open criticism of the Air Force; for he knew that it would be unsafe to do so, and that in any case I should not have listened to anything of the kind; and yet he contrived to make it clear that his energies were no longer devoted solely to the increased efficiency and power of our organization. He spoke much of the villagers, particularly of the elder women and of the children, often commending individuals for the most unlikely qualities, for fidelity that had no rational grounds, for an honesty that was merely the result of habit, for an uncritical acceptance of conditions that were imposed from above. I would often laugh at him, and indeed he found it difficult to defend his new tastes in any coherent manner.

'Somehow,' he would say, 'these people seem to fit better into the country, into the scenery, I mean, than we do', and if we were out of doors he would look over the valley and perhaps stretch his hand out towards it; and I would follow his gaze, often being surprised by the fact that the familiar sight of the ground no longer moved me, for I felt the view restricted, remembering how clean, how remote, and how defenceless this country would seem from a great height in the air.

'What on earth does the scenery matter?' I would ask, and the Flight-Lieutenant would laugh apologetically.

'Well, it's just how I feel,' he would say.

But our most common topic of conversation at this time was Eustasia and, when we spoke of her, I would be frequently amazed to realize the alteration which had taken place not only in the Flight-Lieutenant but in myself. He would talk most enthusiastically of this lady, crediting her with qualities which I was pretty certain she could not possess; for I knew many of the officers' wives, and knew that they were neither faithful themselves nor expected fidelity in others, that their ways of thought were aimless, and that they were almost uniquely interested in clothes, furniture, dances, and physical sensations. But when I listened to the Flight-Lieutenant it seemed to me almost as though I were listening to myself speaking in the old days about Bess; and when I laughed at his enthusiasm, since in its extent it was certainly boring, I could almost believe that it was not I but he that was speaking as he used to speak when he made light, justifiably enough I thought, of my marriage and of my ideas of contentment. What was strange, too, about this affair of his was that Eustasia, so far as I could make out, showed very little interest in him.

'She often speaks of you,' he would tell me, and

after some time he offered to introduce me to her.

'You might put in a good word for me,' he said, 'if you find you get on well with her.'

He smiled, I remember, somewhat sheepishly, and I looked at him in amazement and with some contempt. 'Suppose I like the girl myself?' I asked, and was amused to see a look of fear come into his eyes. He seemed to be forcing the smile to his face.

'Oh, well,' he said, 'all's fair.' And he shrugged his shoulders. 'All the same though . . .'

I remembered suddenly how he had spoken these words outside the hut, and I looked at him sharply. Even though I attached very little importance to this affair, I knew that if I could, without much trouble, do him an injury, then I would do so. He looked at me again, almost with an apologetic air, as though he could read my thoughts, and arranged to call with me on Eustasia on the following day.

She lived in one of the flats for officers' wives that were built at the extreme edge of the aerodrome near the gates opening on to the road. I remember that what struck me first was the extraordinary untidiness of her room. Papers covered with figures were scattered over the floor; open boxes of chocolates and of powder lay about on the divan that extended along one wall; and on the mantelpiece were half-empty bottles of scent and of face lotion. Yet the furniture was both tasteful and expensive. There was a feeling of space about the room, and the chairs and tables were of wood, rather than of metal, unlike the furniture of the rooms which I had so far visited. I felt at once that the occupant must be distinguished in some way from the majority of women at the aerodrome, whose habits were precise and whose tastes stereotyped. And in this view I was certainly not mistaken.

We were left to ourselves for some moments, during which time the Flight-Lieutenant talked to me in a whisper, as though we were in some place of worship, and I answered him in a loud voice, for I was for some reason annoyed by his sheepish air. We heard from an adjoining room the noise of bath-water running out, and soon the door of this room opened and Eustasia appeared, wearing a white silk dressing-gown covered with large purple flowers. She stood for a moment looking at the Flight-Lieutenant and laughing; then she turned her eyes on me and seemed, I thought, for a second the least bit embarrassed. She frowned and tossed back into place a loose lock of hair that had fallen over her forehead. Then she stepped towards me, holding out her hand. 'Sorry to be receiving you in this way,' she said, and smiled again, with her large eyes fixed full on mine.

Later on we both said that in this first look we each had realized what would happen to us after and, in a certain generalized way, this was true. But I saw, too, in her brown eyes, and did not tell her, not only that she could easily be drawn to me, but also, in spite of their bravado, a softness and an honesty which rather depressed me; for I had no mind to take her or any other woman very seriously. For a moment she seemed to me like a child performing with great success the rôle of a sophisticated and self-confident woman. Yet this impression was soon worn away from my mind as she began to move somewhat clumsily about the room, pouring out drinks for us, and talking rapidly in a loud voice about her dressing-gown and the lotion which, after she had served us, she proceeded to rub into her face. Her conversation was interrupted by the Flight-Lieutenant's interjections of agreement or approval, and, whenever she stopped speaking, he would at once speak himself with such a nervous eagerness that nearly everything which he said seemed pointless and unnecessary.

I watched Eustasia closely as she wrapped her dressing-gown more tightly round her and began to do her hair in front of a mirror that hung upon the wall. There was something masculine in the directness of her eyes and in the forward set of her jaw—still more, perhaps, in the confidence and assertion of her voice; yet her ears and hands were remarkably delicate, and her body, though tall and upright, suggested a certain frailty, seeming too soft to be athletic. I said very little, but looked back and forward from her to the Flight-Lieutenant who, in my opinion, was merely making himself ridiculous; for though Eustasia, as she passed his chair, would occasionally pat him on the head and would also occasionally show that she had listened to one or other of his remarks, it was quite clear that she felt no affection for him whatever.

After a time she had completed her toilet and came to sit on the divan at my side. 'I've been looking forward to meeting you,' she said, 'because I've heard such a lot about you from my husband. You've got yourself a very good reputation already.'

'It's nothing like his,' I said, thinking of the demonstration of aerobatics which I had seen.

Eustasia laughed. 'No, of course not. He's very, very famous. But being very successful isn't everything, is it?'

I was not so sure. Her large eyes were turned fully

upon mine, as though looking for something there which was difficult to discover. I found myself smiling in a kind of amusement at the sudden seriousness of her expression. The Flight-Lieutenant made some remark to which neither of us replied. 'How do you like being married?' I asked.

She stretched her legs out in front of her with the palms of her hands resting on her thighs. 'Oh, all right,' she said, 'so long as I can get my young men.' She was smiling slowly, and I thought of her as of some huge cat, lazily extending her limbs to the sun. She looked up, not at me, but at the Flight-Lieutenant, whose face wore an expression of almost idiotic anxiety. 'Go and get us some cigarettes,' she said, and he hurriedly left the room.

After he had gone we sat for some moments in silence. I kept my eyes on the pattern of the carpet, a decoration of small intertwined snakes among ivy leaves, and for some reason my mind went back to the time when I had been sitting on the bed with Bess's mother and had so closely examined the patchwork quilt. Now I felt the same intensity in the atmosphere between the two of us, the certainty that some word or action of extraordinary significance was impending, but this time I was master of myself, and I watched Eustasia out of the corner of my eye, since I felt no urge in myself to make the first move. She was sitting with her head thrust slightly forward, and on her broad determined face was a look of such softness that I was startled; for all the stubbornness and self-will and strain seemed to have gone from her face, leaving it with a strange purity like an April sky, so that she appeared unearthly, a spirit whose whole essence was compassion. Yet I could feel the divan dented by her heavy limbs, and saw the blood just pulsing in a tiny vein above one cheek.

I looked again down at the carpet and smiled, for I found the excitement exhilarating and knew that I would not give myself away. When she stretched out one hand and laid it on my knee, the gesture seemed the most natural and inevitable one in the world, and at once the vague intensity that had surrounded us began to find a habitation in the limbs and in the mind. I turned towards her and put my hand on her thigh and noticed her eyelids tremble as my fingers pressed upon the warm flesh. For a second or two we looked at each other. There was still the same softness in her eyes, but her lips had begun to smile. Suddenly her eyes lit up with a flash of gaiety; she put her arms round my neck and kissed me on the mouth; then with her hands locked behind my head she leant back, looking mischievously at me, and said: 'Now you know.'

I pulled her towards me and began to kiss her the more ravenously, and with the greater pleasure because this affair had started so easily, was so simple, and seemed so unlikely to affect the general conduct of my life. The vigour and assurance of her love-making both surprised and delighted me, so that for some moments I was, as they say, speechless with desire, although in a part of my mind I was secretly amused by what was happening and, even when our lips were pressed tightly together, I told myself that whatever might come of this I was certainly determined not to be hurt myself. Yet, in spite of these feelings, the sudden warmth of her seemed to melt something in me and, when we drew apart, I looked at her with gratitude.

At some time during these proceedings the Flight-Lieutenant had returned, but neither Eustasia nor I had observed his entry. He now stood looking down on us with one hand in front of his mouth, as though he were about to cough. We looked at him and at each other, and burst out laughing, for his appearance, though some might have found it pathetic, was certainly ridiculous. He noticed that he was observed, but did not seem to notice the effect that he made. To my great surprise he flopped down upon the floor at Eustasia's side and laid his head close to her thigh, gently rubbing his cheek against the material of her dress. I looked at him closely and saw that his shoulders were heaving. Then on the cheek that was turned away from me I caught sight of a tear. Eustasia was patting his head as one might pat, somewhat absent-mindedly, a dog. Sometimes, with a kind of perplexity in her expression, she looked down at him; sometimes she turned to me and smiled, as though claiming my sympathy and asking my forgiveness for the part which she was forced to take in this scene. Once, as she faced me, she pursed up her lips, and I leant towards her and kissed them.

Meanwhile the Flight-Lieutenant was speaking incoherently. He said that she was the only woman at the aerodrome who perfectly understood him; that she alone could sympathize with him in his hatred of the perpetual constraint in which he was forced to live; that there was no one else to whom he dared speak his mind; that he realized that he had lost her, but would still be grateful for any attention, however small, that she could give him. Such was the sense of what he was saying in a confused and broken voice, and Eustasia continued until he had finished to pat the top of his head or the side of his face.

I looked at him with mixed feelings. It would be untrue to say that I experienced no pleasure in seeing him in this broken-down state; but at the same time I was horrified by his abjectness and, what was most strange, in some part of my mind I actually resented it, feeling for a moment that, even in this humiliation, he had somehow stolen an advantage over me. For I knew that I could leave the room now, never see Eustasia again, and still be none the worse for that; but he, it appeared, had discovered in her something that he was most reluctant to lose, and in this discovery he might, for all I knew, be showing a finer insight than any of which I was capable. This thought passed from me in a moment as Eustasia turned her head towards me, raising her eyebrows as though to enlist my help. I knew clearly that I would not exchange his state for mine.

He had become quieter now, but was still mechanically rubbing his cheek against her dress. She pulled his head back by the hair and smiled at him. 'There, there,' she said, 'never mind. You can come and see me as often as you like. Of course, we shall always be friends.'

Then she began to draw away from him, and he put one clenched hand on the floor, pushing himself to his feet. He stood looking at us hesitatingly as a nervous guest might look, uncertain whether or not the hour has arrived at which he may properly depart. I particularly noticed his rumpled hair and the fact that a white thread was clinging to the elbow of his uniform. I raised my eyes to his face and saw that he was looking at me in a very odd manner. There was no resentment or anger in him, I could swear; it was rather as though he were about to excuse himself for something, but was searching in vain for an appropriate form of words, or else that he had a statement to make of so surprising a character that it could only be introduced with the greatest diffidence. I went quickly to the door and opened it for him.

So the Flight-Lieutenant left us and we became lovers. For many weeks I spent some part of every day or night with Eustasia, and in all this time there was no moment of uneasiness, far less unhappiness, between us. Our first love-making had seemed easy, natural, and inevitable. Every later occasion improved our love. For though we had no deliberation, no forethoughts or afterthoughts, and though I certainly thought very little of her when I was on duty at the aerodrome, this very absence of inter-mediate reflection seemed to me to make our meetings more delightful, for every meeting revealed to me some-thing new of the tricks of her mind or her body. And everything was surprising; for I had not seen her from the first as a creature ideally shaped by my own imagina-tion, reflecting back to me the colours of my own desires or fancied needs. Rather it had been the reverse of this; for, since the moment when I first heard the Flight-Lieutenant speak of her, I had thought of her as a person whom I would find to be much like any other of the officers' wives, not to be treated very seriously, or not for long.

Thus I was surprised and almost shocked to find the reality so much exceed the imagination in strength, in warmth, in vividness, and in surety of outline. I was flattered, too, no doubt, by the strength of the feeling which she had for me, and was half-conscious, though without any uneasiness, that my own feelings for her, though strong enough, were of a wholly different order. From her I got joy alone, but from me she seemed to obtain joy and something more, something that would cause her at times to cling close to me as though she were wishing to secure a possession that, however wide the circuit of her limbs and fingers, might without care slip from her; and at such moments there would be a look of passionate concentration on her face, a look which would surprise me, since for my part I had what I wanted at least for the moment in my arms, and had no thought for anything else.

Often she would speak to me about love, and I would listen with interest and perplexity, and sometimes with amusement; for I remembered the time when I, too, was in the habit of theorizing on this subject, while now I felt no need to hold any clear idea of it, and was indeed surprised by the vehemence and sincerity of Eustasia's words. She had never been faithful for long to any one person, and yet her love affairs filled by far the most important place in her life. I would often find myself smiling when she made it clear in our conversation that in comparison with her own sexual life she regarded even the aerodrome and its organization as a thing of quite secondary importance; and I saw that there would be no use in arguing such points with her or in protesting against what seemed to me at this time a charming piece of selfishness. But I would question her about her former lovers and she would speak about nearly all of them with affection, with amusement, and with a kind of gratitude. It did not seem strange to her, far less disgraceful, that she should have deserted them all; indeed she would never have admitted that this was what had taken place; for long after any one of them had parted company with her she took a keen interest in his doings and, as a rule, retained his friendship. To the Flight-Lieutenant in his present distress she showed a kind of sympathy which, while it was not love, was certainly far from indifference.

'It's a pity,' she would say, 'that people should get so upset, but it's inevitable and it soon passes. What's really unforgivable is to pretend to feel love when you've ceased to feel it.'

'How long are you going to feel it for me?' I would sometimes ask her, and as a rule she would laugh and begin to kiss me as a reply; and at such moments I would feel peculiarly comfortable, for I knew that I had not only her in my thoughts, but also the excitement of a most promising career and the ability to attract the affection of other women at the aerodrome, many of whom already seemed to me desirable.

Not that this fact made me any the less happy with Eustasia. I was completely pleased with the position in which I found myself. I very rarely thought now of those few months in the past when I had presumed myself to be happy with Bess, and when I did so I found it impossible to compare my present feelings with the feelings that I had had then. I remembered chiefly the pain of the night before I had entered the Air Force, and began to imagine that in the elation and extravagance of feeling which I could still recall there must always have been present an uncertainty and a dissatisfaction enough to make that period of my life less pleasurable than was my life now.

Eustasia often spoke to me of Bess, for she had heard previously of the whole affair from the Flight-Lieutenant;

and though I was willing enough to talk to her on this or any subject, I sometimes found myself hesitating over my answers to her questions, not because of any timidity in myself, but because of the difficulty in my present surroundings of luxury and confidence to envisage the tin hut above the village, the cheap home-made dresses that Bess used to wear, and the recklessness of my own emotions.

It would be hard also to say whether I was more pleased or displeased by the slighting way in which Eustasia often spoke of Bess. I had heard that, since the Flight-Lieutenant had left her, she had suffered an almost complete collapse, and had seldom left her room in the pub. I had not been altogether sorry to hear this, and yet something in me had prevented me from allowing my mind to dwell too precisely on the state in which she must have been living. Now, when I was content myself, I began to feel a wish, not to assist her, but that in some way or other I might know that she was not unhappy. I remember once saying something of this kind to Eustasia, and I can remember exactly when I said it. It was during one of the dances in the glass ballroom on the Manor roof and, although it was a cold night, we had taken coats and gone out together into the garden, since Eustasia wished to look at the full moon shining on the loops of the river and on the bare branches of those trees in the meadows which had not yet been cut down. We could hear the music pounding behind our backs and, if we turned round, could see high up in the air the figures in uniform or in bright dresses laughing and swaying inside the glass. We sat down on a seat between two juniper bushes whose small starry leaves were silvered over by the moonlight.

I forget how it was that we had begun to talk of Bess, but when I mentioned somewhat vaguely my wish that she should be happy, Eustasia laughed and took my hand inside her coat.

'Don't bother yourself,' she said. 'She'll soon find someone else. Women like that never really know what they want. They're always either up or down. I know the type well.'

I made no reply. I had fixed my eyes on that part of the river where I remembered having bathed on the night when I had discovered Bess and the Flight-Lieutenant together. The incident seemed to me now to have taken place a very long time ago. Eustasia turned her head towards me, but I continued to look down on the river. I felt her press my hand before she spoke.

'Supposing Bess were to love you like I love you,' she said, 'would you like to go back to her?'

As she spoke my body stiffened and I became conscious of the beating of my heart. Her fingers were twining into my fingers, but though I was aware of this my own hand remained limp and unresponsive. Unaccountably I seemed to see myself as I had been nearly a year ago, lying in the mud of Gurney's meadow, with Fred and Mac going away from me into the night. This scene seemed to me infinitely depressing and at the same time almost dreadful, for I could connect it in no way with my present way of life, with the discipline and the dances and the fighter squadron to which I was now attached. I was conscious, too, as I had not been a moment before, of the smells and sounds of the winter night, and could envisage clearly the appearance of the stars between the boughs of the elm trees in the meadow where I had lain. I felt Eustasia move closer to me, so that her head rested on my shoulder.

I turned to her and said: 'All that part of my life seems to have vanished away entirely', and I was astonished at the gravity with which I spoke, for in a part of my mind, whose promptings I rejected, I knew and was shocked to know that what I was saying was untrue. I noticed that Eustasia's face also was unusually grave, and I changed my tone. 'Maybe I've got more sense now,' I said, and smiled as I took her in my arms.

She clung to me then, I remember, as though this were our first meeting after months of separation. More than any night that I can remember there was excitement and a kind of desperation in our love-making that night. Later when we were on our way back to the dance Eustasia held my arm tightly between her hands. 'Some day soon I'm going to tell you a secret,' she said, but in spite of all my efforts refused to say then what the secret was.

CHAPTER XV

Discipline

SHORTLY AFTER THIS I was appointed to a position in the aerodrome to which in my most ambitious moments I could hardly have aspired. I was given the post of private secretary to the Air Vice-Marshal himself; and now, in the light of what followed after, it is difficult to summon up again to the imagination the feelings of pride and satisfaction with which at that time I was filled. There were other feelings as well. I regretted being no longer able to live the life of the squadron to which I had been attached and amongst which I had made many friends. My vanity, too, was flattered by the esteem with which I was looked upon by other ranks; for this was a unique appointment. In the past the Air Vice-Marshal had had no confidential secretary but, with the aid of two or three stenographers and by delegating some of his work to various senior officers, had personally superintended an immense field of activity. Now I was to share his confidence, and the knowledge of this fact and my pride in it easily outweighed every other feeling that I may have had.

When I was first called to his office and informed of my new appointment I remember that together with my pride and my surprise at being selected for such a post, I felt also a kind of reluctance and an extreme diffidence; for I knew what I could do as a pilot, whereas of many of the other and more important activities of the Air Force I knew too that I was almost entirely ignorant.

The Air Vice-Marshal, I think, must have understood the hesitation that my face, no doubt, expressed. He was sitting, I remember, at a long table in his room, and a shaft of winter sunlight through an open window passed behind his head, which was inclined forward, and just touched the edges of the fingers of one hand which rested on the dark wood beside a blotting pad. When he informed me of my appointment and when I had, from a variety of feelings, failed to give an immediate answer, he smiled and at once began to speak again.

'I dare say you remember,' he said, 'the display of aerobatics which some time ago I arranged for you to watch. You will know now that the work which you are doing at present, invaluable as it is as a part of your training, is in itself practically worthless. I should like you to realize that the same is true of any other of our specialized activities. Specialists, of course, we must have, and a sound knowledge of the basis of their work is also necessary for anyone who, like myself, has the duty and the delight of exercising control.'

I noticed that when he pronounced the word 'delight' his lips curved in a smile that in any other man I should have taken as an expression of sensuality. Now he looked up at me quickly, and from the animation of his eyes I could see that he was deeply moved.

'All these people,' he continued, 'are invaluable; and all of them are, in the last analysis, worthless. Even our great mathematician with whose wife, I believe, you are carrying on an affair.'

He smiled again, and looked at me intently. Uncertain of what attitude I should adopt, I found myself smiling also. He leant back in his chair and said: 'Good.

I congratulate you. She is an estimable woman. I am glad that it is not too serious. You must remember' (and here his face changed so that he was looking at me with an expression of extraordinary gravity) 'you must remember what your duty is and what is more than your duty, what is the whole purpose of our life.'

Here he paused, keeping his eyes fixed on me as though he were expecting an answer, and I again hesitated, for, to tell the truth, I was not exactly certain as to his meaning, whether he was speaking of our duties in the Air Force or of something else. He might have been prompting me in a part which I had momentarily forgotten as he continued in a low voice: 'To be freed from time, Roy. From the past and from the future. From shapelessness.'

He had never before, I think, and certainly not since I had joined the aerodrome, called me by my Christian name, and this fact impressed itself now more forcibly on my mind than did the sense of his words. However, he had either not noticed that he was speaking to me more familiarly than usual or else attached no significance to what form of address he used. His eyes had left mine and he seemed to be staring fixedly at the edge of the table. His lips continued to move though no words came from them, and there was a look of such concentration on his face that I could not believe that he was any longer aware of my existence. As I watched him I noticed for the first time the long lines that ran from his cheekbones to his chin, giving him in this brief moment of withdrawal from the outside world a haggard appearance which in some way I was shocked to see. For an instant I was reminded of the Rector's face as I had seen it in his study when he was confessing aloud the murder of his friend.

The Air Vice-Marshal did not remain for long in this state. Quite suddenly the tension of his face relaxed. He raised his eyes from the edge of the table and looked at me sharply. Then he pushed his chair back, smiled, and began to tell me about my hours of work and some of the duties which I should have to perform, and as he spoke I became amazed at the confidence which he was bestowing on me and at the extent of the responsibility of my new work.

At this first interview I was only told in the roughest outline of the tremendous aims which the Air Vice-Marshal had set before himself and before us; indeed, much of what he said to me at that time seemed to me then almost incomprehensible, almost fantastic; for I had not yet learnt how detailed and meticulous were the means already arranged for each far-reaching end. It was only gradually, as a result of many hours of routine work and many long conversations, that I began to form in my mind anything like a complete picture of the scope and the ambition of our operations. Then I realized the importance to us of those large sections of the aerodrome staff who were engaged on work which had previously seemed to me to have little or nothing to do with flying. There was, for example, not only the enormous propaganda department, but there were other departments whose work consisted in an investigation of such subjects as banking, agriculture, fisheries, and factory organization. And though our aerodrome was far the largest and most important in the country, there were many others large enough to contain corresponding specialist departments, with all of which we were in constant touch.

I remembered that at the time when the Air Vice-Marshal had addressed us in the chapel he had informed us that our aim was not only to protect but to transform the country, and I remembered the contempt with which on various occasions he had alluded to judges, lawyers, politicians, industrialists, agricultural and factory workers —to all those in fact whose professional life is usually held to constitute the fabric of civilization. Now he would speak to me of such people with even greater acrimony and with more precision.

'I should like you to understand,' he would say, 'that it is by no means sufficient to blame society for its inefficiency, its waste, its stupidity. These are merely symptoms. It is against the souls of the people themselves that we are fighting. It is each and every one of their ideas that we must detest. Think of them as earthbound, grovelling from one piece of mud to another, and feebly imagining distinctions between the two, incapable of envisaging a distant objective, tied up for ever in their miserable and unimportant histories, indeed in the whole wretched and blind history of man on earth. Religion, which for many centuries did exercise an ennobling, if a misleading, effect, has gone. The race which we, of all people, are now required to protect is a race of money-makers and sentimentalists, undisciplined except by forces which they do not understand, insensitive to all except the lowest, the most ordinary, the most mechanical stimuli. Protect it! We shall destroy what we cannot change.'

And as I listened to him I would feel that I understood more clearly now than before, when I was in the chapel, what it was at which we aimed. I remembered how from the air the valleys, hills, and rivers gained a certain distinction but wholly lost that quality which is perceived by a countryman whose day's travel is bounded by the earth of three or four meadows, and whose view for most of his life may be constricted by some local rising of the ground. In the air there is no feeling or smell of earth, and I have often observed that the backyards of houses or the smoke curling up through cottage chimneys, although at times they seem to have a certain pathos, do as a rule, when one is several thousand feet above them, appear both defenceless and ridiculous, as though infinite trouble had been taken to secure a result that has little or no significance.

I began to think now in the same way of those inhabitants of the earth who had never risen above it, never submitted their lives to a discipline like ours, a discipline that was unconnected with the acquisition of money or of foodstuffs. Many of these people, I knew, were miserable; many were content; but both their misery and their happiness seemed to me at this time of my life abject and pointless. From this class of people, I thought, could never come the initiation of any grand idea, and I began to detest those organizations that were outside our own, for I saw that they were aimless and that their power was accidental.

But we had an aim which was nothing less than to assume ourselves the whole authority by which men lived, and we had a power that was not an affair of cyphers, but was real and tangible. We were set to exercise our brains, our nerves, our muscles, and our desires towards one end, and to back the force of our will we possessed the most powerful machines that have been invented by man. It was not only our dexterity with these machines, but the whole spirit of our training which cut us off from the mass of men; and to be so cut off was, whether we realized it or not, our greatest pleasure and our chief article of pride.

As I began gradually to understand the elaboration and the grandeur of the Air Vice-Marshal's plans, I realized that already we were equipped at any moment to take over the direction of the country whose servants nominally we were. In some of the key posts of administration we already had our own men; as for the other posts we could fill them at a moment's notice with officers who had already been trained for the purpose. And at the centre of this vast organization was the Air Vice-Marshal himself. He alone was in contact with the leaders and sub-leaders of the numerous groups connected with each other through him. Nor was this all; for it was only he who could exercise complete and unquestioned control over others who, without him, would certainly have disputed among themselves for pre-eminence. As it was I never knew of his authority or of his decisions being at any time questioned; and this was natural enough for, talented and resolute as were many of his subordinates, there was none of them who possessed that seemingly certain vision of the future that made the Air Vice-Marshal so uniquely able to inspire confidence.

It was not long before I became aware that I was being entrusted with secrets that were not shared even with the highest of these officials; and my surprise at being selected for such a post of trust was equalled by my determination to show myself worthy of my position. I would work day after day and late into the night, keeping always in the forefront of my mind the aim and certainty of our conspiracy. Indeed, I did not think of our purpose as a conspiracy, but rather as a necessary and exciting operation. We constituted no revolutionary party actuated by humanitarian ideals, but seemed to be an organization manifestly entitled by its own discipline, efficiency, and will to assume supreme power. Outside us I could see nothing that was not incompetent or corrupt, and I remember as on various occasions I piloted the Air Vice-Marshal's plane from one aerodrome to another I would look down on the hills and forests, the coal mines and factory towns over which we flew, and would wonder with a kind of joyful trepidation how much longer we would have to wait before the word was given to us to seize into our own hands all the resources and all the power that we traversed with our wings.

But it was not with our ultimate aims that my day-to-day work was chiefly concerned. There was still much to be done in the village which we had recently occupied, and indeed in this small province of our activity there was already something disquieting. For there was no doubt that, after the initial surprise of our occupation and the excitement which it caused, the mood of the villagers had changed to one of hostility, and there were signs that this hostility, sluggish and undetermined as it was, might grow to dangerous proportions. Already one of our junior aircraftsmen had been murdered in the meadows by the river where he had been walking with the young daughter of one of the men whom I remembered in the past as having been a bellringer. In spite of a strict inquiry we had been unable to find the murderers, and although the girl's father and the girl herself had been dealt with under military law, and a large fine had been levied from every household in the village, we could not but feel that, since the real criminals were still at large, our punitive measures had not been wholly successful. It was certain that the villagers had felt the same thing. I remember that for a week or two following this incident there were reported a number of cases of slackness and insubordination, trifling in themselves, but indicative of a dangerous tendency. All these cases were dealt with severely so that complete discipline was soon re-established; and yet it was somewhat disturbing to us to have to realize that it was still necessary to devote a certain proportion of our time and energy to the task of suppressing discontent in our immediate neighbour-hood.

Most of the reports on this subject from our police officers passed through my hands, and it soon became evident to me that among several centres of disaffection the circle of people who surrounded the Squire's sister and the Rector's wife was one of the most important. It appeared to me that the hostility towards us of the village women was more bitter and more homogeneous than was that of the men, and there was no doubt of the influence which many of these women exercised on their husbands, relations, and lovers. They seemed to have formed some sort of club which, under the name of sewing parties, mothers' league, or other such titles, was constantly meeting for malicious gossip either in the church or in the house shared together by the Squire's sister and the Rector's wife. The Flight-Lieutenant often attended these gatherings, but the reports which he gave of them seemed both to the police and to me also, singularly feeble and unconvincing. Moreover, in the course of his sermons he had on several occasions made remarks that might be construed in a sense prejudicial to our organization; nor was his apparent interest in the church itself a thing which commended itself to any of us.

I remember that when I put before the Air Vice-Marshal these reports and my conclusions upon them, he surprised me by appearing somewhat more worried with the facts than the situation demanded. I was used to quick decisions from him, and on this occasion had expected him to order some immediate action, perhaps the transportation of the two ladies to another part of the country, and perhaps the relegation of the Flight-Lieutenant to some less important post. But for some moments after I had concluded my report he remained silent, leaning back in his chair and tapping the top of the table with the knuckles of one hand. I noticed particularly his strong and delicate fingers curving upwards, tense as though he were holding a foil. When he spoke he said: 'I imagine that of these two ladies the younger is the more dangerous. I mean the sister of the Squire. She, I believe, is a little younger than her friend.'

I was surprised at the accuracy of his knowledge, for I had forgotten myself which was the elder of the two. 'Yes,' I said. 'The other lady is more difficult to understand, but she seems to have a much more placid temperament.'

The Air Vice-Marshal smiled at me, and it struck me that he was smiling in approval of the fact that I had not mentioned my mother by name. As it happened I had made no conscious effort to comply with his wishes in this respect, for, although if I had been asked, I should certainly have admitted that the Rector's wife was, indeed, to the best of my knowledge, my mother, I had long ceased to regard this fact as important.

The Air Vice-Marshal went on speaking. 'As for that young man,' he said, 'he must be told what his duty is. I can't understand what has happened to him. He was never brilliant but he used to be competent enough.' Here he frowned and looked at me as though I could enlighten him on this subject. The keenness of his eyes and the directness of his look were almost embarrassing to me, and I felt something like relief when he smiled again, looked hurriedly at his watch and rose to his feet. 'Come,' he said. 'You and I will go to church. There is, I believe, a service in progress or just starting.'

I had grown accustomed to unexpected decisions, but was surprised at this one. He had not visited the church since the day of the Rector's funeral, and it was something of a shock to me now to remember that occasion when I had been indignant at his interruption, and then to reflect on how radically my feelings had altered. As we left the office and entered the car I thought it strange that the Air Vice-Marshal should be willing to waste an hour of his time in a personal inspection of the Flight-Lieutenant's activities and perhaps a few minutes' conversation with the Squire's sister. It seemed that he had read my thoughts, for when we were in the car, he said: 'It would really be somewhat ridiculous to have to arrest two old women and a boy. It should be sufficient to scare them. We shall see.'

He did not speak again until we reached the church. Then, as we stood still in the porch listening to the singing beyond a red curtain that separated us from the congregation, he turned to me and smiled. 'Some of these tunes,' he said, 'I can remember quite well.' And he looked away from me with his lips tightly pressed together.

As I followed him into the church I found myself wondering, as I had never done before, what sort of a youth and upbringing he had had; for he had never in my presence alluded to the period of his life that had gone by before he joined the Air Force.

We took our places almost unobserved at the back of the church, and saw that, as the last verse of the hymn was being sung, the Flight-Lieutenant had left the reading desk where he had been standing and was walking slowly towards the pulpit. To our surprise he was not wearing uniform, but was dressed in a cassock and surplice. So far as I knew he had no authorization whatever to wear this costume, and I guessed from the movement of surprise in the congregation and the faces turned towards each other that he was giving this performance for the first time. I could just see the faces of the Squire's sister and the Rector's wife who were standing in a pew to the right and a little in front of us. They had looked into each other's eyes and smiled while the Flight-Lieutenant was on his way to the pulpit, and when after the brief prayer which he pronounced the congregation had resumed their seats, I observed the heads of the two ladies slightly tilted backwards in an attitude of respectful attention such as I had often seen in the days when the place which the Flight-

Lieutenant now occupied had been filled by the man whom he had shot. I leant back in the pew and listened as the preacher began to speak, but before many words had been uttered I turned in surprise to the Air Vice-Marshal; for it was clear at once that the Flight-Lieutenant was greatly exceeding or actually transgressing the instructions which had been given to him.

He looked, I thought, remarkably young and handsome as he stood there in his surplice; and yet his looks and whole bearing had altered greatly since the days when I had first become acquainted with him. He had almost lost that careless and irresponsible air which I had so admired. When he spoke now there was a diffidence, almost a timidity, in his manner, and it seemed that he was afraid to let his eyes rest long on any single object. He looked round the congregation absent-mindedly, being quite unaware, I am certain, of the Air Vice-Marshal's presence; but when he spoke it was in a voice of strange solemnity.

'Isn't it true,' he began, 'that you and I, that all of us, are, in comparison with what we desire, poor fools, incapable of directing either our own lives or those of others? We all want to be happy; we all know that if the world were good then the people in it would be happy. We can imagine goodness and we can imagine happiness. Why is it that we are neither happy nor good? Our very love divides us as often as does our hate. As for our work, are there many of us here now who find pleasure and fulfilment in our jobs?

'Yet we read in old books of the peace which passeth understanding, of joy and love and tranquillity, which the world cannot give. So far as we can discover, this joy and this peace have actually been experienced by people living on the earth. How is it that we do not experience them? What is it that we have lost? These are questions that I must ask, but which I cannot answer. I can only tell you that when I read of these things I realize that something of the utmost value is being mentioned, something which I have never known, something with which you, perhaps, who have only recently come under the control of an impersonal force, are better acquainted than I am.'

Here the Flight-Lieutenant paused and licked his lips. There was a look of such desperation in his eyes that it was impossible to question his sincerity. It was evident that, in this mood, he could be of no use to us whatever, and I looked again at the Air Vice-Marshal who was leaning back in his pew, the tips of his fingers pressed together below his chin. He was frowning as though in perplexity, and I was surprised to see him so.

'It seems to me,' the Flight-Lieutenant continued, 'that it is only honest for me to say that in my opinion you were much better off, so far as the things of real value are concerned, in the time before your village was occupied by the Air Force.'

At this extraordinary and daring statement a hush fell upon the congregation, and I could see that the limbs of the people stiffened as they leant their heads farther forward as though to be certain of hearing the speaker's next words. I felt a movement at my side, and saw that the Air Vice-Marshal had risen to his feet and stepped past me into the middle of the aisle. Those in the pews in front of us began to turn round, and their movements excited the notice of others, so that in a short time the attention of the audience had been diverted from the Flight-Lieutenant to the slight tense figure of his superior officer. The Flight-Lieutenant himself gripped the edge of the pulpit with one hand and licked his lips. He stretched out his other hand in front of him in a kind of appeal, vague both in itself and in its direction.

The Air Vice-Marshal spoke slowly and distinctly. 'This religious service,' he said, 'is at an end. The church will be closed until further notice.' Then, looking directly at the Flight-Lieutenant, he spoke more sharply. 'You, sir, are under arrest. Be so good as to come down from that pulpit immediately.'

He stopped speaking and in the short silence that followed I looked at the Flight-Lieutenant and saw, what surprised me, that he was evidently deliberating whether or not he should obey the order that he had received. His face was very pale and his lips quivered as he looked down at us. But the shocked silence which had succeeded the Air Vice-Marshal's words was now broken by voices from the front of the church. People out of sight, both men and women, were muttering together angrily. I could see fists brandished above heads, and heard one man shout: 'Throw him out! Make an end of the lot of them! There are enough of us!'

The Air Vice-Marshal looked away from the pulpit and in the direction of this voice. He drew his revolver from his side and, as he did so, I and two or three of our special police who were sitting at the back of the church took our places beside and behind him.

'Silence!' he shouted, and such was the authority of the man that the complete silence which followed his command did not appear to any of us as surprising.

He added in a quieter voice: 'The first person who leaves his pew will be shot.'

The Flight-Lieutenant had now left the pulpit and was standing by the chancel steps. He seemed about to address an appeal to someone, but whether it was to the Air Vice-Marshal or to his congregation it would have been impossible to say. Before he could open his mouth, however, the Air Vice-Marshal spoke again. 'Go to the vestry,' he said, 'and report back here to me in uniform.'

The Flight-Lieutenant took a step forward, towards us and not in the direction of the vestry. I noticed the concentration of his eyes upon the revolver which the Air Vice-Marshal held in his hand, and I felt a quick pang of terror, something that was almost an impulse to move forward myself to prevent what I feared might happen. I glanced at the Air Vice-Marshal's face, and saw that it was strangely tense. When he opened his mouth, as though about to speak, I was extravagantly relieved.

Yet before he spoke our attention was distracted to a new quarter. There was a sound of scuffling from the pews to our right, and I saw that the Squire's sister had torn herself free from the Rector's wife who had evidently been holding tightly to her arm in an effort to restrain her from some action. Now she began to speak in a high voice that was almost a shout. Her hair was disordered where it was uncovered by her hat, and one lock had straggled down her neck on to her shoulder. There was a fierce light in her eyes, and I remember that I was suddenly and unreasonably struck with the thought that in her youth she must have been a remarkably handsome woman.

She turned her head to the Air Vice-Marshal and cried out: 'Leave my son alone!' Then, before anyone had had time to grasp her meaning or to be startled at it, she stretched out her arm towards the group of us and cried out again, 'Listen! Listen all of you.' And she stepped into the aisle with her finger still pointed at the Air Vice-Marshal and her mouth open and distorted as though she were in a frenzy.

He fired his revolver at once and she, I observed, turned up her eyes to him with a look that seemed to show more of surprise than of any other feeling; she fell on to the fibre matting that carpeted the aisles. A murmur of fear and of horror filled the church and soon came the sound of women sobbing. Many of the congregation sat down in their pews covering their faces with their hands. I saw the Rector's wife move forward and then, as the Air Vice-Marshal caught her eye and waved her back, collapse in a faint where she had been standing. But the Flight-Lieutenant had run towards us uninterrupted, and was now kneeling by the side of the dead body. He was holding the limp hand and staring into the distorted face, seeming to be unaware of the danger in which he stood.

I looked at the Air Vice-Marshal and was startled both by the pallor and the severity of his face. He was staring fixedly not at the body nor at the Flight-Lieutenant, but at a portion of the young man's surplice which was already stained with blood. There was complete silence in the church except for the intermittent sounds of choking or sobbing which came from some of the pews.

After a moment or two the Air Vice-Marshal looked

up at me, and I was astonished to see something like a smile on his face. Then he turned to the police officers. 'Take him away,' he said, pointing towards the Flight-Lieutenant, and I just saw them lay their hands on the elbows of the surpliced figure before I followed the Air Vice-Marshal from the church.

When we reached the car he turned to me again, and I was almost ashamed to meet his eyes, so dreadful to me had been the scene in which we had taken part. 'Go and have a drink at the club, Roy,' he said. 'I shall return by myself.' As I raised me eyes to his I noticed a strange expression of kindliness on his face. 'This has not been pleasant for me either,' he said, and I could see from a sudden contraction of his lips that he was speaking the truth.

CHAPTER XVI

The Secret

SOMEHOW IN THE club that morning I was unable to join as readily as usual in the conversation and joking of my friends. I had walked to the club house slowly and found, when I arrived there, that one of the special policemen who had been present at the church had preceded me. He had already recounted what had happened and the discussion which was now proceeding was what I might have expected; yet I could neither join in it nor regard what was said as being at all appropriate.

The action of the Air Vice-Marshal in shooting a woman was a source of considerable amusement to everyone. Promptitude and decision were what we expected of him, but in this instance the result could not but appear slightly disproportionate to the effort expended.

'One old woman shot down in flames. Not so good!' people said; though at the same time everyone was aware that what might have been a dangerous riot had been wholly and entirely quelled; and, though most officers jested about the affair, most of them too felt both gratitude and relief at the fact that our authority in the village had been once more unequivocally demonstrated. The responsibility for anything that might be considered displeasing in what had happened was unanimously laid at the door of the Flight-Lieutenant. Of him no one had a good word to say, and indeed I could not see myself in what way his conduct could possibly be defended.

And yet with the tone of this discussion I felt myself

to be wholly out of sympathy. I could not help thinking that what had taken place was more important and, in a way, more significant than my brother officers believed. Whether this feeling of mine was due to my having known the Squire's sister in my boyhood or to my old friendship with the Flight-Lieutenant, I do not know. It may have been perhaps that I had sensed in the Air Vice-Marshal's own attitude something that gave me reason to suppose that he himself had regarded this affair by no means lightly. However it was, I know that during this conversation at the club I felt continually ill at ease, and found it difficult to express myself clearly when asked, as I was from time to time, for my opinion. It was true enough that the death of an elderly woman and the disgrace of a young man were little things when compared with the authority of the Air Force and the greatness of its aims; but something in the identity of this woman and this man disturbed me. Had I known by hearsay only of the event which had taken place, perhaps my feelings would have been different. As it was, I was almost superstitious enough to imagine some fatality that seemed to bind me to these characters from my past, so that I had not been able to avoid being actually present at scene after scene of violence and stress in which they had been the chief actors. And these scenes, however much I might consider myself a mere spectator, still strangely moved me.

I remember thinking, oddly enough, that the Air Vice-Marshal himself would feel as I did on this point, and would have wished, if he had been weak enough, to escape the necessity of the action which he had taken I recalled the moment in the church when he seemed to have been on the point of shooting the Flight-Lieutenant, and how he had refrained from doing so. What had happened afterwards had happened suddenly and left him no choice but to act as he had done. Yet both the shooting and the refraining from it seemed to me now more significant than was apparent to the officers in the club who had not seen the Air Vice-Marshal's strained face or the blood staining the surplice.

Before long I grew tired of their conversation and left the club house. I stood for some moments in the road beneath the black boughs of the chestnut tree that extended over the wall of the Rectory garden, uncertain whether to visit Eustasia or to return to my office. As I stood there I noticed with something of a shock the first signs of spring. The chestnut buds above my head were sticky and swollen with their load of folded leaves. Already along the river I knew that some of the willows would be out, and in the hedges the first migrant birds would soon be singing. I thought of what day of the month it was, and reflected that nearly a year had passed since the disturbing celebration of my supposed birthday. Now I had little or no curiosity either as to the exact date of this event or as to the circumstances which had attended it.

As I walked up the village street I allowed my mind to dwell idly upon the past year, idly and without perturbation, for I felt secure in my loyalty and easy both in my work and in my pleasures. Indeed, I found myself in this way relieved from the perplexity of my thoughts about what had recently happened. I began to recall to my mind my interview with the landlord's wife and, though I could still feel within me the stirrings of the agitation into which that interview had thrown me, the sensation was now not unpleasant, for I seemed, even after this short space of time, to be looking back on myself as I had been in a vague and irresponsible boyhood, full of pain but without direction or significance.

When I came to the pub I glanced across the wall and observed a few men standing inside the door waiting their turn to be served with drinks from the bar. Some of them turned their heads towards me, and I recognized one or two of my old friends, and realized more sharply than ever that they were friends no longer; for the interest I took in them now was solely concerned with their reactions to what had taken place that morning in the church. If there had been any hostile demonstration I should have had the pub closed; as it was the men were looking at me in a somewhat sheepish manner, and I conjectured that the Air Vice-Marhsal's action had been from a disciplinary point of view wholly successful.

I had my revolver with me, and wondered for a moment or two whether to enter the pub, but I had decided not to do so and was on the point of passing on when I saw the landlord's wife come towards me past the group of men. She appeared to me at once as both older and less self-possessed than she had been at our last interview, and though for some weeks after that time I had avoided conversation with her, now I was by no means displeased to see that she evidently wished to talk to me; for I still retained for her the affection of my childhood, and did not fancy that she could reveal anything else to me that could disturb the serenity in which I lived.

I stepped inside the gate to meet her and remember taking both her hands and smiling at her, for I was pleased to see her and, perhaps because I had grown so unused to the company of any people except airmen, did not notice at once that my gesture was insensitive and inappropriate. Her hands were limp in my hands, and her face wore a harassed expression that showed that she was in no mood for laughing. I dropped her hands and stepped back a pace, once more upon the defensive, for I fancied that the reason for her distress must be the event which had just taken place in church, and I was not prepared to discuss this with her. Perhaps she read my thoughts, since before speaking she shook her head as though to free me from some misconception.

'It's Bess,' she said. 'She's in a terrible way, my dear.' And she stood looking at me for some moments, while I found myself so profoundly and variously moved by her words that I was unable to make any reply.

When she had first spoken it was as though I had been pierced with a sudden dart or shaft of pain and fear. The feeling was both involuntary and irrational; in a moment it was succeeded by an impulse, though the word is too violent for so lethargic a feeling, to be away from here, to be left alone. 'What was to be done?' I wondered, and 'What, in any case, could I do? Why must I be disturbed by women?' For a second I felt not unpleased that Bess was in some danger or trouble, and the thought presented itself to me that if together with a number of my other past friends she were to die, I should enjoy a greater peace of mind than I had at present. Then instantly and with a sudden overwhelming force, as though such ideas had never occurred to me before, I seemed to see Bess as

I had known her a year ago, and I was conscious of nothing but terror and of a kind of tenderness that was the fiercer through being unconnected with any organized practice or theory by which I now lived. Apart from this feeling my mind was blank so that I listened as a child might listen to what was being said, without making any effort to show the landlord's wife by any comment or exclamation of sympathy how her words were affecting me.

She told me that for some time past Bess had been tired and dispirited. This I was prepared to hear, since I had known that ever since the Flight-Lieutenant had left her she had been in a weak nervous state. I had seen her myself often with her eyes red from weeping, and I now recalled to mind how diffident had been her smile when I had seen her last. I felt my muscles contract as though I were shrinking from some source of pain when I reflected that the sight of this smile of hers had neither distressed nor displeased me.

'But now it's terrible,' the landlord's wife was saying. 'You wouldn't know her. She's gentle and quiet as can be, and yet she isn't herself. It's as though she wasn't there. Oh, I can't explain. I can't tell you how sweet she is, and yet not in a way that I would have her so. She seems not to be there at all, and yet she talks quite sensibly, except sometimes when she seems to have something on her conscience and says she wants to die. And she does want to die, Roy. That's what's so terrible.'

She stopped speaking abruptly, and looked at me almost as though beseeching an answer to some question. I saw that she had suddenly wondered whether the information which she had given me about my relationship to Bess had been disregarded by me, and had I not been so deeply moved by her words and manner I should have smiled to think how totally she had misunderstood my reaction to her story. As it was I had formed in my mind a picture both of what Bess must look like now and of what she must be suffering. The distaste at being called in to deal with an affair which I considered no longer to concern me, even the agony of tenderness which I had felt a moment ago, passed clean from my mind.

I began to think wholly of what could be done to cure or to alleviate a misery which I imagined to be even greater than any that I had felt myself; and I questioned the landlord's wife minutely, for I intended to take back as good an account of her condition as possible to Dr Faulkner, the chief medical officer of the aerodrome, whom I hoped to be able to persuade to visit her. I wished to see her myself, but was dissuaded from doing so, since it appeared that even the mention of my name was apt to distress her; and indeed it had already occurred to me that her illness might be due in part to a sense, whether conscious or unconscious, of the criminality of our relationship. I do not know how it was that now this thought aroused in me no feeling of resentment whatever; nor can I account for the fact that from this time onward I found myself capable of thinking clearly and distinctly of her, without any of those conflicting and irreconcilable feelings that I had had when I listened to the landlord's wife's first words. It was as though one uprush of pity and of tenderness had swept away the rest; yet now this pity and tenderness, too, had gone, leaving me only anxious to see to it that the best possible course of action should be pursued.

Soon I left the pub to go to the aerodrome. I would return later, I said, and if possible would bring the doctor with me. Bess's mother was, I could see, pleased at having spoken to me, and before I left she smiled and complimented me on playing the part of a real brother to her daughter. For a moment I was shocked by this remark, so indifferent had I become to the existence of any kind of relationship that was not willed; but as I walked away I began to find a curious satisfaction in the words which she had used. For I felt now not only the impulse, but a kind of right to be of service to Bess, and, worried as I was about her condition, there was something pleasant in the thought that I was doing what I could to make it better. Seldom or never before when she had been in my mind had I been tranquil, but now I could think of her calmly and continuously, omitting nothing that I knew from the current of my imagination, and holding her dear in everything that I imagined. Now I demanded nothing from her, and was thankful for rather than convinced of my own right to give her anything of mine. Indeed, the service which I wished to render her was, in any case, a small one. Yet my desire to render even this small service filled me with so deep a joy that I could think consciously of hardly anything else but of the urgency of what I was doing and of this new-found and irrational happiness. For that my feelings were irrational there was no doubt. If I had been uniquely concerned with her state of health there was every reason for me to be sad. If I had suddenly decided that I was still in love with her I should have had still less reason to be pleased with myself. Yet the happiness was in me and was intense, more intense, I think, than any feeling which

I had known, although it was intermingled with much anxiety and much deep-seated perplexity that the thought of its own novelty aroused. It was as though there had been something in me like snow and ice which were now melting and gradually revealing a landscape whose outlines I had not seen for some time and barely remembered.

So I hurried on towards the aerodrome, eager to obtain an interview with the doctor as soon as possible; but before I could do so I was to receive more news to surprise me. My way to the doctor's house took me past the block of flats where Eustasia lived, and while I was still some distance off I noticed her standing in front of one of the ground-floor doorways, not looking in my direction, but staring up the road that led to the airfield and the big hangars. She was wearing a red costume which I had not seen before, and looked almost a stranger, I thought, as she stood averted, waiting perhaps for me, perhaps for her husband. Yet I had half a mind to go round by a different way, for I regarded my present business as the most urgent thing and had no wish to be distracted from it. But while I was thinking in this way she suddenly turned round and waved to me. I noticed when I approached her that there was an unusual brightness in her eyes and a more than usual warmth in her smile. She stretched out one hand towards me invitingly, and there was something frail and winning in the gesture. I thought that I had never seen her look so beautiful.

'I've been waiting for you,' she said. 'Come in. There's something important I want to tell you.'

I took her hand and said: 'Can it wait for an hour?' and was about to continue when she interrupted me, displeased as she always was if any of her plans were in any way thwarted.

Over her strong face passed quickly an expression of sulkiness, as though she were a child. 'No, I can't wait,' she said, and then, smiling again to show that she was not really angry, she added: 'What is your important business that makes you in such a hurry?'

I began to tell her about Bess, feeling somewhat uneasy as I spoke, for I could not convey to her my own sense of the urgency of what I was doing, nor pretend that, so far as the facts went, there was any need for me to be so determined not to waste an instant before seeing the doctor.

She listened to me impatiently and soon interrupted me. 'That's not important,' she said. 'Or is it that you're still in love with the girl? She's certainly not in love with you.'

I was unreasonably angered by this remark, not, I think, because of its inaccuracy (for my feeling for Bess was certainly not what I should have recognized as love), but because Eustasia's manner seemed to indicate that she regarded herself as having some kind of proprietary right over me, and I was unwilling to admit such a right. I looked hard at her and found, to my surprise, that I was looking at her with a certain distaste. 'Of course I'm not in love,' I said. 'Anyway, haven't I told you that she's my sister?'

'You don't even know that,' she said, and stared at me angrily, challenging me to reply, but I made no answer and, as I looked at her, observed that tears were beginning to form in the corners of her eyes. No doubt my own expression must have softened, for she stretched

246

out her hand again and said, 'Come upstairs for a minute or two. I must speak to you', and I followed her somewhat reluctantly and somewhat ill at ease, for I saw that what she had intended to be a pleasant meeting had started inauspiciously on the verge of a quarrel.

When we were in her room I sat down on the divan and she sat in an armchair facing me. Her eyes were bright again with suppressed excitement, but I was still anxious to be gone and I fancied that she sensed my feelings and was distressed by them. But she smiled more than ever, and spoke in a voice that was even more than usually confident, as though her own assurance were calculated to make me speak and feel as she wished me to do.

'I told you I'd got a surprise for you, a secret,' she said. 'Well, now I'm going to tell you. I'm going to have a baby.' She paused and looked at me eagerly, as though to estimate precisely the effect of her words. Then her eyes left mine and she stared at the floor with a small smile at the corners of her mouth. 'Are you angry?' she said, without looking up at me.

For some moments I found it impossible to answer her question. Certainly my first feeling after hearing this piece of news had been one of horror at the prospect of seeing my career in the Air Force irretrievably ruined. My mind went back to the scene in the chapel when as a mere recruit I had listened to the Air Vice-Marshal's address, and I could even now see his confident face in front of me and his lips moving as he pronounced the words: 'No airman is to be the father of a child. Failure to comply with this regulation will be punished with the utmost severity.' I knew that I could not hope to retain

247

for another day the position of trust which I now occupied when once it became known that I had permitted myself to be an accessory in the breaking of this rule, and I knew that it would be useless to attempt to hide what had taken place.

Yet together with this horror and shame I could not help feeling at the same time a certain satisfaction. I had never once envisaged the possibility that I might become a father, and it was a pleasant sort of excitement to discover that I was now on the way to being what I had never imagined. I thought of the many agreeable hours which I had passed with Eustasia and, when I looked at her, I could see that she herself was pleased with what she had no doubt deliberately arranged. 'No,' I said. 'I'm not angry. I'm rather pleased', and as I spoke she left her chair and put her arms round my neck gladly and with a kind of triumph, as though I had surrendered to her something of great value.

As for myself, I had been shocked to listen to the words which I had just spoken, for they seemed to show that I was willing to renounce the loyalty which I had sincerely believed to be the foundation of all my activities. I asked myself how I could possibly declare myself pleased at this event, when I was aware that once it became known I should infallibly forfeit the confidence of the Air Vice-Marshal and of my brother officers. I might say that this particular regulation, though valuable for others, was not of so much importance in my case, as, however many children Eustasia might have, my own work would not be affected by them. Yet I could imagine how the Air Vice-Marshal would look if I attempted to make to him so puerile an excuse for my direct disobedience to his clearest instructions. No: I saw nothing for it. My career was evidently at an end, and I was startled to find that I was, though distressed enough, much less distressed at this prospect than I could have imagined possible.

Could it be, I wondered, that all this time I had been engaged in a pursuit for which my enthusiasm had been in a way forced and not natural? Had I not had my heart in my work? For now I began for the first time to wonder what was the point of our tremendous programme, what lasting satisfaction was to be obtained from the acquisition of power over men's lives, what were the precise qualities of the new race of men which we designed to promote and for which we were asked to sacrifice what had already begun to appear to me something of importance.

I saw that Eustasia was watching me closely. Her large eyes were fixed on my face and there was an expression of eagerness in them, as though she were attempting to drag to her my thoughts from behind my forehead. 'You'll have to leave the aerodrome,' she said. 'We'll go away together.'

I looked at her in surprise and a kind of consternation, for it appeared that she was convinced that I should accept this proposal without objection, whereas in reality I knew that I had no wish whatever to ally myself with her in any permanent sense. Indeed, I began to see now that what I had chiefly enjoyed in our relationship was the feeling that it could at any time be ended. I fancied that we had both conducted ourselves in accordance with the best traditions of the Air Force. We had given and received pleasure, but had undertaken no responsibilities each to each. Now she was speaking in a manner with which I had no sympathy at all.

'We can go away to another part of the country,' she was saying. 'I've got enough money. We might even get married if I can get a divorce. Really I've always wanted to leave the aerodrome. Oh, I'm so glad that you were pleased.'

Here she broke off and looked at me with a kind of dismay, for she could no doubt see in my face that I had none of her enthusiasm for the life which she had set before herself. Indeed, I could not imagine her outside the aerodrome, and knew that if I were forced to leave I would much sooner leave by myself. I was conscious of feeling some distaste for her as I reflected that this was the first occasion on which she had ever expressed a wish for my undivided attentions, and that of all occasions this was the one when I was least likely to regard such a prospect as either possible or desirable. Yet I felt somewhat awkward as I told her that to my mind her plan seemed impracticable; that I had never contemplated marriage; that after having left the aerodrome it did not seem likely that we should meet very often in the future; that the love which we had shared was the creation of a particular time and place.

As I was speaking I saw that her eyes were filling with tears, but soon she brushed them from her eyes with the back of her hand in a gesture that seemed to me curiously childish and when she spoke she spoke angrily. She said: 'So you never loved me at all', and then looked at me as though she were horrified by what she had said.

In a flash I remembered how I had used these very words to Bess in the hut upon the hill, and I was secretly pleased that it was not I who was using them now. I felt a mounting anger, though I was conscious that this anger was both cruel and irrational. I had no wish to hurt her, but was hurt and irritated myself by her expectations from me. Had she not already got what she wanted, I asked myself. How could she imagine that I had failed her? We had promised each other pleasure, never any kind of devotion.

'Love?' I said. 'It covers a lot. But certainly I loved you, and still do.'

'Liar,' she said, and I looked at her in surprise, for there was no trace of anger in her voice. Her large eyes were wide open and there was a softness in them, a generalized compassion that made me feel that I was looking at a religious picture rather than at a woman whom I had offended. 'With me,' she continued, 'it has grown and grown. With you it never started to increase. You don't know what love is, unless perhaps you were in love with that mad girl. But I would do anything for you.'

Her eyes and the corners of her mouth were trembling as she looked at me with no reserve whatever in her face. So, I remembered, the Flight-Lieutenant had looked at her on the occasion of our first meeting; so I myself perhaps had looked at Bess in the course of our last conversation in the hut. There was nothing attractive in the hopelessness and abnegation of such expressions of the face, yet I knew now the misery that lay behind them, and the thought of Eustasia with her gaiety and generosity, a woman who had given me nothing but pleasure, being plunged on my account into this misery was a thought that was unspeakably painful to me. I knelt on the carpet by her side, holding her in my arms and kissing her. And as we made love I felt perhaps as wretched as she did, for we were both of us aware that something new had come into our relationship, throwing suddenly out of all proportion what had previously appeared so symmetrical; or else that in a moment there had become apparent some flaw, hitherto unnoticed, and yet of so serious a kind as to reduce almost to nothing the value of something which had seemed precious.

I had no anger for her now, as she had none for me, and her love-making had been rather sad than desperate. We said little to each other, even pretending perhaps in words that no great alteration between us had taken place. Her extreme gentleness made me wish not that I could ease her suffering but that I had never acted in such a way as to have become the occasion for it. It seemed to me then that the Air Vice-Marshal had been right, that by some law of nature a love affair must end in pain.

When I left I was aware that there were tears in my eyes, for I knew how weak was my pity when compared with Eustasia's much stronger feelings, and I began to wonder what necessity it was that made my very unwillingness to hurt her more painful to her perhaps than anything else.

CHAPTER XVII

Bess

NOT LONG AFTERWARDS I was walking back to the village from the aerodrome with Dr Faulkner. Some time soon, I knew, I should have to face an interview with the Air Vice-Marshal, which could be agreeable to neither of us, but of this I did not think much, nor even much of Eustasia and of her news. My thoughts were again with Bess, and as I walked I looked from time to time at my companion, wondering how much I should tell him of my old relationship, for I wished him to be in possession of all the facts that might help him in dealing with the case.

I had found him very willing to accompany me, although in doing so he was losing the short time of the day in which he was accustomed to rest, and now I looked at him with gratitude, almost as though I were seeing him for the first time. Actually, since I had taken on my new appointment I had seen him nearly every day, for he was on terms of great intimacy with the Air Vice-Marshal; indeed was perhaps his only friend who was not directly concerned with the organization of our final aims. When they were together they would hardly ever talk of the aerodrome, but would discuss such subjects as music, literature, and the general principles of medicine or psychology. These conversations were, I could see, a valuable form of relaxation to the Air Vice-Marshal, and there was no doubt that he valued the Doctor's company very highly. For this reason perhaps the Doctor occupied a unique position in the Air Force. Though he wore uniform, he seemed to have no precise duties, and was given every encouragement to follow his own inclinations in his work. He was recognized as our leading authority on cases of injury to the brain, and had a number of the most remarkable cures to his credit; but in spite of his great reputation and his singular position he was so unassuming as to be almost inconspicuous, for neither his appearance nor his manner were at all remarkable. He was a short stout man with an almost bald head, rather older than the Air Vice-Marshal, I should imagine. His eyes were deep set and keen, but when he was not looking directly at one his large red face made him appear placid, contented, and even lazy, although in point of fact he was capable of working all day and night without a rest, and was as rapid in his thinking as the Air Vice-Marshal himself.

There was so much in him that inspired confidence that I determined now to tell him the whole story of my relationship with Bess, and so ready was his understanding and pertinent his questioning that in a very short time I had done so. I had never before related the whole story continuously to anyone, and as I spoke I found myself curiously moved by recollections of the past. It was not that I felt now any shame or much pain at what had taken place; nor had I any definite desires at all for the future. But I thought constantly with extreme pain of the state of mind in which Bess must be now, and was determined so far as possible to help her. This determination was not due to a wish to redress any wrong which I may unwittingly have done her, nor was it an example of any kind of altruism. It was an impulse so strong that I was neither able nor inclined to account for it, and it so far dominated my thoughts that I was at this time indifferent to the trouble and disgrace which, I must have been aware, awaited me in the immediate future.

When I had finished my story the Doctor looked at me, I thought, rather oddly. 'I take it,' he said, 'that you have no desire to continue your old relationship with this girl. I believe you are quite content elsewhere.'

'I don't even think of it,' I said, and remembering my recent interview with Eustasia, I did not reply to the second part of his statement.

He looked at me again rather as though he were examining me in an official capacity. Then he looked away and began to speak with a curious hesitancy that at the time surprised me. 'It is quite possible,' he said, 'that this girl is suffering at least in part from a sense of guilt. Unfortunately, we judge ourselves much more harshly than others could judge us. However impossible it may have been for us to estimate the effects or even the nature of our actions, we still in the deepest part of us are self-condemned if later events prove us to have been mistaken. This girl believes that she has married her brother, and though at the time she could not possibly have suspected that she was doing so, she none the less cannot forgive herself.'

I listened without much interest to this diagnosis, which indeed seemed to me sufficiently obvious. After a few moments' silence the Doctor looked at me again. He was frowning as though his mind were concentrated on a subject of unusual difficulty. He appeared to be about to make some important pronouncement, opening his mouth and looking sternly at me; but in a moment looked away from me and said in a careless voice: 'The affair is also complicated by her infidelity to you. The case is, in fact, absurdly complicated.' Again he stared at me as though he were attempting some difficult work of classification. 'I know quite well,' he said, 'what I ought to do. The question is, can I do it? And if I can do it, can I rely on you?'

I was mystified by this remark and by the manner, half embarrassed and half conspiratorial, in which he made it. But he refused either to answer my questions or declare himself satisfied with my assurance that I would do everything that he wished me to do in order to assist Bess's recovery. He shrugged his shoulders, as though he had lost interest in the conversation. 'Let's see the girl first in any case,' he said, and quickened his pace towards the pub.

We soon arrived there and were received in the front parlour by Bess's mother, who proposed at once to show us upstairs to the room in which Bess was.

'Perhaps she won't speak to you, Doctor,' she said. 'Many a time I've been with her and she's stared through me as though I were a ghost. She just sits in her chair looking out of the window and crying. She must lose her strength that way, mustn't she, Doctor?'

The Doctor nodded and proceeded upstairs. I was in doubt whether or not to accompany him, and Bess's mother, too, seemed to wish to detain me below; but he took me by the arm and said: 'Come up for a minute or two. I'll send you down soon', and as I followed him up the narrow stairway I had to grip tightly the thin iron rail to keep myself upright, so great was the trepidation that had spread over my limbs.

The Doctor paused for a moment at the top of the stairs, for he was somewhat short of breath. Then he rapped with his knuckles on the door that faced us, and without waiting for a reply turned the door-handle and entered the room. I followed him, but was no longer aware of him at all after I had crossed the threshold and could see Bess sitting in a long chair by the window with her face turned from us in profile staring, it seemed, at the wall and at the corner of the window. It was neither the pallor of her face nor the thinness of her hands nor the despair of her posture, that so deeply moved me, though all these features I noticed in a moment. I was filled, I believe with the most contradictory feelings, a profound pity for her condition, and an extreme delight at finding myself once more in her presence. I stepped forward quickly and knelt on the floor in front of her, looking up into her eyes which were still averted from me and noticing how large, wide-open, and expressionless they were, or rather how constant was their expression of hopelessness. Very slowly she let her gaze fall from the cord of the window to the top of my head and there her eyes seemed to pause as though reluctant to receive a new impression. It seemed a long time before they rested on my eyes, and I saw in them a slow gleam of recognition and a hint of surprise. Perhaps I was gazing on her too wildly, for soon she began slowly again to raise her head to the position which it had held before and to stare again at the wall and the window by the wall. I saw that she was crying to herself, softly, noiselessly, and almost restfully, without knowing for what she cried, or perhaps even that she was crying at all.

The innocence of her face was too unearthly to be called childlike, for it was no confidence in the world but a total resignation to despair that gave her that look of unapproachable peace. But I could not bear not to approach her, and so I took one of her hands in mine and let my head rest in her lap, and so remained for some time. She had some early primroses on her lap, a gift perhaps from a visitor, which lay unregarded on the rough material of her dress. I fixed my eyes on the pink and hairy stalks of these flowers and was conscious for some moments of nothing else but of them.

Presently I felt her other hand moving to and fro in my hair, uncertainly in the way that a blind man might use if he were examining some object of whose identity he was uncertain. As I felt her hand and looked at the primroses on her lap, I remembered suddenly and vividly the moment in the past when we had been together in the field listening to the larks singing, the time when I had decided easily and gladly to abandon myself to her love. The promises and ambitions of that time may have been stupid and ill-considered. I had believed them to have become null and void; but I saw now that the feeling that had prompted them could never be recalled. It was not that I had any more a desire to possess her. Such an idea would in any case have been absurd; but I knew in a moment and with certainty that compared with her health and happiness the aerodrome and all that it contained meant nothing to me at all; and in my own mind I insisted on my own right to secure for her what health and hapiness I could. I wished to hold her in my arms and perhaps would have done so, regardless of her frailty, had I not felt the Doctor's hand on my elbow and heard him speak.

'Wait for me outside,' he said as he pulled me to my feet, and I went to the door and paused there for a moment to look back into the room. He had pushed forward his chair to Bess's side and had begun talking to her at once.

'Listen, my dear,' I heard him say. 'I'm a friend of yours. I used to know your father quite well, and I'd like to talk to you about him. I used to know Roy's father also, and I'll tell you about him, too, if you like.'

He spoke slowly and cheerfully, without letting his eyes leave her face. I saw her large eyes turn to him and a gleam both of comprehension and of fear momentarily light them up. Then I opened the door softly and went downstairs, my mind too full of my own feelings to allow me to speculate on what story the Doctor was proposing to tell.

When I reached the bottom of the stairs I found that Bess's mother was serving in the bar. From behind the door I could hear the voices of men whom I used to know, and these voices were strangely attractive to me, although I knew that the men themselves had little liking for the aerodrome and had already proved themselves incompetent in the work which we had set them to do. I thought of the Flight-Lieutenant's remark – 'Somehow these people seem to fit better into the country than we do' – and I began again to wonder what particular merit there was in being expert in the kind of work we did, and for the first time I began to realize the nature and the extent of the sacrifices which we were required to make. Constantly before my mind was the imagination of Bess lying in the upstairs room like a sleeping beauty, with no hint of hapinness to bring back life and gaiety to her wide eyes. I thought, too, of Eustasia and of her disappointment in my love; of the Flight-Lieutenant as he had knelt in the church above the dead body of the Squire's sister; of the Rector's funeral and of the Rector's face when he had confessed to God the murder of his friend. Against these scenes I set the hours of liberty which I had enjoyed with Eustasia, the drinks and easy conversation at the club, the pleasure in becoming expert with a machine and the greater pleasure of sharing in the control of the operations of men. In return for the ease, the security, and the excitement of this life what we had been asked to renounce had seemed to me at the time of little importance. It had been no sacrifice to me to give up my parents when I neither knew certainly nor cared greatly who they were. I had been willing enough to make certain of pleasure in my love affairs rather than risk again the distress which had seemed inseparable from an excess of love. And it had been gradually, almost insensibly, that I had lost touch with the country where I had been bred, looking down on it from the sky with a kind of contempt, indifferent to the changes of climate and of seasons, the rising and falling of the ground, except in so far as these things affected the readings of my instruments or the immediate purpose of the hour. Now I thought with longing, and with shame for my neglect of them, of the meadows whose soil I had not touched for so long, of the clumps of hazel in the spinneys beneath which the primroses and wood anemones would be flowering. And I saw again the stalks of the primroses in Bess's lap, and it seemed to me certain that there was more life even in her despair, even in the Rector's rankling conscience, even in the Flight-Lieutenant's perplexity and in Eustasia's disappointment, than there was in the ease, efficiency, and confidence of our ways. In contrast with the villagers, with women, with clergymen, and squires, we were simple, carefree, and direct, having made ourselves the servants of a single will and imagination, constituting as a result an instrument that could shape like clay, cut through like butter the vague, amorphous, drunken, unwieldy, and unsatisfactory life that was outside our organization.

Yet I began to see that this life, in spite of its drunkenness and its inefficiency, was wider and deeper than the activity in which we were constricted by the iron compulsion of the Air Vice-Marshal's ambition. It was a life whose very vagueness concealed a wealth of opportunity, whose uncertainty called for adventure, whose aspects were innumerable and varied as the changes of light and colour throughout the year. It was a life whose unwieldiness was the consequence of its immensity. No skill could precisely calculate the effects of any action, and all action was dangerous. The fumbling conventions that had centred around church, manor, and public house had been the efforts of generations of the dead to establish some basis of security in the middle of a mystery which to many of them had been delightful as well as startling. We in the Air Force had escaped from but not solved the mystery. We had secured ease for ourselves, discipline, and satisfaction. We had abolished inefficiency, hypocrisy, and the fortunes of the irresolute or the remorseful mind; but we had destroyed also the spirit of adventure, inquiry, the sweet and terrifying sympathy of love that can acknowledge mystery, danger, and dependence.

So I thought as I gazed over the valley while waiting for the Doctor, yet perhaps not so distinctly as I have set it down here, for at the back of my mind was continually the thought of Bess and my anxiety for her. I did not at this time inquire into the reasons for my anxiety or the sources of my deep and still undefined feeling; but I reproached myself with my own conduct to her when I reflected that it was my pride rather than my lack of feeling that had led me to abandon her so entirely and had thrown me into a profession in which it had become almost impossible for me to think of her at all.

I was recalled from my thoughts by hearing the Doctor's steps on the stairs. I turned round to meet him and was dismayed to notice the gravity of his face. Hesitating to question him lest there should be no comfort in his reply, I was surprised when he looked at me wearily and said: 'She'll be all right. It will take weeks, perhaps months, before she's perfectly well. But she'll be all right. No question of it.'

The pleasure which my face must have expressed awoke no response in his. He looked hard at me and said: 'I only hope I've done right. Remember that I'm depending on you.'

I followed him round the corner of the house and into the road, mystified by what he had said, and as we walked I noticed the anxious and worried expression of his face. Presently he smiled somewhat grimly and turned to me.

'Often one wonders,' he said, 'whether it may not be best to leave ill alone, but I know that my own small accomplishments consist in restoring health, and I know that I must attempt to do so, however inconvenient the results of my efforts may be. Now listen carefully.'

We had come to a gate in one of the fields below the aerodrome, and here we stopped, leaning against the gate, while the Doctor continued. 'It is necessary, of course,' he said, 'to convince this girl that her relationship with you was a perfectly innocent one. What will cure her is for her to be able to recognize that she is still in love with you, as indeed she is, but she is prevented from recognizing this by the deep feeling of the criminality of what you have done together. I have already succeeded partially in convincing her that you are not her brother. I happen to know that you are not, and this may be a fact that will surprise you. There is no need for me to go into any explanation of this. You have chosen your career and you know the views of the Air Vice-Marshal on this subject. You will simply have to take my word for the fact that I knew your father. He was a remarkably distinguished man, but died young. He had nothing whatever to do with Bess's mother. Let us leave it at that.'

Here he looked at me sharply as though to make sure that I would obey his instructions and not question him further. My face, no doubt, was calm enough, since I was waiting for what he had next to say. He can have had no idea of the mental agitation into which his speech had thrown me.

'Now,' he went on, 'the important thing to decide is how to act when she has recovered her health. We have to consider two people, her and yourself. The burden of acting correctly will fall naturally on you. I can see that you have no wish to injure her any further. Let me remind you of how you can avoid doing so. First of all she will be, in all probability, much more inclined to fall in love with you than she ever was before. She will be aware that, however childish your affection for her may have been, it was at least more genuine than anything she has ever known, and she is now in a position to value it. That is somewhat unfortunate, for you have succeeded admirably in your career and are no longer in a position to give to her what you once gave. She has already had enough of our Air Force convention of making love and you might well do her some lasting damage if you were to give her a fresh experience of it. Any kindness you can show her at this stage will be of great value; but you must not go further than this.'

He paused again, and turned his sharp eyes upon me. I could not help smiling at his flushed face and at his serious air, for it was evident that he completely misunderstood my feelings. He appeared somewhat embarrassed by my smile, and continued speaking with greater vehemence.

'There is, of course,' he said, 'one other alternative. It may be that the strong associations of the past together with the girl's exceptional good looks may turn your head. That would be a tragedy for all concerned. It might even lead to the end of your career. I should find it very difficult to forgive myself if I found that I had contributed to such a result. As you know, I am bound to the Air Vice-Marshal not only by duty but by affection. You have been singularly fortunate in attracting his notice and even his regard. Neither you nor I must leave him in the lurch.'

He was looking sternly at me as though waiting for a reply, and I found it difficult to meet his eyes, for I knew his devotion to the Air Vice-Marshal and indeed I still partly shared it in spite of my recent reflections. I knew that the Air Vice-Marshal had reposed such trust in me that I was perhaps after himself the person with the fullest knowledge of our calculations and of our aims. He would regard my dereliction of duty and my present way of thought not only as weak and unworthy, but actually as traitorous. It would appear to him that I was prepared to sacrifice his esteem and the certainty of power for something as insubstantial as a dream or shadow which I had not defined clearly even to myself. For a moment or two I was in two minds whether or not to tell the Doctor that in any case my expulsion from the Air Force was certain; but I saw that if I did so and told him of the reasons for this certainty, he would, in the first place, assure me that I should find it easy to persuade Eustasia to get rid of her child, and if I declared my unwillingness to do this he would assume that it was Eustasia who, in his phrase, had turned my head.

But the situation was too complicated to be analysed by such directness of thought. So far as love went, the love that is a concentration of all the feelings on a single person, I knew that for all my life I should never love anyone but Bess; nor at this time did I anticipate much happiness from my connection with her, since her own state was so far removed from happiness. But there was other love, too, a myriad shapes of it, shapes that blended into each other, were interlocked or were irreconcilable, a bewildering and rich confusion where it was easy for one's way to be lost. Yet it was one thing to lose one's way, another to proclaim, as the Air Vice-Marshal had done, that no way was to be found. And unless I was prepared, as he was, to reject and despise the whole world of time and movement, colour and alteration, I had no right and could have no desire to attempt to exercise any control over Eustasia in a matter which concerned her so nearly. She, it seemed to me, had accomplished something wonderful in breaking the bondage of sterility which had been imposed on her and on the wives of all our officials, though she had made a mistake in taking me seriously, and I a much greater mistake in shrinking from the infinite implications of all love.

The mistakes had been made, and I could see no means of redressing them. But least worthy of all means was what would be recommended to me by the Air Vice-Marshal and perhaps the Doctor, to deny wholly the relevance of the world of time and feeling where such mistakes were only too easy to make, and to erect in contrast with it our own barren edifice of perfection, our efficient and mystical mastery over time.

I had hesitated for long in replying to the Doctor, and he, thinking perhaps that I had been offended by his mere mention of the possibility that I might desert the Air Vice-Marshal, slapped me on the back as though to make amends for any indiscretion that there may have been in his speech. He smiled, and again I observed that he was looking at me curiously, though with a twinkle in his eye, as if I were some patient on whom he was glad to bestow his attention.

'Things work out very curiously,' he said. 'Very curiously indeed.'

We began to walk on, and I was at a loss at this time to interpret the meaning of his remark.

CHAPTER XVIII

New Friends

THERE WAS NOW so swift a succession of events, and
these events were of so surprising a character, that it is
almost impossible for me to describe accurately the transformation in my mind and in the minds of others which
was, if not exactly caused, certainly accelerated and concluded by what took place in the week or two that followed my conversation with the Doctor. First, perhaps, I
should mention the several interviews which I had with
the Rector's wife during this period, not that these interviews were of great importance in themselves, but because
they led up to what was for me the most surprising and
important event of all.

It was on the day after I had first visited Bess with the
Doctor that I had occasion to walk down to the club house
and, as I left the aerodrome, observed the Rector's wife
standing in the road outside the main gates. Something in
her manner when she greeted me seemed to show that she
had been waiting there expressly to see me and I remember, so changed was I already, that I felt some distress
when I reflected that my profession had set such a barrier
between me and the lady who had brought me up with
much care and kindness and who was, to the best of my
knowledge, my mother. Since, however, there was no
certainty about my parents, I was not debarred from
entering into conversation with her, and I experienced a
strange feeling of relief and of elation when she agreed
willingly to my proposal that we should walk down to the

village together. She admitted that she had come to the aerodrome in the hope of seeing me, and told me that ever since the shooting of her friend she had been anxious for news of the Flight-Lieutenant.

As she spoke I watched her from time to time, and admired as I had not done for long the calmness of her speech and gestures, the grace and delicacy of bearing which she still retained in spite of age. Scenes from the past which I had forgotten recurred to my mind, scenes of childhood and boyhood, and the scene in the Rectory after the celebration of my birthday when both she and I had listened to her husband's confession. I began to wish for certainty as to whether she were my mother or not, and was surprised that she herself seemed content to allow me to be in doubt, though I felt no resentment at this, for I fancied that if she were indeed my mother her attitude would have been determined by some weighty consideration or might be a deliberate sacrifice in order to help me in my career. I had nothing with which I could reproach her, but rather, as we went down the hill together, reproached myself for my neglect, which seemed to me equally culpable whether she were my mother or not.

I listened eagerly to her questions about the Flight-Lieutenant, and was glad to be able to answer them, for only that morning the Air Vice-Marshal had been discussing his case with me, and I knew that he was to be released that day, reduced to the ranks, and employed as a mechanic in one of the sheds. I had been surprised that he had not been expelled from the service and had indeed suggested this course, believing that this would be what he wished himself, and that in any case he was not likely to be of much use to us. The Air Vice-Marshal had astonished me not by the severity of the punishment which he inflicted (for the Flight-Lieutenant's work would be extremely arduous and his pay greatly reduced), but by the evident consideration which he still showed for the young man.

'We will give him one more chance,' he had said. 'He may have something in him after all.' And he had looked at me as though he were the slightest bit ashamed of the leniency which he imagined himself to be showing.

For my own part I knew what must be the Flight-Lieutenant's state of mind, since I shared it myself; but I had made no comment, though I felt uneasy at the part which I was still forced to play; for I had decided to wait for some days at least before telling the Air Vice-Marshal of my own state. I did not know what would be the result of my confession, whether I should be discharged outright or perhaps be sent under guard to some other part of the country with restrictions placed on my movements, and I wished for some days at least to mark the progress, which the Doctor had regarded as certain, in Bess's condition.

I was able then to tell the Rector's wife everything which she wished to know about the Flight-Lieutenant, and she appeared relieved to hear that he had met with no worse punishment.

'I am only sorry,' she said, 'that he's still attached to the aerodrome', and here she looked at me somewhat apologetically as though certain that her words would displease me. 'I know that you are doing very well there, Roy,' she said. 'I always hoped that you would do well, though now I'm afraid I'm not so certain about it all. You can't think that I should feel very friendly to the aerodrome when I've seen all these changes made, and when I remember Florence.'

She saw, and I think was glad to see, that her words, so far from offending me, had been welcome. Now she smiled somewhat sadly and said: 'I was really as foolish as a young girl might be when I thought that I should like to see you in the Air Force. I thought it was romantic, I suppose, and manly.'

I was thinking of the scene in the church when the Squire's sister had been shot. 'What did she mean,' I asked, 'when she called him her son?'

The Rector's wife looked up at me quickly and began to speak at once. 'It was true,' she said. 'He is her son, though he never knew it till recently. He was educated abroad. It was the one quarrel which Florence ever had with her brother, for he refused to have the child brought up in his house. He had known the father of the child, and he wished, I think, to protect his sister. Perhaps he was quite right. Florence knew his love for her, but she hated being separated from her child. You can imagine how pleased she was to find him again. She did not know him at first and only came to do so after the boy himself had changed and had begun to feel unhappy in his life at the aerodrome. Just a chance remark of his one day told her who he must be. They were very fond of each other.'

'What about the father?' I asked.

She shook her head gravely and said: 'He disappeared altogether. Perhaps her brother was quite right.' She looked at me almost shamefacedly, although there was a gentle smile on her lips. I fancied that this expression was caused partly by a feeling that she had been indiscreet in revealing the secrets of her dead friend, partly by the

270

pleasure she found in us being able again, after so long, to hold an intimate conversation. For a moment or two I hesitated whether or not to ask her about my own birth, but I saw that if she had a secret she was entitled to keep it; and so I determined to allow her to enlighten me or not, as she chose, unless it should become necessary for me to obtain some certainty on this point. Instead I spoke to her of the aerodrome, and soon found that I was confessing to her my dissatisfaction with it. I accompanied her to her home and before I left had told her about my feelings for Bess and my joy in the fact that there seemed a good prospect for her recovery. I arranged, moreover, to call upon her on the following day and felt, I remember, a keen sense of pleasure in the making of this arrangement.

This was the first of several meetings in the course of which I told her of my marriage and its failure, my early ambitions in the Air Force, the position of trust in which I had been placed, and my present conviction that neither those ambitions nor my present way of life was worth the having. I said nothing of Eustasia to her, partly because I did not wish to distress her with thoughts of the danger which I now ran, partly because on this subject my own mind was still undetermined and confused. I met her not only at her own house, but also sometimes at the pub, for she would call there often to leave fruit or flowers for Bess and later on books, magazines, and newspapers.

Each day for more than a week the Doctor would visit his patient at least once, and as a rule I would accompany him. He would sit with her for perhaps an hour and would then call me upstairs, and from day to day I wondered and was delighted at the change which his skill and perseverance was bringing about in her. Even now the incidents of that time and the feelings which they evoked in me are so fresh and vivid in my mind that I find it difficult or impossible to write of them. I remember how her memory which had contracted to the period of her childhood gradually lengthened and deepened until it included all the past. I remember how she first recognized her mother, the Rector's wife, and myself, and how, when she did recognize me, there was no trace in her eyes of the uneasiness, the fear, the guilt, or the reluctance which I had known. It was as though we were meeting each other for the first time, and yet together with the shyness and sensitivity that must spring from such a feeling there was a confidence, or the certain beginnings of it, an assurance which seemed to unite us more fully than anything had united us in the past. Neither of us at this time thought coherently of love. She was still too weak for it, and I too conscious of my impending disgrace which might result in imprisonment or in exile to another part of the country with restrictions on my movements. But there was, I think, in this time of her convalescence a tacit understanding between us that if there was anything in the past on either side to be forgiven it was forgiven, if there was anything in the future that could be shared then it would be shared. More and more, though at first with difficulty, she began to direct her mind into the future, and I was sad to think that, however she thought of me, her thoughts would not hit the real truth of the danger in which I stood.

The Doctor would sometimes leave us alone together, and sometimes remain with us after his visit had properly concluded, in order, I supposed, that he might see how his patient conducted herself with other people. On one occasion the Rector's wife called when we were all three together and was shown up to the room. I was sitting with Bess at the window, and I remember that in the middle of our conversation I turned my head to look at the others and saw them conversing together earnestly and in whispers in a corner of the room. I could not help remarking the look of dejection and irresolution on the Doctor's broad face, and this look surprised me. The Rector's wife was speaking to him with her usual calmness, but it appeared that there was something urgent in what she was saying. I turned back again to Bess, paying little attention at the time to this scene which yet remained fixed in my memory, for I was too happy just then to think of much more than of her gradual recovery of health and the gradual revelation to me of her confidence and her heart.

On our walks to and from the aerodrome the Doctor would say little to me of the case beyong his frequent assurances that her complete recovery was certain, and I was reluctant to question him much, for I feared that he would revert to his prescriptions as to my conduct when once the cure was finished. As it was he, too, seemed anxious to avoid this subject. Once he said: 'There is no doubt that you two do each other good', and he shook his head in perplexity as though uncertain whether to condemn or to approve of this fact, then he would often speak to me of my duties at the aerodrome, though somewhat half-heartedly as though he were performing some necessary but not particularly pleasant task.

As for myself I was solely grateful to him for his willingness and success in the cure which he had undertaken, and was in no mood to sympathize with him in his perplexities. Indeed, I had enough perplexities of my own. From day to day I put off what I knew that I should have some time to do—inform the Air Vice-Marshal not only that I had disobeyed his express instructions but, what was perhaps even harder to say, that I had no longer any interest in his ambitions or desire to share in his success. And all this time I would work late into the night with him, preparing and co-ordinating plans for the stroke which I believed could not be much longer delayed.

At this critical stage of our venture, the Air Vice-Marshal was as calm and precise as ever, but beneath the surface there was a suppressed excitement and in his eyes an elation that seemed to me to show that important events were impending. This elation in which he lived must have concealed from him what otherwise he would have noticed as my comparative lack of enthusiasm, and his conferences with officers from other aerodromes and with chiefs of departments were so numerous in these days that except during the evening and night I had plenty of time to myself.

I was able to visit Eustasia frequently, and though there was no longer between us any of the careless happiness that there used to be, though we never again made love, I know that in my heart I loved her more during these days than I had ever done before. Previously we had taken each other as we found each other, irresponsibly and gladly, as was the way at the aerodrome. Now we found, though in different ways, that our natures had driven us into responsibilities outside the complete circle which the Air Vice-Marshal had traced for his subordinates. Eustasia believed that she had injured me by jeopardizing my career; I knew that I had injured her by following in her case, though not in another, the advice which we had been given as recruits. Nothing in the past could be changed or could be retracted. Neither of us, we thought then, had much that was certain to which we might look forward in the future. We had the will to help each other beyond the circle of irresponsible enjoyment, and we recognized that with all the will in the world neither of us could give to the other just that one thing needed to be helpful. She was demanding from me now what she had perhaps never thought of before, a kind of love that was wholly different from what was encouraged in the Air Force, the love which I felt for Bess, the love which the Flight-Lieutenant felt for Eustasia and which at the time she had rejected. In this kind of love pleasure is shared with an added intensity, but is an epiphenomenon and still not the essence. Pain may disrupt the surface and even colour the depths, but can never alter the material. Had we in the past even acknowledged the existence of this thing we should either never have loved at all, or loved differently; and our mutual knowledge of this fact, though we rarely spoke of it, made our conversations at this time, sad as they were, more affectionate and sympathetic than they had ever been.

It was in Eustasia's room that I saw the Flight-Lieutenant for the first time after his release from imprisonment. He was now wearing the uniform of a mechanic and his face, curiously enough, seemed to have regained some of the gaiety which it had lost during his tenure of the position of Rector. I found him in conversation with Eustasia when I arrived, and from the first moment of our meeting it became apparent, rather to the surprise of each of us, I think, that we had rediscovered the friendship which used to exist between us. We talked eagerly and without reservations. Though we said on this occasion nothing of the aerodrome or of the death of the Flight-Lieutenant's mother, it was plain to us that we were on the same side, and in later conversations he hinted to me of his plans for escaping altogether from the Air Force, and of going into hiding in some place where he could not be tracked down as a deserter. Knowing the efficiency of our police organization I discouraged these plans, though, while I feared for his safety, I admired once more the recklessness and the gaiety with which he made them.

Eustasia, too, seemed much more glad of his company now than she ever had been in the past and after this first meeting we met frequently in her rooms. He would also accompany me sometimes on my visits to the Rector's wife, and in returning from one of these visits I told him of Eustasia's condition and of my intention to seek an interview with the Air Vice-Marshal on the following day. The conversation had started, I remember, by his warning me of the danger which I ran in being seen so often in his company and in making calls at the houses of those who were known to be opposed to the Air Force.

To set his mind at rest I had told him that a little more or less danger could not under my present circumstances make much difference to me, and had then given him the whole story.

He looked very grave while he listened, and when I had finished, he asked: 'But why tell the old man about it now? Why not wait a few weeks?'

It was a question which I had often asked myself and found difficult to answer. Partly it was because I disliked playing any longer the part which I was forced to play; for though I had convinced myself that the life and the ambitions of the Air Vice-Marshal were not my life and my ambitions, I had too much respect and even affection for the man to enjoy giving day by day the impression of loyalty which I no longer felt. But also I was disturbed by the change which was taking place both in Bess and in myself. Her recovery was now so far advanced that the Doctor had pronounced it permanent, and had hinted to me that the need for my collaboration in the cure had now ended. I did not care what his thoughts or his doubts of me might be, but I saw that it could not be long now before the love which both Bess and I knew was shared between us would be expressed openly, and before this happened I wished, for her sake as for mine, to find out exactly how I should be punished or menaced by the authorities. It might be that I should be prevented from seeing her again. It might be, as I hoped, that I should merely be discharged from the service. It was the uncertainty of the thing that made it impossible for me to look straight in her eyes or to join as I wished to do in her tentative inquiries of the future.

The Flight-Lieutenant nodded his head from time to time as I explained to him the reasons for my decision. We had reached the gates of the aerodrome by the time that I had finished and he made no comment on what I had said. I remember that before saying good-bye we, for some reason, shook hands, and I remember the affection I felt for him as I looked into his face and saw it to be more certain than it had been, graver than when I knew him first, but again with the gleam of recklessness and daring in the eyes. There were many things that I wished to say to him, and I looked forward to future times when we could talk of his mother, of his feelings for Eustasia, of the address which he had so unfortunately delivered in the church. He, too, I think, was looking forward to our next meeting. I remember that we seemed to hesitate as though reluctant to leave each other before we went in different directions, he to the barracks for the mechanics, I to my room in the Air Vice-Marshal's house. Yet we could neither of us have known that we should not speak to each other again.

On the following day I asked for a private interview with the Air Vice-Marshal somewhat before the hour at which I would normally report to him for duty. When I entered his room he looked at me gravely and in such a way that I was half inclined to suspect that he knew already what I was about to tell him. This impression was strengthened by the manner in which he heard me. He was leaning back in his chair with his hands relaxed on the desk in front of him. His lips were pressed tightly together and his eyes watched me closely. The expression of his face showed no surprise as I was speaking. It showed nothing indeed but a concentrated attention to my words and to my face; and this attitude of his embarrassed me much more than would any display of anger or of consternation. I had prepared something of a speech, but was unable to deliver it with any conviction. As it was I told him only the facts of my relationship with Eustasia, of its result, and of how things stood at present. Ending my account somewhat lamely I waited for his reply.

For some time he said nothing, but remained in exactly the same position as he had held while I had been speaking, with his eyes still fixed closely on my face. If I had expected him to show either anger or disappointment, I had been wrong. There was no animosity and nothing of reproach in his look. I began to think almost that he had not understood my words, and in my embarrassment to feel the need to speak again, though I had nothing material to add to what I had said already.

At last he began to speak, and there was, I thought, a lack of energy and a weariness in his voice. 'I know the lady in question very well,' he said. 'Some years ago I was intimate with her myself.'

He stopped speaking, and looked at me sharply. I realized that had my feelings for Eustasia been other than they were, had they been, for instance, like those of the Flight-Lieutenant for her, this revelation (for she had told me nothing of any previous connection with the Air Vice-Marshal) would, however unreasonably, have distressed me. As it was, I felt nothing at all but some slight surprise.

This, I think, the Air Vice-Marshal must have noticed, for he smiled quickly as though I had said or done something to please him. His face then took on an expression of severity and he spoke with a greater energy than hitherto. 'It is impossible for you to escape some responsibility for this,' he said, 'although I don't propose to suggest that you are by any means entirely to blame. There is only one thing for you to do, and that is to ensure that this child is not born.'

He waited for my reply, looking at me steadfastly from beneath his brows. I felt that he was making to me what appeared to him as a remarkable concession, and I felt the full inhumanity of the organization which he had constructed with such an expense of will and which seemed to me now, not only in this instance, to be designed to stifle life which, however misused, was richer in everything but determination than our order.

'How can I do that?' I said.

He appeared surprised by my reply. 'Do you mean,' he asked, 'that she will be unwilling? That is ridiculous. She has her duty just as you have, and you must both do it. Surely you have sufficient address to be able to persuade a woman, who in any case is infatuated with you, to do the obvious thing?'

'I've no right to do so,' I said. 'I've given her enough pain already', and, seeing that the Air Vice-Marshal was smiling, I added: 'Besides, I don't want to.'

He lifted one hand from the table and brought it down quickly again. His words were harsh and rapid. 'Are you mad?' he said. 'Pain, whether yours or hers, is neither here nor there. What on earth are you thinking of? Do you want to have a child?'

His present agitation surprised me as much as had his calmness at the beginning of the interview. What surprised me, too, was that there was in his voice a note not only of anger, but almost of supplication. He was prepared not so much to punish me for my neglect of duty as to implore me to repent of what I had done. It seemed that his very consideration for me, and the affection and respect which I still felt for him, made it the more impossible for me to resign myself to his will. I was about to speak again, but he rose to his feet, interrupting me.

'Listen, my boy,' he said. 'I have no more time to waste on this idiocy. You may have three days in which to think things over and in these days you will be released from your duties. At the end of that time please bring me a satisfactory account of what you have done. In your case, with your responsibilities and your prospects, any neglect of your plain duty and your honour would be intolerable to me. Say no more now. You'll only make a fool of yourself. Let me tell you this. If I had a son I would rather see him dead at my feet than persisting in the kind of folly in which you have landed yourself.' He paused and looked at me more calmly. 'I still have confidence in you,' he said, 'and to show you that I have I will tell you that the time for which we have been all waiting is now very close.'

As he looked at me his eyes flashed and for a moment infected me again, almost against my will, with his own enthusiasm. I wished to speak, but he would not allow me to do so. 'Three days!' he cried, and I left the room in dejection, knowing that, days or years, time would not alter my mind.

CHAPTER XIX

The Decision

BUT I WAS to meet the Air Vice-Marshal before my leave expired, and this interview took a form which I could never have anticipated. Perhaps I would of my own initiative have asked to speak with him again before the three days had elapsed, for I had made up my mind as to what attitude I should adopt and the generosity, according to Air Force standards, which he was showing me made me most reluctant to deceive him any further with thoughts that I should ever again be a willing helper towards his aims; but, even supposing that he would consent to see me, I thought it best not to disturb him on the following day, for I knew that he and Eustasia's husband and several other heads of departments were to fly that day to the airfield of a neighbouring town, where an important conference was to be held.

Normally I should have accompanied the Air Vice-Marshal, and I could imagine that in his view it was already a sufficiently grave punishment for me not to be able to do so; for this conference might well fix a date in the near future upon which our long-matured plans would be put into operation. I remember well that early in the morning I noticed on the airfield near the Air Vice-Marshal's office the large twenty-seater passenger aircraft which was to fly the officers to the conference. It was surrounded by mechanics, and among them I recognized the Flight-Lieutenant working on one of the wings. As I watched him I saw him straighten his back and look at his wrist watch. I was about to wave to him, but he turned round quickly, while the other mechanics were busy on the further side of the aircraft, and walked away with long strides towards his barracks. I fancied that he had gone to fetch some tool which he had forgotten, and I watched him until he was out of sight. Then, since Eustasia's apartment lay somewhere in the same direction, I went slowly after him, for I had promised Eustasia that I would, if I were able, tell her about my interview of the preceding day.

I should perhaps have been in time to see her and him, too, if I had not met on my way the Doctor, who hurried towards me across the flying field, evidently bent on a conversation. Indeed, I soon learnt that it was at the Air Vice-Marshal's own request that he had come to speak with me, and I saw that he was performing his task with a certain amount of unwillingness; for, while both his duty and his friendship made him support the Air Vice-Marshal's side of the question, he had become also, I knew, very friendly both with me and with Bess during the hours which we had spent together, and there was a lack of assurance now in his repetition of the Air Vice-Marshal's views. I felt sorry for him as I looked at his harassed face, and at the same time I was aware of my gratitude to him for his attention to Bess and his kindness to myself. So without any dissembling I told him of my true state of mind—my shame at having brought Eustasia into a position where I could be of little use to her, my devotion to Bess which would continue whether or not Eustasia's child should be born, my conviction that the code under which I had been living for the past year was, in spite of its symmetry and its perfection, a denial of life,

283

its difficulty, its perplexity, and its suffering, rather than an affirmation of its nobility and its grandeur. Even the tortured existence of the Rector, I said, even the self-sacrifice of the Squire's sister, seemed to me nobler and richer than the Air Vice-Marshal's undeviating success.

'You yourself,' I said to the Doctor, 'who have spent your time in saving life and sanity indiscriminately, you must agree with me.'

I fancied that he nodded his head as he smiled at me, with a remarkable kindness in his eyes. But his words expressed nothing but perplexity. 'Why on earth,' he said, 'did you ever join the Air Force? Don't you realize that if you say such things to the Chief you will be shot?'

It was a thought that had occurred to me myself, since it was obvious that no high official of our organization would wish me, with the knowledge I had of our plans, to be at large and opposed to them.

The Doctor patted me on the shoulder, seeming afraid to make the gesture, but relieved when he had done so. 'It is no use my saying more,' he said. 'I would help you if I could, but I fear the consequences of anything I might do.' He smiled again and shook hands. This time it was not so much the kindliness as the irresolution of his face that impressed me.

I continued on my way and remember that at one point I had to step back hurriedly against the wall of a building as six motor-cyclists of our special police force came round a corner at high speed, and proceeded out of the gates of the aerodrome and along the main road. At the time I attached little importance to this incident but was soon to know what the object of the policemen was, for when I had arrived at Eustasia's apartment I found the doors open and the rooms deserted. The place was no more untidy than usual, but the sight of the open doors caused me to experience a momentary shock, a premonition that I should discover something unexpected and perhaps alarming. I went hurriedly from room to room, and finally noticed on the divan a note scrawled in pencil and addressed to myself. It was to inform me that Eustasia had left that morning with the Flight-Lieutenant, and I realized at once that they could not have started greatly in advance of the police squad who had, no doubt, been sent after the fugitives with instructions to bring back the Flight-Lieutenant as a deserter, dead or alive. I went on reading the letter. 'We both hope,' she had written, 'that if we manage to escape you will benefit from it. The Air Vice-Marshal is very fond of you, and it would be so easy to pretend that the child is not yours. You will know that this is not a love affair that I am embarking on now. We are just anxious to escape, and he is certainly very good to me.'

So I continued to read and as I read I wished with all my heart that they might be safe and happy, though I dreaded any moment to hear news of their capture. I hurried down the stairs as though my haste could have been of some assistance to them, and walked quickly to the main gates of the aerodrome where I stood for some minutes, and I do not know whether anxiety or admiration for the fugitives was the feeling uppermost in my mind. They seemed to me to have done something noble and desperate in making this deliberate escape along the white and dusty road that would take them almost immediately into a world of towns and villages where our standards no longer applied, or had a less certain application. I thought of Eustasia's generosity and independence, of her love which I had returned, but not fully. I thought of how my feelings for the Flight-Lieutenant had changed from admiration to contempt, from contempt to respect and affection. I was thinking of them as of my closest friends when I heard in the distance the sound of a motor-bicycle engine, and soon saw from the distant corner of the road one of the cyclists approaching.

As he slowed down at the gates he recognized me and when I raised my hand he stopped, thinking perhaps that I was bearing a message to him from the Air Vice-Marshal. He was a young man who had only recently been recruited and I thought, when I questioned him, that his face looked pale. 'What's happened?' I asked, and he replied, 'A nasty mess. We caught them at one of those narrow stone bridges. The car's smashed to bits. So were they. One of our fellows injured, too.'

He must have been surprised at the consternation in my face, for he added, as though apologizing for this achievement, 'Those were our orders, anyway.' The phrase came lamely from his lips, and he spoke again hurriedly. 'I've got to make my report,' he said, and starting his bicycle he went on by the road that led to the Air Vice-Marshal's quarters. By now one of the other cyclists was in sight, but I did not wait to question him. Instead I began to walk back on the way by which I had come, my mind for the moment numbed by the news of which I could still hardly think, and at the back of my mind a dull hatred for the organization which had caused these deaths.

I hardly noticed, until I was face to face with him, the Doctor, who was standing again in the spot where I had left him previously. He put his hand on my arm to stop me going by and I observed the worry and strain of his expression. His eyes appeared to be questioning me, and I gathered that he, too, had heard the news and was now anxious to see how I had been affected by it. He took my arm and said: 'It's a bad business. I can imagine what you feel.'

I made no reply, and he went on to speak as though he were frightened and ashamed of the words he used. 'There's only one thing that isn't so bad about it,' he said. 'You needn't quarrel with the Chief. You can keep your job now.'

He looked at me pathetically, knowing well, I think, that his words would shock rather than impress me. I turned on him angrily, as though it were he who was responsible for what had happened.

'Keep my job!' I said. 'I wouldn't keep it if my life depended on it.'

Neither my words nor my manner had offended him. 'Wait a bit, my boy,' he said. 'Don't be in a hurry. I may be able to help you', and I was astonished at the sadness and resignation with which he spoke. He smiled at me, but very gloomily, as though he had come to some momentous decision which greatly depressed him. I was about to ask him what either he or I could do in the case, when we were approached by an orderly who saluted, and informed me that the Air Vice-Marshal wished to see me immediately. I turned to follow him and the Doctor looked round him in a kind of desperation, as though in search of some person who was not present. Then he walked away from us hurriedly, nodding to me before he went. His manner was so strange that at another time

I should have sought to explain it to myself. As it was I could think of nothing but of the death of my friends and my approaching interview which I knew would be decisive.

I found the Air Vice-Marshal in his room, not sitting at his desk as usual, but standing with his back to the window. He smiled at me as I entered and with a gesture invited me to sit down. He seemed full of life, even of gaiety, that morning, and there was no severity in his voice when he spoke.

'I shall be able to take you with me to-day, after all,' he said, and then, sitting on the corner of his desk and looking down on me, he began to speak more gravely. 'You may or may not have heard,' he said, 'of what happened this morning.'

I nodded my head, and must have shown by my expression that the news had affected me more deeply than he had imagined possible. When he continued to speak there was the same assurance in his voice, but a greater urgency.

'From some points of view the affair was regrettable,' he said. 'Particularly regrettable was the fact that one of our airmen could be found capable of desertion and, I should imagine, of infatuation. But from your point of view the advantages of what has occurred are obvious. You must see to it that you avoid similar mistakes in the future. Another time you may not be so lucky as to escape so easily from their consequences.'

As he spoke the thought occurred to me, and almost with the force of a conviction, that it was he himself who had given instructions that the two should be killed and not merely arrested. The thought was terrible to me, for in spite of my certain knowledge that I detested his organization and no longer shared in his ambitions, I still retained an admiration for his accomplishments and a gratitude for the consideration which he had shown me. These feelings, combined with the assurance of everything he said and did, made it difficult for me to express myself at all intelligibly. Instead of stating what my feelings were, I now asked: 'Was it you who ordered them to be killed ?'

He looked at me steadily and was well aware, I knew, of my suspicions. 'In the ordinary course of events,' he said, 'the death of a woman and of a deserter would be a matter of complete indifference to me. In this instance old associations made my task a somewhat unpleasant one. But I am glad at least that you have profited from what has taken place.'

I felt myself overwhelmed by a momentary despair. It was not only the strength of the man, but his utter insensibility to what lay outside his organization that seemed to me now to make any speech of mine useless. I covered my face with my hands and for a second or two was, I think, almost insensible until I felt the Air Vice-Marshal's hand on my shoulder and heard him speakinge in a voice that, for him, was curiously soft.

'I can understand your feelings,' he said, 'and I can assure you that they will soon pass. You will realize even more than you do already how treacherous and undependable the heart is, and so are all our actions that are not guided by our will towards a certain aim. What you feel is natural, but it is weakness. I should like to see you think more of what is immediately before us, and of how splendid your own success may be.'

I took my hands from my face and rose to my feet. There was a strange look in the Air Vice-Marshal's face, almost as though he were ashamed of having made such a concession to me as to have shown sympathy with my weakness; but I hardly noticed this look, for when he spoke of my success and of the splendour of it I was filled suddenly with the saddest thoughts of how desirable to me would be the most ordinary of lives if I might but escape from this iron ring into which I had forced myself. As though I were speaking to myself aloud I said:

'I hate the success which I have had here, which has destroyed my friends and may destroy me. There is nothing splendid about it.'

I saw the Air Vice-Marshal's eyes flash with anger. It seemed to me then that my words had insulted him personally, had stirred his indignation to an extent far greater than I could have anticipated. He sat down again at his desk with his hands extended, the muscles of his arms taut, and his fists clenched. He appeared to be labouring under emotion so strong that he required time to master himself sufficiently to speak. I stood facing him, and for the first time felt capable, if not of holding my own, at any rate of expressing myself in words; for his sudden anger had seemed to me to support the truth of my own conviction.

At length he spoke, and though his voice was calm enough, it was evident that he was not speaking without effort. His lips were unusually compressed, and his eyes levelled at me in a look either of hatred or of exceptional concentration.

'If those are your real feelings,' he said, 'you have succeeded very well in deceiving me. You cannot suppose that I shall allow you, thinking as you do and with the knowledge you possess, to remain alive.'

I thought suddenly of Bess, and of what had seemed to me the miracle of her return to health. My hopes for her future and for mine were as yet undefined, but our feelings were hardly disguised although they had not yet been openly expressed. I knew that the Air Vice-Marshal meant what he said, and was about to reply to him when he spoke again. 'Think carefully,' he said, 'and be sure that your life will depend on the conclusion you reach in the next half minute. There is an effort of the will of which I know you are capable, and which can place you for ever on my side with the most brilliant prospects before you. I would not give this opportunity to anyone else but you.'

He was still looking at me fiercely, but I thought I saw in his eyes an expression of indetermination, a reluctance to carry out the threat that he had made. Though I knew well that this reluctance would not deter him from acting as he thought fit, nevertheless the presence of the feeling encouraged me to stand my ground. He saw, I think, what kind of reply I was about to make, for he pressed his lips together and made a quick impatient gesture with his hand, as though he were urging himself to some unpleasant or dangerous task. But before I could speak or he could express himself further I heard the door at my back open and caught a glimpse of the Doctor's bald head, which quickly was withdrawn, although the door remained wide open. Instinctively the Air Vice-Marshal and I looked at each other, for we shared in the surprise at such an intrusion.

Our surprise, however, was much greater when the

Rector's wife entered the room, hatless, and with the hair dishevelled on her forehead. Behind her came the Doctor, who closed the door carefully behind him and then stood awkwardly by it, though in spite of the awkwardness of his posture his face was determined and his eyes met firmly the look of anger which the Air Vice-Marshal directed at him.

'Sorry, Antony,' he said. 'I must try to stop this if I can.'

When he pronounced the name 'Antony', a name by which I had never before heard the Air Vice-Marshal addressed, my mind reverted instantly to the scene in which I had heard the name spoken before with such agony, and I seemed to know already what I would soon hear. I remembered that the Doctor's name was Faulkner, and that this, too, was a name that had occurred in the Rector's confession. The details of the story now to be explained were still unknown to me, the story itself would have seemed incredible; yet already I was certain of its main outlines and pleased with the certainty, in spite of the trepidation and excitement with which I listened to the speakers and the danger in which I knew that we must all be placed.

After the Doctor's speech the Air Vice-Marshal had stretched out his hand towards a bell, but the Rector's wife had stepped quickly between him and it. 'No, Antony,' she said, 'you must hear me first.'

She spoke with a power and a determination that I had never seen her show before. For a second or two the Air Vice-Marshal stared at her with an expression of both anger and contempt upon his face. Then he sat back in his chair, leaning his elbows on the armrests.

'Very well,' he said. 'Say quickly what you wish. Try to remember, at least, some of the promises which you have made.'

'I would never have made them,' she said, 'if I could have known what you are capable of doing. You have killed one of your sons. I have come to do what I can to save the other, my son as well as yours.' And she stepped towards me and stood at my side, holding my hand.

Somewhere at the back of my mind I had known already that these words would be spoken, yet when I heard them finally pronounced, I was filled with all the agitation that is felt by one who receives utterly unexpected news. I looked from one to the other of those whom I now knew to be my parents, and I pressed my mother's hand.

The Air Vice-Marshal, whom I now knew to be my father, the lover of my mother before her marriage, the Rector's friend believed to have been murdered, looked coolly and with a strange dispassionateness at both of us. When he spoke his voice was so cold as to seem to me inhuman, and yet I could not look at him without feeling, even in this moment of danger, a sympathy and an affection for him.

'You have come to do what you can to save him,' he said. 'I have, against my own principles, been attempting exactly that. He seems, however, to have inherited some of the infidelity and unreliability which I first noticed in you, afterwards in every woman. I have no further use certainly for you nor, I think, for him.'

My mother flushed, and I could see that his words had made her angry rather than alarmed. 'Infidelity!' she said. 'I would never have married if I had not been certain that you were dead and if my husband, knowing all the truth, had not consented out of his goodness to be the father of your child. Even after you had come back and reproached me for what I had done and had immediately made love to my friend and left her, taking her child from her, even after that and for years I thought of you as my lover and thought well of you while you were living on your hatred and your pride. Now I see where these have led you. You have killed Florence with your own hand. You have ordered the murder of her son and yours. Now you have no further use for me and for our son. God knows that I wish that I had never had any use for you.'

The Air Vice-Marshal turned away from her and looked steadily at me. 'Listen, Roy,' he said. 'Though it may be useless to attempt any more to recall you to your senses, I should like to explain to you once again what is the result of living the life that these people lead. Consider the record of crimes, hypocrisy, and irresolution in this woman's family. She falls in love with me and her fiancé, instead of recognizing this fact, attempts to murder me. He never realizes that he has failed to do so, but makes himself miserable for the rest of his life because he cannot face the consequences of what he deliberately willed. As for your mother, she marries before I can recover from my injuries and return to claim her. Whether her conduct is due to conventionality or to mere self-seeking I cannot guess. She does not love her husband, and in consequence he pays his addresses to another woman. He deserts the child who is the result of this connection, but his sense of honour is so fine that he will not allow you, after you have grown up, to think of him as your father. By so doing he also deprives you of your mother. Here he acted un-wittingly for the best. Finally he is killed accidentally by another son of mine, whose mother, thanks to her brother's care, has lived a life of extreme respectability, though in the end, so attached is she to this way of living, she places me in a position where it is necessary for her to be shot. What a record of confusion, deception, rankling hatred, low aims, indecision! One is stained by any contact with such people. Can you not see, and I am asking you for the last time, what I mean when I urge you to escape from all this, to escape from time and its bondage, to construct around you in your brief existence something that is guided by your own will, not forced upon you by past accidents, something of clarity, independence, and beauty?'

He was speaking with great emphasis and in a louder voice than usual. In his eyes there was a look almost of frenzy, so that it seemed that his words were addressed to himself as much as to us. I contemplated as he bade me the long record of crime and deception into which I had been born and had lived, but saw in that no reason to change my mind. If there had been guilt in the village, there had been guilt also at the aerodrome, for the two worlds were not exclusive, and by denying one or the other the security that was gained was an illusion.

Dr Faulkner, whose presence had been forgotten, I think, by all of us, stepped forward. 'It is you, Antony,' he said, 'who must change your mind, not your son.' He spoke with great deliberation, as though he were replying to a question on which he possessed expert knowledge. 'Let him be happy in the way in which you failed to be happy. Let him at least attempt it. Remember that I saved your life. Save his for me in return.'

My father looked at him blankly. 'You are mistaken,'

he said, 'if you imagine that I am likely to be affected by your sentimentality. Your own life, after what you have done, is in considerable danger. You will be lucky to get off with that.'

My mother stretched out her hands to him and I saw that there were tears in her eyes. 'Antony,' she said, 'why must these crimes and cruelties continue? You have the power to put an end to them.'

He looked at her gravely, and said: 'These crimes, as you call them, must continue so that the world may be clean.'

Then he looked at his watch and turned quickly to me. 'Are you coming with me to the conference, Roy?' he said. He spoke casually, and yet we knew what might depend upon my answer.

'No,' I said, 'I cannot', and I looked at his expressionless face with an affection that I had never felt for him before.

He kept his eyes on my face for a moment and then rose to his feet and locked the side door of the room. 'You will all remain here till I return,' he said. 'Guards will be posted at the doors with orders to shoot if anyone attempts to escape. I will see you later.' And he went quickly to the door, locking it behind him.

We stood for some moments without saying a word. My mother took my arm and I smiled at her, feeling, in spite of our predicament, happy and assured as I had not been since the night, that now seemed so long ago, when the Rector had spoken at the dinner party. The Doctor looked at us sadly. He was rubbing the sleeve of his uniform against his ear. As though by common accord we went to the window overlooking the airfield and watched the Air Vice-Marshal, the Chief Mathematician, and many others of our chief officers climbing into the aircraft that was waiting for them. If I had been accompanying them I should have piloted the plane. As it was I noticed that the Air Vice-Marshal himself was taking his place at the controls.

We watched, still silently, the preparations made for the start.

Almost absentmindedly I allowed my eyes to follow the aircraft as it gathered speed over the field and took off into the air. So surprising had been the events of the last half-hour that I hardly thought of our danger. Indeed, my mind was curiously calm, as I considered what might be the results of the conference which my father was attending. I noticed, I remember, that the aircraft was not gaining height as rapidly as I might have expected, and I felt half-consciously the pressure on the stick that would be needed to bring the nose up. Then suddenly my mind became all attention and anxiety. The aircraft had responded to the pressure that I had imagined, but it had responded unnaturally, and was rising as though handled by a novice. What happened next happened quickly. One of the wings, the one on which I had observed the Flight-Lieutenant working that morning, became detached from the fuselage, and the aircraft plunged downwards to the ground. Obviously nothing could save it.

The noise of the impact shook the windows of the room where we stood, and in a moment the wreckage was hidden from our eyes by sheets of flame. We saw the fire-parties rush over the field towards the conflagration, but for long they could neither quench it nor approach it. It was some time before we turned and looked with inquiring glances in each other's faces, not thinking then of what might have happened to us, or of what must happen now, of how the new order, resting as it did on the desperate will of one man, had been broken and the old order could never be restored, of the vices and virtues of each.

CHAPTER XX

Conclusion

NOR WOULD IT be right for me to end this story, as so many stories are ended, merely with a description of my marriage, and of the relief that must be felt when danger has been escaped, of explanations given to each other by various characters and of their mutual understanding.

True that in the days following the accident many such explanations were made. From Dr Faulkner, in particular, I learnt more of the early life of both my parents than I had known before. He told me, among much else, the full story of the failure of the Rector's crime: how he had himself recovered the battered body of my father, and of the lucky accident that had broken the fall from the precipice; how for some days after this my father had been in full possession of his faculties and had persuaded the Doctor into the trickery of the funeral and into hiding his knowledge of the attempted murder. Dr Faulkner had accepted the risk of this deception since he had been from youth a friend both of the Rector and of the Rector's friend. He had been convinced that the interests of both would be best served by carrying out the plan that my father, before his relapse into serious illness, had designed in every detail. After his friend's slow recovery from this illness he had been less certain of the wisdom of the course which he had taken. At first there had seemed to the Doctor something of Quixotism in Antony's decision to efface himself. But in the long days of his convalescence it became evident that it was not self-effacement but a change of identity at which the young clergyman was aiming, and that the news of the Rector's marriage had seemed finally to determine the shape of character into which would grow the Air Vice-Marshal whom I had known. Dr Faulkner had remained with him throughout his career, at times sharing enthusiastically in his work since over him, as over so many others, the scope and brilliance of my father's plans had exercised a kind of fascination that was irresistible.

It had been only gradually, over a period of years, that the full scheme of his ideas and of his ambitions had taken form. Dr Faulkner, as a scientist and philosopher, had followed closely and excitedly the growth of plans that extended from a profession to a policy, from a policy to a revolution not only in his own country, but in the whole nature of man. Nor, until recently, had there seemed to the Doctor anything necessarily inhuman or monstrous in the tremendous ambitions of his friend. 'That the world may be clean' were some of the last words which the Air Vice-Marshal had spoken, and there was no doubt in our minds that this had indeed been his ambition, though he had stained his hands with the blood of his son and mistress, and would, in all probability, have destroyed another son and another mistress had his life not been ended by an accident.

Now he was gone, and shortly the whole organization which he built up would, through the death of all its leaders, be ineffectual in the direction for which it had been planned. But it was not as though he had never been, for none who had met him could forget him; no corner of the country that had felt the force of his ideas could afterwards relapse wholly into its original content.

I, least of all, could remain indifferent to his memory. I knew that my mother from hearsay only (for since her one angry meeting with him after her marriage, she had not met him till the day of her husband's funeral) had been so swayed by his confidence and his success that she had wished for nothing more than that I should serve under him. I knew that my guardian, the Rector, had lived all his life in agony at the thought of a crime which he had in fact been unable to commit. I knew that, but for accidents of various kinds, I should myself have followed in my father's path and repaid him perhaps for the care which he had shown more to me than to any of his subordinates; for, though I lacked his great qualities, the impulses of my mind had been the same as his. Now I had found my parents and I had found that I was both united and at variance with them both. In so doing I had also found myself.

I think now, when I recall those past days, of another scene which took place in the same meadow to which I had retired drunk after the party at which the Rector had mystified me by his speech. I remember sitting there with Bess, some days after our second marriage, on an evening not unlike the evening which I have described already. The gigantic elms were there as I knew them in my boyhood, but the sky was clearer than on the evening of the dinner party, for it was not long after sunset. We were happy as we had never been, for we were each confident of each. Bess had regained her health and her vitality. I, too, had regained what I had lost, a desire to see the world as it was and some assurance of the ground on which my feet were treading. It was not for me, I knew now, to attempt either to reshape or to avoid what was too vast even to be imagined as enfolding me, nor could I reject as negligible the least event in the whole current of past time.

We had been talking, I remember, of the lives of our fathers and of ourselves. Nothing of any great profundity was said by either of us, but, as we talked and looked from time to time in each other's eyes, it seemed to us that between those two enemies there was something binding and eternally so. Something, too, which would bind their children together in confidence though never in certainty; for the future was too vast for that. It might be said that we anticipated, both of us, that now at least the circle of sin might be broken, that, with what we knew, we might live to avoid murder and deception. Yet this would be to put our feelings too simply.

I remember that night as we looked over the valley in the rapidly increasing darkness that we were uncertain of where we would be or what we would be doing in the years in front of us. I remember the valley itself and how I saw it again as I had seen it in my childhood, heard a late-sleeping redshank whistle from the river, and thought of the life continuing beneath the roofs behind us.

'That the world may be clean': I remember my father's words. Clean indeed it was and most intricate, fiercer than tigers, wonderful and infinitely forgiving.

ELEPHANT PAPERBACKS

Literature and Letters
Stephen Vincent Benét, *John Brown's Body*, EL10
Isaiah Berlin, *The Hedgehog and the Fox*, EL21
Philip Callow, *Son and Lover: The Young D. H. Lawrence*, EL14
James Gould Cozzens, *Castaway*, EL6
James Gould Cozzens, *Men and Brethren*, EL3
Clarence Darrow, *Verdicts Out of Court*, EL2
Floyd Dell, *Intellectual Vagabondage*, EL13
Theodore Dreiser, *Best Short Stories*, EL1
Joseph Epstein, *Ambition*, EL7
André Gide, *Madeleine*, EL8
John Gross, *The Rise and Fall of the Man of Letters*, EL18
Irving Howe, *William Faulkner*, EL15
Aldous Huxley, *After Many a Summer Dies the Swan*, EL20
Aldous Huxley, *Ape and Essence*, EL19
Aldous Huxley, *Collected Short Stories*, EL17
Sinclair Lewis, *Selected Short Stories*, EL9
William L. O'Neill, ed., *Echoes of Revolt: The Masses,
    1911–1917*, EL5
Ramón J. Sender, *Seven Red Sundays*, EL11
Wilfrid Sheed, *Office Politics*, EL4
Tess Slesinger, *On Being Told That Her Second Husband Has
    Taken His First Lover, and Other Stories*, EL12
B. Traven, *Government*, EL23
B. Traven, *The Night Visitor and Other Stories*, EL24
Rex Warner, *The Aerodrome*, EL22
Thomas Wolfe, *The Hills Beyond*, EL16

ELEPHANT PAPERBACKS

Theatre and Drama
Robert Brustein, *Reimagining American Theatre*, EL410
Robert Brustein, *The Theatre of Revolt*, EL407
Irina and Igor Levin, *Working on the Play and the Role*, EL411
Plays for Performance:
    Aristophanes, *Lysistrata*, EL405
    Anton Chekhov, *The Seagull*, EL407
    Fyodor Dostoevsky, *Crime and Punishment*, EL416
    Georges Feydeau, *Paradise Hotel*, EL403
    Henrik Ibsen, *Ghosts*, EL401
    Henrik Ibsen, *Hedda Gabler*, EL413
    Henrik Ibsen, *The Master Builder*, EL417
    Henrik Ibsen, *When We Dead Awaken*, EL408
    Heinrich von Kleist, *The Prince of Homburg*, EL402
    Christopher Marlowe, *Doctor Faustus*, EL404
    The Mysteries: Creation, EL412
    The Mysteries: The Passion, EL414
    Sophocles, *Electra*, EL415
    August Strindberg, *The Father*, EL406

ELEPHANT PAPERBACKS

American History and American Studies
Stephen Vincent Benét, *John Brown's Body*, EL10
Henry W. Berger, ed., *A William Appleman Williams Reader*, EL126
Andrew Bergman, *We're in the Money*, EL124
Paul Boyer, ed., *Reagan as President*, EL117
Robert V. Bruce, *1877: Year of Violence*, EL102
George Dangerfield, *The Era of Good Feelings*, EL110
Clarence Darrow, *Verdicts Out of Court*, EL2
Floyd Dell, *Intellectual Vagabondage*, EL13
Elisha P. Douglass, *Rebels and Democrats*, EL108
Theodore Draper, *The Roots of American Communism*, EL105
Joseph Epstein, *Ambition*, EL7
Paul W. Glad, *McKinley, Bryan, and the People*, EL119
Daniel Horowitz, *The Morality of Spending*, EL122
Kenneth T. Jackson, *The Ku Klux Klan in the City, 1915–1930*, EL123
Edward Chase Kirkland, *Dream and Thought in the Business Community, 1860–1900*, EL114
Herbert S Klein, *Slavery in the Americas*, EL103
Aileen S. Kraditor, *Means and Ends in American Abolitionism*, EL111
Leonard W. Levy, *Jefferson and Civil Liberties: The Darker Side*, EL107
Seymour J. Mandelbaum, *Boss Tweed's New York*, EL112
Thomas J. McCormick, *China Market*, EL115
Walter Millis, *The Martial Spirit*, EL104
Nicolaus Mills, ed., *Culture in an Age of Money*, EL302
Nicolaus Mills, *Like a Holy Crusade*, EL129
Roderick Nash, *The Nervous Generation*, EL113
William L. O'Neill, ed., *Echoes of Revolt: The Masses, 1911–1917*, EL5
Glenn Porter and Harold C. Livesay, *Merchants and Manufacturers*, EL106
Edward Reynolds, *Stand the Storm*, EL128
Geoffrey S. Smith, *To Save a Nation*, EL125
Bernard Sternsher, ed., *Hitting Home: The Great Depression in Town and Country*, EL109
Athan Theoharis, *From the Secret Files of J. Edgar Hoover*, EL127
Nicholas von Hoffman, *We Are the People Our Parents Warned Us Against*, EL301
Norman Ware, *The Industrial Worker, 1840–1860*, EL116
Tom Wicker, *JFK and LBJ: The Influence of Personality upon Politics*, EL120
Robert H. Wiebe, *Businessmen and Reform*, EL101
T. Harry Williams, *McClellan, Sherman and Grant*, EL121
Miles Wolff, *Lunch at the 5 & 10*, EL118

European and World History
Mark Frankland, *The Patriots' Revolution*, EL201
Clive Ponting, *1940: Myth and Reality*, EL202